Little Lavender

Little Lavender by CE Parker

Published by Catharine Parker

Royalty Free images & other art and textures provided by

pixabay.com & wildtextures.com

ISBN: 978-1-7776691-0-2

To all of the
silenced voices throughout history;
this one's for you.

Content Warning

THIS BOOK CONTAINS SCENES WITH THE FOLLOWING:

Mild violence, (non-explicit/graphic) sexual intimacy, period-typical homophobia and racism, alcohol abuse, coarse language, trauma, PTSD, suicidal thoughts, and depression.

Reader discretion is strongly advised.

DISCLAIMER!

This book is a work of fiction. Even though I, the author, take historical accuracy very seriously, this story will not be historically accurate as it is a reworking of history in which John Laurens lives beyond the Revolutionary War. I highly encourage all readers to look into the actual history themselves if anyone is interested in it. This book is for entertainment purposes only.

Even though there are points of this series that may be historically accurate, please still assume this is just a work of fiction.

If you are interested in the real-life relationship of Alexander Hamilton and John Laurens, I highly recommend starting with reading their correspondence letters on the "Library of Congress" website since there is a lot of actual historical proof of their relationship not being platonic—but rather, romantic in nature.

This book is my personal take on an alternative version of history. I am not a historical expert—I am a writer who just really likes history.

Thank you, and enjoy!

CE Parker

Little Lavender

C E PARKER

Part 1

In The Beginning

September 2, 1782

Charlestown, South Carolina

My Dear Uncle

I apologize for the lack of correspondence on my end this previous year as I had been hard at work, fighting the good fight for America's countenance and ensuring Her freedom & Liberty. I pray France is treating you well—as I am quite aware of the scrupulous conditions of your health being unbearable in this South Carolinian heat. I am also to rid myself from the wretched humidity to join my good friend, Mr. Hamilton—you met him once two years ago if my memory is still sufficient—in New York City as our impetus to build the new foundations of America align with each other immensely.

I am wary of admitting my fallacy as a Lt. Col. this past month. I have been *'freed of my wartime responsibilities'* as Gen. Greene had so humbly phrased it, and I am to set sail upon a ship New York-bound in a few days from the date in which I write this. I would never divulge this to anyone else, but I confess that I had done something quite reckless, dear uncle, and I fear others learning the veracity of the incident. But know that I am alive and well and I promise to continue my Law studies in NY. I cannot relay verbatim what had transpired during the early hours of the 27th of August, but know that my actions were deplorable. I could blame the fever or the lack of sleep, but in full candor, my mind has been clouded with an ineffable melancholy for many years—as you know—and I know not

10

what I shall do to rid myself of this great burden.

I do not arise to be so blunt with this letter, as it be against my quintessential characteristicks, but I fear if I do not speak my truth now, it may come to haunt me into the future. My arm grows far too tired as I write, so I must bid you adieu, my dear uncle, but know that I aim to write as often as I am able from this point onward. I had almost lost far too much in so little time, and staring at the Carolinian stars whilst bleeding out in the soft grassy field and fearing that my sins may consume my soul—damning me to Hell for all eternity—I vow to follow through with the promises I have made, starting with my promise to my most affectionate friend, Mr. Hamilton, and joining him in the war for our country after the war for our freedom.

I plan to write again after I settle in New York. I hope to hear from you again soon.

Yr. most humble nephew,

John Laurens

PS. I also inuire upon the health of my wife and child. If you hear from my girls, please forward anything Martha might possibly send to you as it had been quite some time now since she had writ to me last. Perhaps I may have miscarried her correspondence? I may have married her out of pity & honour, but it be my duty to invite her and our child into my life as soon as we are able

Chatpter 1

New York Harbour
Tuesday, September 23, 1782

THE FOAMY GREEN WATERS RUSH OVER the ocean walls of New York Harbour as the bell upon the ship chimes to notify passengers they anchored the ship. John Laurens looks up from the report relaying his honourable discharge from the Continental Army and folds it methodically into his inner waistcoat pocket, eager to flee this claustrophobic ship.

With his luggage awkwardly piled underneath his arms, he stumbles down the skewed, ridged ramp onto the harbour docks. His coat, dredged by the saline waters of the sea, clings to his form. His queue has fallen brazenly askew in the breeze as he adheres to the line of travellers into the befoul roads of New York City. The warmth irritates his sweat-coated skin, yet still less daunting than the sweltering heat of South Carolina.

Inside a newly freed America, John still finds his thoughts whirling with lingering regrets and melancholy. He still hears the echoes within his mind's damp and cold caverns, mocking his plan and tarnishing his dream.

Fool. Worthless. Imbecile.

Dandy.

With the sanction of the Philadelphia and South Carolinian congress at his side, his friends and neighbours had held him back, ridiculing him for such a preposterous proposal. His dream battalion stays but a daydream, now stained with gritty realistic pessimism as he sways, finally settling upon the earth and away from the suffocating ship. Sizzling nausea grips at his innards, but he swallows to retain his pride and propriety.

John blinks dizzily as sweat trickles into his eyes and he nearly drops a few suitcases and grunts whence the satchel hanging over his right shoulder irritates the sore muscles from multiple inflicted wounds from the war. Once he's away from the direct path of the people bustling through the ports, he places a few bags down hastily to catch his breath and fix upon his tangled mane. John had lost his hat on his travels, it having been picked up by the wind and blown directly into the sea to his misfortune. A small boy laughed with deep mirth at his increment and he could not help but smile along.

His pale blue coat rides up slightly as he reaches to assemble his queue in an orderly manner, and he pauses in his ministrations when he makes direct eye contact with those intensely desirable violet eyes that he had only been able to dream about for the past year since *The Battle Of Yorktown*. John cannot help the enraptured grin encompassing his features as the man gallops towards him, hastily gripping his hat as it nearly catches in the wind.

John barely has time to open his arms for an embrace as he is nearly tackled to the dusty road, laughing brightly and forgetting his aching bones and wobbled centre of balance as the shorter man holds him close to his rapidly beating heart. John folds his arms around him and squeezes in return, blinking away oncoming tears threatening to attack his eyes.

"Alexander..." John whispers as he reluctantly pulls away; reminded of their environment when a horse sneezes nearby and garbled noises come flooding from the New York crowds passing by them.

"Oh, John, how I missed you, so!" Alexander says breathlessly, nervously straightening his bark-coloured coat. He gives him a once-over and all of the heat centralizes within John's freckled cheeks. "Where is your hat?"

"I imagine a wicked sea creature owns it now," John quips with a sheepish grin.

Alexander bursts into boisterous laughter, the crow's feet in the corners of his eyes more prominent and his auburn curls bouncing as he pulls back to breathe between his giggles. "Ah, of course. I know just the man who we may commission you a new one."

"Oh?" John folds his arms over his chest with a quirked brow.

"An old friend, Hercules Mulligan," —Hamilton pauses for effect— "yes that be his true name."

John nods. "I believe I have heard of him. I've not met him, however." John blinks, shaking his head as a new thought crosses his mind. "How did you become aware of my arrival on this date? I was not expecting to see you until tomorrow."

Hamilton's freckled cheeks tint a rosy colour as he side-glances around them. "I, ahh— I may have come here to see you off the ship for the past few days. Only three days have gone by now that I have, uh, rather *happened* to walk by the harbour—to see if any ships from South Carolina have arrived?" He phrases this as if it is a question and John finds himself smiling with amusement.

"Aye, it was a *happenstance*, of course."

"Of course," Hamilton repeats slowly, adding a

wink. There is a moment where they only soak each other in, unspeaking, unmoving, and smiling like two fools. "Well, sir. I would rather you not burn your head in this sun without a hat. Perhaps we may retire at the house? You look exhausted."

John sighs with relief and offers a bag. "Help me carry my luggage? I am far too exhausted from my trip and wish to let the depth of unconsciousness consume me."

Alexander readily accepts the bag before leaning over to pick up another. "Shall we, then?"

"Aye," John replies with a toothy grin; he shifts the satchel to his left arm as his right shoulder is already sore from the excursion.

"Oh, you will adore the place I have obtained, John! It is barely outside of the city so you should not feel too terribly crowded," Alexander boasts as John flags down the driver of an empty carriage parked on the side of the road. Luck surely has been paying him well, recently. A lingering thought inside of him twists uncomfortably at his insides, chilling his blood and churning his stomach; a dark melancholic voice hissing; 'too good to be true... You know this only be temporary, you fool,' within the crevices of his mind like an incessant South Carolinian mosquito.

"Sounds wonderful," John comments rather late with a forced grin before turning to the driver of the coach. Hamilton furrows his brows but says nothing on Laurens' behaviour. "Sir, is this coach occupied by another travelling party?"

"Nay. Do you require a ride?" The man replies with a thick Irish accent, his eyes searching the two young men.

Another rush of coldness swirls through John's stomach but he promptly ignores the internal chill. "Aye, if you do not mind."

Hamilton offers the address of his home and they are off, watching the city streets melt sluggishly into the countryside as lesser buildings paint the environ-ment beyond the tiny carriage windows.

Laurens catches Hamilton's gaze multiple times and wonders if he is purposely trying to steal John's attention span. His mind wanders to Alexander far too often, and having him be so near after a year apart is *intoxicating*. His fingers twitch for Alexander's skin; as if he pulls John towards him like a tidal wave in the ocean.

The ride is not tediously endless; Laurens had slipped his pocket watch out after they had departed and holds it now as they arrive to find they only travelled for the better half of an hour. He also finds it was not detrimental to sit in such close proximity with Alexander's knees bumping against his own from the opposing side of the carriage.

The only thing that has deterred him from enjoying the trip was having Alexander so close, yet not being able to do anything about it without causing suspicion from the driver of the coach.

The carriage abruptly yerks into a sharp halt, rudely interrupting his stream of thoughts and causing John to fumble forward and grip Hamilton's knee to resist gravity from tossing him onto the smaller man entirely. The pocket watch had landed on the floor of the carriage during their abrasive halt and Hamilton bends over to grab it, delicately returning it into John's vacant left hand. Their faces are mere centimetres apart, and the tantalizing lips of the fiery man before him quirks upward slily. Alexander proffers a few quick pats upon John's hand before retreating from the carrier.

John swallows deeply as he slips the pocket watch into his coat and pulls himself out with a low grunt, his muscles and bones permanently sore from many years at war, but the stiff carriage ride was not of any aid to his aching bones by any means.

The brick building in front of him is humble and modest. It appears to be two homes conjoined in one building and the four other buildings on this dead-end street seem to not acquire the same architectural layout. John wagers that it must be a uniquely fresh design—one he surely has never seen before—perhaps to save money and space.

He turns and procures his purse, pulling out a few extra coins for the carrier rider. The man grunts in appreciation and grips the money in his clammy hands before shoving them haphazardly into his waistcoat pocket. "Godspeed, sirs."

Hamilton pulls the last of John's luggage from the boot before giving a few hearty pats upon the dark steed. "You as well. Thank you for your troubles."

The man tips his hat and flicks the reins, steering the horse around into a casual trot down the way he came.

John picks up two bags as Alexander carries the others. "Allow me to show you the house!"

John's expression melts into one filled with pure fondness as he follows Alexander towards the house. An older woman outside of the adjoined home tends to the flora sitting upon the windowsill and she turns at the sound of the men climbing their shared porch.

"Hello, Mr. Hamilton," the woman says kindly, the wrinkles on her face become more prominent as she grins sweetly at the man. As they approach nearer and she turns towards them, John notices a faded burn scar riding up her left neck. It partially covers half of her face and blends into her deformed ear; he smiles politely like the gentleman his father raised him to be, and allows no cruel thoughts to invade his mind as a lesser man would be so inclined to do.

"Good day, Mrs. Rosmund. This is my friend, John Laurens. John, this is Mrs. Rosmund," Alexander introduces as he pulls his keys from his pockets.

"Is Mr. Laurens visiting for long?" Mrs. Rosmund queries with a quirked brow, her earthy-green eyes flickering towards the luggage.

"I will be living with Mr. Hamilton whilst we complete our law studies in New York," John replies. "T'is a pleasure to make your acquaintance, ma'am."

She grins deviously. "Mr. Hamilton, you never informed me that a handsome southern gentleman was moving in. If I'd known, I would've dolled myself up."

"Nonsense—you're already a doll, Mrs. Rosmund," Hamilton replies with a flirtatious wink; he finally tugs the door open.

She chuckles lightly and John cannot help the grin taking over his features. "Oh, you are a shameless flirt, Mr. Hamilton. Go woo a woman your own age."

Hamilton fondly rolls his eyes before retreating into the depths of the home. John nods respectfully towards his new neighbour. "Take care, ma'am."

"You as well, Mr. Laurens," the kind old woman replies sweetly before returning to her task.

John steps inside the home and closes the door behind himself. "Mrs. Rosmund owns the home and lives in the other half. I believe it used to be one house but then she had it split in half," Hamilton elucidates with a shrug. "She is a kind landlady and I fear she is greatly under-charging for this place." John puts his luggage beside the other bags Alexander put down.

"Well, come in. Allow me to show you the home!" John follows the man in question as he eagerly beckons him over.

"Here we have the parlour," Hamilton begins with a bright smile.

"Right next door is the dining room, quaint but functional," Hamilton says as they enter the room from a door in the parlour.

They enter the corridor again and Hamilton smiles brightly. "Our study," he continues, opening the door to show the room with bookshelves installed into the two far walls and a window at the back—two desks are pushed together so the occupants may face each other whilst working.

"Our study?" John inquires with a playful grin.

"Aye. There is only one study...and we work well together, anyhow," Hamilton replies with a cheeky wink.

John follows him further down the hallway; behind the staircase. "This is the cleaning room. I wash the laundry and take baths in here," Hamilton says, leaning against the doorframe. "There is a rather convenient water pump right outside the back door that leads to the well in the garden."

"Wait but a moment," John backtracks. "You clean everything yourself?" he asks incredulously.

Alexander furrows his brows. "Must I remind you that I am not the son of a plantation owner, John? I cannot afford to hire a maid."

Laurens shakes his head, embarrassed. "Right. My apologies."

Hamilton raises a curious brow. "Will this be a nuisance to make your own food and clean your own mess? Or are you far too pampered for such tasks?" Alexander sounds quite teasing, rather than truly mocking—but John remains flustered.

Laurens shakes his head and grins, his embarrassment swelling within his chest. "T'is not an issue at all. Besides, this arrangement is only" —temporary. He swallows, unable to finish his sentence. He clears his throat. "Well, you know..."

Hamilton hums and points over his shoulder at the door directly beside the cleaning room. "This is the kitchen." John smiles, silently thanking providence for the change of subject matter.

"T'is somewhat detached, so be careful with the step in the morning. I've tripped on this step far too many times. There is a door to the back garden from both of these rooms. There be a dirt path leading to the outhouse that I am sure will not supply us well when it rains." John's lips quirk amusedly at the thought of Alexander slipping on his way to do his business after a rainy day. He hides his amusement with a curt nod in understanding.

Alexander hurries down the hall they came and grabs half of the luggage. "I wager we will be going upstairs, now?" John asks conversationally as he follows close behind, grabbing his remaining luggage before they begin their trek up the narrow staircase.

John watches their feet upon the creaky stairs and lifts his head at the most inopportune time; his forehead smacks against the low hanging wooden beam above the stairwell and he hisses in pain, rubbing the spot tenderly before ducking to continue his ascent.

"I am aware that this house is rather...paltry—but it was all I could afford after resigning from my commission," Hamilton mumbles self-consciously as they approach the top floor—which appears to be a narrow corridor adjacent to the one below with three doors.

"Alex, it's perfect," John replies with a smile.

Hamilton's brows furrow in question. "You will have to be conscious of your head ascending and descending the stairs."

"Aye. It be akin to my experiences in the attic

at Valley Forge, if you recall," John replies, his eyes scrunching as he grins fondly at the memories of early mornings whence he would smack his head against the ceiling. It had only been a few years ago but they were quite young back then; rather naïve.

Alexander snorts and shakes his head with a crooked grin. "Oui, mon imbécile chéri. I would very much wish for you to keep your head intact, John."

John chuckles and blushes at the sight of Alexander's eyes twinkling brightly. Laurens coughs indiscreetly and enthusiastically explores through two of the bedroom doors, promptly averting the subject matter. "So, which room be mine?"

Hamilton flushes and pushes the door behind him open. "Why, the biggest room of the house, of course..."

John follows him into the master bed-chamber and pauses when Hamilton shyly places half of his luggage in front of the second wardrobe in the room. "Why must you make me walk to the opposite side of the room to put my clothes away?" John inquires in a low, gravelly tone.

"Because I already claimed the other wardrobe," Hamilton replies with a playful grin.

John gazes at the large bed and looks down at Hamilton as he places his luggage upon the hardwood floor. "And this is my bed?"

"Our bed." Hamilton's breath tickles John's lips. "We finally have a place of our own..."

"Aye," John mumbles with a dopey grin. His smile falters as the fleeting reminder of 'temporary' flickers through his mind. Alexander catches his change in mood and John delicately cups his face with both hands, leaning down to place a chaste kiss upon his chapped lips. Hamilton responds eagerly, wrapping his arms around John's back and clawing his hands up between his shoulder blades.

John reluctantly retreats for air and Alexander follows his lips with a low whine. John chuckles warmly and holds his lover at an arm's length. "This home is perfect, my dear boy. Thank you for inviting me to stay with you."

Hamilton huffs rather indignantly, sliding his arms around Laurens' waist to rest his hands upon his hip bones. "You speak as if I had considered sharing this home with anyone other than you, my dear Laurens."

John flushes and ducks away from Hamilton whilst biting his nails. He leans like a swaying tree as he grabs his suitcase and places it onto the bed. He tucks stray hairs falling from its queue behind his ear before piling his clothes into the wardrobe. "The rest of my belongings should be here within the next few days, they said." John pointedly avoids gazing in Alexander's direction. "Not everything, of course—but I will have everything I would ever need to be here."

"John—"

"I do greatly look forward to studying at King's College with you. Mind you, Middle Temple was located in London and I had only chosen that school to stay away from my father if I be honest—and what now with the war being won, I could not possibly resume my law studies outside of—"

"John!" Alexander grabs John's face and halts him in his nervous ministrations. He had been hastily putting things away, barely taking a breath between his words—rambling like a nervous schoolboy. Laurens simply cannot believe that he is here with Alexander. Many years ago, the idea of this was simply but a dream to him—not something to be considered as a reality for men like them. "My dear, are you alright?"

He purses his lips and gingerly pulls Hamilton's hands away to thread their fingers together at their chests. "My sincerest apologies. I only ramble with pure adrenaline at the prospect that we truly are here...doing this..."

Alexander's smile is like the moon; bright and irresistible to look away from. "Aye, sir." John swallows. "I am utterly delighted to have you in mine company," —Alexander exhales a breath and leans up to ghost his lips to the shell of John's ear, causing him to tremble— "all alone. All mine."

John is unable to suppress the croaked whimper from his slightly parted lips as heat swells into his groin. Hamilton hums with approval and lifts a tantalizing brow before grabbing John's cravat and tugging him into a deep, passionate kiss.

John blindly reaches out behind him to swipe the suitcase off of the mattress before tugging Hamilton upon his lap as they fall to the bed. They bounce with the landing and Alexander begins exploring John's neck with his lips and teeth.

John sighs deeply as Alexander unties his cravat hastily and tosses it carelessly over his shoulder before leaping in to suck the nape of John's neck. Laurens tilts his head and Hamilton hums in satisfaction as he gains more access to kiss, lick, and nip as he pleases.

"I missed you so much," Hamilton whines into John's shoulder, his arms securely wrapping around his back as if he is about to float off into the ether.

"Aye," Laurens replies breathily, turning his head to place a gentle kiss upon Hamilton's cheek. "Being apart from you constantly throughout the war was an irritating hindrance."

Hamilton smiles wickedly and pulls back to look into Laurens' eyes properly. "I do not know if I will be able to keep my hands off of you during your stay."

"I would hope not," John growls, sensually sliding his hands to grip Alexander's thighs with vigour. "Pray tell, what would you desire for us to do when our studies be not in session?"

Hamilton's grin widens and he pushes Laurens onto his back; he cradles his elbows on either side of John's head and locks his legs around his sides to cage him upon the mattress. "Perhaps I may be inclined, rather, to show you?"

"Proceed," John replies heavily, swallowing deeply before his lips are fiercely captured.

All of John's reserves float away whilst every crevice of his body is ignited by Alexander's fiery passion. As Alexander kisses the spot below his ear, he unabashedly moans before catching himself with a sheepish expression. He smacks his hand over his mouth and Hamilton chuckles heartily, utterly amused.

"Why must you cover your mouth, John? We aren't two soldiers hiding in the night any longer, my dear," Hamilton inquires with a playful quirk of the brow.

"But our neighbour!" John hisses in retaliation. "The walls be adjoined—surely she could hear," —John halts when Alexander's finger presses lightly onto his lips, hushing him with a low giggle.

"Mrs. Rosmund cannot hear us. Her home has a different layout so her bed chambers are nowhere near ours." He punctuates his sentence with a peck on the cheek. "And the wall between the two homes be far thicker than the walls within the singular home," Alexander replies, pecking John's opposite cheek. "Also, she is far older than us and partially deaf. We will not alert her, I am sure."

Laurens huffs indignantly but relents when Hamilton places a chaste kiss onto his lips. "You worry far too much, my dear."

John tilts his head away when Hamilton dips downward for another kiss; he sits up, leaning on his elbows, and nearly knocking Alexander off of his lap with the sudden actions. "Hamilton, I am serious upon this matter. If we were to be caught whilst we were engaging in such a sinful affair—"

"Sinful?" Hamilton slides off of John's lap and runs his fingers through his unruly hair that has escaped the hastily tied ribbon during their illicit endeavours. "John, I had thought you did not think we are—"

"I don't," Laurens intercepts swiftly, leaning closer to Hamilton, placing his hand underneath his chin. John maneuvers his face towards his own and searches his deep, violet eyes. "Darlin', you know where my sentiments lie. I believe our love to be pure—I only remind you of the world outside these walls. We cannot give anyone a moment of suspicion so that I may protect your life and your legacy, my dear boy."

Hamilton sighs defeatedly, his shoulders slumping with resignation. "I'm sorry. I know you only," —he purses his lips and closes his eyes, ducking his head away from John's calloused fingers— "I only wish for you to feel safe in being yourself when we are here, Jack. We do not need to hide here."

Laurens quirks the corner of his lips and runs his fingers through Alexander's hair, carefully taking the loose ribbon out with his fingers and placing it upon the bedside table. He holds the nape of Hamilton's neck and pulls him forward into a hungry kiss, sucking and lapping his tongue upon the supple pink flesh as if his life depends on it. Hamilton moans softly and falls backwards, his copper hair haloing his freckled-ivory skin.

Now it is Laurens who cages Hamilton beneath him and he smirks at his dear boy as he squirms wantonly underneath his weight. "John," he breathes like a prayer upon his parted lips, his eyes closing and his head digging over into the pillow. "Please..."

Laurens lowers to barely tap his lips against the lobe of Hamilton's ear. "For you, my darlin', I would do anything for."

Alexander sighs in a high-pitched tone and smiles blissfully; Laurens takes this as his opening to consume Alexander, their bodies moving in tandem, and their noises being only somewhat repressed out of respect for John's fears.

***

A shockwave sends John flying backwards and he awakens with a painful twitch, wheezing like an accordian. He fumbles for flint in the bedside drawer, lighting up the candle and sighing with relief when he can see his surroundings. T'was only but a nightmare.

He breathes deeply, sliding his legs off the side of the bed and burying his face in his hands. He had not dreamt this particular nightmare in three months. The dream occurs less frequently now, but when it returns, it shakes him to his very core. He cannot recall who the people were, why they were there any longer—if it was ever real or a terrible dream from the horrors of war— but regardless, it frightens him to the bone.

He shivers when a hand strokes his back and he melts into the touch, sighing as a warm body engulfs him in a protective embrace. He smiles fondly as soft and warm lips press against the juncture of his neck and shoulder; he tilts his head to give more access to the assailant.

"John," he whispers slowly into John's skin, and Laurens melts into his chest.

"Alexander," John replies in a low voice, turning

his head to face him. "My sincerest apologies if I had awoken you, my dear boy."

"Mmm, I mind not, my darling," Alexander sighs into John's cheek, his lips quirking into a grin against John's sweat-coated skin. "Are you alright?"

"Aye. Merely a nightmare."

Alexander's face falls. "Which one was it this time?"

John shrugs, rubbing his face with a low groan. Alexander places a few kisses on his shoulder, emitting a few chuckles from John. He turns properly to capture Alexander's lips. He moans into it, clinging onto John's shirt with growing intensity. John reluctantly pulls away and rests his forehead upon Alexander's. They say nothing for some time, only holding each other and breathing languidly. Alexander anchors him to reality. The nightmares mean nothing when he is there to hold John.

"I suppose now is a decent enough time to rise for the day, hmm?" Alexander suggests, leaning back to look John up and down. "We have a big day today."

John smiles and cups Alexander's cheek, stroking his thumb across the expanse of freckles splayed out like the constellations in the night's sky. "Aye. We could dress ourselves for the day."

John leaves the statement to hang in the air and

Alexander smirks deviously, lightly tugging John back to lay upon his chest on the bed. "Dawn has not creased the skies yet, my dear Laurens. We could perhaps make better use of our time, instead?" Alexander teases in a light tone.

John traces patterns into Alexander's chest and smiles fondly, nuzzling his head into his nightshirt. "What do you have in mind?"

Alexander chuckles and the vibration of it soothes John, nearly lulling him to sleep again. He laces his fingers through John's honey-gold hair, smoothing it over his shoulder. "Mmm, I could lie here and hold you close to my heart for the rest of my life and be perfectly content, my sweet Jack."

"My heart is yours, Alexander." John smiles. "Always."

Laurens raises his hand to clutch Alexander's shirt—his nightmare long-forgotten albeit for one lingering sentence dripping in the recess of his mind like a droplet upon a blooming flower.

"All I ask of you is that you live, John. Living will leave the impact you so desire."

Chatpter 2

LAURENS CANNOT DENY THE TRUTH;
he *adores* living with Hamilton. They have a routine they
have followed for a month now; very akin to the one they
followed in the war.

They wake before dawn and lie together until the
sun peeks through the window. They dress, occasionally helping the other with a button, hair, or a shave since
they do not have a mirror in their bed chambers as of yet.
John purposely does not buy one so he may shave Alexander, and so Alexander may shave him—he clings onto
these intimacies and wonders if Hamilton reciprocates
these sentiments since he's also not purchased a mirror.

They retreat down the steps, Laurens having to
duck his head to not smack it against the wood panelling
hanging low above the staircase for his stature. They eat

breakfast and leave to go off to King's College for a few hours for their law studies, always being sure to say good morning to Mrs. Rosmund who typically is tending to her flora or mending clothes in the rocking chair upon the porch at this time.

They typically pay attention in school, but Laurens still taps Hamilton's foot under the table as if they are aides-de-camp yet again. They usually eat in the town, buying food from a local vendor and chatting enthusiastically before their next class. Once they return home in the late afternoon, they greet Mrs. Rosmund before locking themselves into their home and making special use of their space and privacy; having been frustrated all day from being unable to touch the other outside of their home.

John rather enjoys the ritualistic patterns of each day and hums with satisfaction as he helps Hamilton cut up vegetables for their suppertime stew. Their home truly be their safe-haven and John offers a lopsided grin when Alexander playfully bumps their hips together, chopping side-by-side within their humble kitchen.

Their life is quite domestic—Laurens pauses his motions as this thought strikes him like a cannonball. He is humbly at peace and desires to do this every single day until they turn old and grey. He has never thought so far in his life before, but with Alexander, all he can think about is the future. All he can see is a tired man with silver-streaked copper hair smiling sweetly at him, telling him he loves him, and that he would run away with him if it came to be.

The gentle eyes of a kind young woman and a faceless daughter an ocean away flicker into the forefront of his mind, reminding himself that he shan't become too comfortable here with Alexander. T'is only temporary.

John nearly drops the kitchen knife whence a light knocking comes from their front door. He and Hamilton wipe their hands with the cloth and retreat down the narrow corridor, chuckling like young boys as they struggle to fit in the hallway beside each other.

Hamilton opens the door and Laurens leans his arm against the frame, both looking down at their neighbour. She smiles upon seeing their faces, and Laurens cannot help but return the grin.

"Hello, boys. I hope I am not interrupting anything?" Mrs. Rosmund says cheerfully.

Hamilton shakes his head. "No, not at all. We were only preparing supper when you had knocked."

"We're making stew," John adds with a childlike smile. "An old family recipe from my mother."

"Ah, so this is a perfect time," Mrs. Rosmund replies as she removes the cloth from the object within her frail hands. "I had tried a new recipe and so I made two just to be certain I had gotten it correct and...well, they're both perfect, however, I do not require so much food for myself. I was wondering if you two would like to have this second loaf?"

John and Alexander exchange a curious glance before returning their gazes to their kindly neighbour, smiles warming into a fuzzy fondness for the older woman. "Aye, if you insist," Hamilton says whilst accepting the perfectly baked loaf. It appears to be baked with herbs from Mrs. Rosmund's garden.

"What do we owe you for the loaf?" John queries with a lifted brow.

She also lifts a curious brow and shakes her head in befuddlement. "Oh, no, sir—no payment required. All I ask is that you eat it. If you dislike it, however, you are more than welcome to throw it away," she says timidly. "This be a gift, Mr. Laurens, from one neighbour to another. I do not expect any repayment."

John blinks owlishly, pressing and releasing his lips like a fish out of water. Alexander, thank the stars, speaks for him. "Thank you, m'dear. This was a very kind offering. We will gladly enjoy it this evening with our stew." He opens the door further and gestures with the loaf of bread towards their narrow entranceway. "Would you care to join us for supper? The Eleanor Laurens stew is absolutely delectable and I urge you to at least taste it."

Mrs. Rosmund smiles and looks to Laurens as if silently asking for his permission to enter. He nods enthusiastically and shuffles backwards to give more space for her to enter. "Why, thank you. You really do not have—"

"This is a gift, Mrs. Rosmund, from one neighbour to another," John echoes with a cheeky grin; she chuckles, wagging a finger at him before lifting her skirts to step inside their home.

Hamilton takes the loaf into the kitchen whilst John holds out an arm for Mrs. Rosmund to hold. "I can walk on my own, Mr. Laurens," she mutters before grabbing his arm and allowing him to walk with her.

"Oh, certainly, ma'am—t'is only my upbringing. A habit I am unable to break," he replies with graceful mirth. He releases her after they step down into the kitchen and she wanders to the large black pot hanging over the fire.

Alexander stirs their recently cut ingredients into the stew before offering the spoon for her to taste. She smacks her lips together after sipping the thick broth, making a grand performance out of it, and smiles brightly at them. "This is delicious. I did not take you two as cooks."

"I am no cook, ma'am," John replies sheepishly. "I had only relayed the recipe to Alexander and he did most of the work."

"Oh, hush. You are getting better at cutting vegetables," Hamilton replies swiftly, flicking the cloth at John before retreating towards the stew to continue stirring. "Will you stay with us for supper, Mrs. Rosmund? I am certain your bread will go wonderfully with it."

"Aye, of course, Mr. Hamilton." She sits gingerly at the small kitchen table, making herself at home. "It would be my greatest pleasure."

John looks out the window at the oak tree in their back garden, right beside the fence that separates their garden from Mrs. Rosmund's. The leaves fly from the tree with the breeze and John averts his gaze, returning his attention to the stew.

***

The hazy sun shines and the day is fresh and oversaturated with a magenta fog. John is with his brothers Harry and Jemmy, and he has been in constant contact with Francis. What could possibly go wrong?

John smiles at Jemmy waving to him from the tree. He waves back and chuckles before returning to the correspondence he had received early morn from Francis. His heart skips a beat in his chest as he opens the letter and soaks up the words like a fine wine. As his eyes dance along with the beautiful writings, he takes pause as the letter changes course, causing his blood to boil.

His chest heaves and he frowns. With handwriting so marvellous, the words are unmatched and Laurens wishes to burn this parchment as it stands. How could he believe something so abhorrently wrong? What monstrous beliefs are being spilled into his mind's eye? All he can see is mind-controlling upon the page and John simply cannot believe that Francis, his Francis, would say such—

SNAP!

CRACK!

John's head whips up at the sound of blood-curdling screams and tosses the letter carelessly whence he sees Jemmy lying upon the grassy floor beneath the large tree. He runs but his feet stick to the grass like it's become a swampy marsh, holding him back from reaching Jemmy sooner.

He finally approaches Jemmy and collapses beside him, his tears stinging his cheeks. His face is obscured with so much crimson liquid, pouring onto the green grass and staining it until the small boy lay within a pool of his own blood, staring up at John with glassy eyes.

"Jah-k—"

"Shh, Jemmy, shh. Don't speak," he coos between harsh sobs. The small boy whines when he attempts to move and John cradles his small head, holding him perfectly still. "I am here, Jemmy. I am right here. I promise I will not go." He looks up at Harry, his eyes be crazed and red-rimmed. "Go find help. Now!"

Harry nods as if finally being unfrozen like the winter has surpassed his form and he hurries down the hill, past the letter, beyond the foggy frame of John's vision. He rambles about nothing and everything, keeping his brother distracted. He sings and cries and talks about their mother, telling him to stay strong for her—to stay strong for him.

"John," Jemmy says in a startlingly deep voice, very unlike his own childish whimpers from before. As if he be a grown man with a firm grip upon John, anchoring him to the ground, sinking—sinking—sinking— further into the blood-soaked earth, surrounded by bones and warm iron liquid, thick and coarse.

"John, wake up," the voice echoes from a distance as John spirals into darkness, still holding the face of the corpse below him.

"No, no, don't go," John cries desperately, lightly tapping his brother's porcelain cheeks and staring into the greyed eyes that are left utterly soulless, staring blankly up at nothing.

"John, t'is only a dream, my dear. Wake up!"

John blinks and shoots up, gasping for breath and clawing away the heavy duvet. The room be dark, one lone candle lit upon the far night table beside—

"Alex," John sobs gratefully, lunging towards his lover with such tenderness and clings to him like a lifeline in the sea of his grief.

"Shh, I'm here with you," Alexander whispers soothingly as he rubs gentle circles into John's back. His nightshirt clings to his sweat-coated skin and his hair has gone askew, sticking to his forehead in odd places and tangling behind his back. "You're safe, now."

"I couldn't save him," John sobs into Alexander's shoulder, hiccuping between his breaths.

"There was nothing you could do, John," Alexander replies patiently. "You were young. You did the best you could."

"I was responsible for him," John shudders violently. "My father will resent me if he discovers this."

Alexander closes his eyes and tugs John a little closer, rocking him back and forth. "Stay with me, John. Do not drift away, my dear. Repeat after me; It is seventeen-hundred and eighty-two."

"But my father—"

"Repeat after me, John," Hamilton interjects in a soft tone.

John's breath wobbles and he nods. "It be seventeen-hundred and eighty-two."

"Good, now; I am in New York City," Hamilton says firmly.

"I am in New York Ci-City," John garbles sleepily, his eyes drooping as Alexander sways him peacefully. His heartbeat simmers and his tears stop.

"Good, that is good my dear Demosthenes," Alexander coos sweetly, to which John snorts amusedly.

***

John awakens far past sunrise and becomes further surprised when he discovers the other half of the bed to be vacant. He instantly gains a whiff of something cooking downstairs and smiles endearingly to himself.

He dresses swiftly and rushes down the stairs, ready to—

SMACK!

John rubs his head grouchily and ducks to further retreat down the steps. He grumbles upon entering the kitchen and Alexander smiles knowingly at the tall honey-haired man tenderly rubbing his forehead.

"Happy birthday, my dear," Hamilton declares

with great enthusiasm. John only responds with a grunt as he sits at the small kitchen table, grabbing the Rivington's Gazette laying upon the table, the date on the front reading: Monday, October 28th, 1782. "You are one year older and apparently one inch taller," Alexander quips cheekily as he places John's breakfast in front of him.

John flickers his gaze above the paper to squint glaringly at Alexander who only chuckles lightly in response and places a mug of coffee in front of John. He looks back to the paper and absently picks up the mug to take a minuscule sip to test the temperature.

"You are twenty-eight today, correct?" Alexander says conversationally as he sits beside John at the table with his own plate and mug.

"Aye," John affirms stiffly, keeping his eyes on the paper.

" 'Ave you received any letters from your siblings or your father?" Hamilton inquires innocently enough, his native accent narrowly slipping into his speech as he drowsily reaches for his mug of black coffee.

"I had received a letter from my Uncle James this week previous, wishing me well for my upcoming birthday," John mumbles in response. "My father mainly asked how my studies were going and mentioned my birthday in a footnote, only to remind me that I am his eldest son and that I have responsibilities to upkeep our good family name."

Alexander nods carefully, squinting at his mug as he places it down upon the table. "What of your wife?" he says quietly, barely over his breath. "Has she writ anything to you since—"

John sighs and places the newspaper down, disturbing the plates and cutlery with a shuddering clang that causes Alexander to twitch within his seat. "Let us not discuss this," he grits through his teeth. "We must complete our meals and continue our studies for the day." John punctuates the end of the conversation by grabbing a slice of Mrs. Rosmund's infamous herb bread upon his plate and begins to eat.

John does not wish to give Alexander the silent treatment, but his lingering embarrassment from the night previous whence he had awoken from such a terrible nightmare has drained him. Somewhere in the crevices of his mind's eye, a recurring dream has told him time and time again of his untimely demise. He wonders if he is overstaying his welcome on this planet and should never have been able to arrive at this age on this day. His muscles be sore with years of strain and his heart lies with the man by his side; he is to only study with Alexander until he inevitably has to face reality and his family tucked away across the sea.

"I do not mean to sour our good fortune with this limited time we have together, John, but the lack of correspondence only worries me so—"

"Why shall it worry you?" John hisses, banging his fist by his plate. He flinches away as coffee spills on his skin.

Alexander furrows his brows. "As much as I desire for you to stay with me forever, my dear, I also must worry about your family since they are a part of you."

"They are not," John replies with despondency before resuming his meal.

Alexander huffs angrily. "That little girl is your child, John, whether you like it or not." John looks over at Alexander wearily as his voice rises in volume. "You shall not abandon her and her mother! Do not condemn them to such a cruel fate!"

John swallows painfully as realization dawns upon him. "My dear boy, I apologize. I had not realized you—"

"Oh, piss off!" Alexander yells furiously, tossing his cloth on the table and standing up abruptly, the chair scraping abrasively across the floor. "Do not make this about me you inconsiderate bastard! Write to your family, dammit!" Alexander grabs his food and mug and slams the kitchen door with his foot on his way out.

Akin to a fragile glass, the façade of their life is now shattered. John sighs in resignation; how could he allow himself to fall into Hamilton's web of fantasies yet again? He is aware that this is temporary, but when he had arrived in New York, Hamilton had made him perceive that he was to stay forever.

As the river may flow, so does their life. America may be free, but John Laurens will forever be trapped in the constantly flowing stream, his happiness always to be out of reach. He aggressively tears the bread apart with his teeth. "Happy birthday to me."

***

After his meal is complete and dishes have been cleaned, John cautiously enters their study, staring longingly at Alexander who writes furiously at his desk, his food untouched.

"I apologize, Alexander."

He scoffs in response, his gaze unmoving from the parchment he is scrawling upon. "I am not the one you should be apologizing to." He dips the quill into the inkpot. "How long has it been since you have written to your wife?"

John sighs, leaning against the doorframe. "I cannot recall for certain. Perhaps five or six months?"

Alexander stops writing, his eye twitches. "Why

have you waited so long?"

John marches to his desk. "I can write to her now if you so desire—"

"That not be the point of the matter, John!" Alexander snaps, harshly dropping the quill into its placeholder. He rubs his face, exhaling in defeat. "I'd assumed you were in continuous contact with her. Do you have any inclination of when she will return to you? Is she even set to return to you anytime soon?"

John chews the inside of his cheek with indignation. "Last I had writ, I had informed her that I planned on completing my studies with you in New York—just as we had previously discussed— and wished to meet with her when I finished. She had not written back since."

Alexander raises a curious brow. "She has not written back?" He blinks, perplexed. "John, when was the last you heard from her at all?"

John squints, his insides swirling as he considers this. He struggles to recall the contents of her last letter, and when he does remember, it does not soothe his icy nerves. "I believe I've not heard from her in a year. Perhaps her correspondence could have miscarried?"

They stare silently at each other and startle painfully as a knocking upon their front door interrupts their heated conversation. Alexander waves at John to sit down and retreats from the study, leaving John to worry his bottom lip between his teeth as he considers how truly strange it is that he had not heard from Martha in a year. The sweltering knot inside his chest grows; his guilt is beginning to truly eat away at him.

He had been focused on his black battalion plan and peacefully closing off the war. He's yet to even mention to Alexander that his resignation was false, in that he was actually honourably discharged for—

"T'was Mrs. Rosmund. A letter for you had been put into her mailbox again," Hamilton announces as he re-enters the study with the object in question gripped in his hand. "It appears to be from your sister. Perhaps she had timed her letter perfectly to reach you nearer to your birthday."

John stands, gratefully accepting the letter, and opens it with the small knife laying upon his desk. He unfolds it and smiles because: yes, this be Patsy's handwriting! John's eyes eagerly scroll effortlessly through the words upon the page, but as he reads further on, his smile all but fades into oblivion.

Alexander takes notice of John's stature and hurries to his side when John collapses into his chair, his eyes wide and his trembling hand wearily covering his mouth.

"What is it?"

John says nothing, only hands the letter to Alexander, his eyes unmoving as they begin to grow glossy with unshed tears. Hamilton accepts the letter with great hesitance and begins to read aloud.

"My dear brother, as you had not replied to my past correspondence from June, March—or December of last year—I am inclined to believe they had gone missing upon travels as I hear the ships going between America and Britain has had many issues this past year with the end of the war." He pauses, chewing his fingernail absently.

"I apologize if you had not received the news previously, that this letter may not be rather merry for you to receive on or near your twenty-eighth birthday..."

Alexander flickers his gaze to John momentarily to see he has completely covered his face now. He reads on. "Sarah Manning Vaughn, your beloved sister-in-law, has been kind to keep a close eye on Frances as you continued to fight the good fight for America. We had received your letter to Martha and decided it would be best now that since you no longer be a soldier in war, for me to sail the sea with your beloved daughter. We have spoken very highly of you to her and she greatly looks forward to finally meeting you..."

Alexander nearly falls over as he reads the next sentence. "She has been quite forlorn since this past September first when your love, Martha, had passed away—she had lost her last breath at Lisle in France. I am so, truly sorry, my dear brother for your loss."

Alexander holds the parchment with trembling hands as he continues. "Mr. Vaughn had writ to Mr. Franklin last November that *'the effects she left are few & trifling, but the magistrates of the place still refuse hitherto to suffer the operation of her will, till the Cols. pleasure is known.'* This be why we so inclined to believe you had not received our letters since post-mortem. Perhaps a misplaced letter upon the ships? Or they have simply fallen into mud towards your headquarters? We hope that uniting you and your daughter will brighten your spirits, even if our poor Martha has been taken from us far too soon..."

Alexander looks up again to see John crying softly into his hands, his shoulders shaking, and his sniffles deafening in the silent room. "Dear God."

John looks up, his eyes red-rimmed and his lightly freckled cheeks tear-stained and blotchy. "I am vile."

Alexander's breath hitches. "How so? This is the first you are hearing of this."

John stares into Alexander's eyes and nearly retches his breakfast at the prospect of what he had done. "I had ruined her, forced her into a loveless marriage, and longed for her to simply disappear so that I may live on with" —*you*. John shakes his head. "She's been gone since last September, Alexander, and I had not known! I am a terrible husband and a vile man who is nothing but a sinner!"

Alexander stares at the letter for a moment before simply saying, "this was sent months ago. She states that she and your daughter are to board the next available ship to New York. They may already be on their way over here as we speak, John."

Laurens thinks of an oak tree. He thinks of a small boy he had been responsible for and had failed, simply because he was distracted—*by a man.* John rushes out of the room as his breakfast truly begins to rise from his stomach at the thought of his five-year-old daughter being sent his way to raise all by himself—whilst he had been living with another man!

He lurches out the back window in the cleaning room, shivering and sweating as his nerves spark like a flame, licking his insides and burning him alive with nothing but fear and melancholy. John shivers again when a warm hand presses onto his back, rubbing up and down soothingly as he spits out the remaining acid from his stomach. He painfully grips the windowsill and stares at the oak tree as nearly every single leaf has fallen by now.

"What the hell am I supposed to do?" John whispers hoarsely.

"I know not, John," Alexander replies soothingly. "But we will figure this out" —Hamilton turns John's face so their eyes may interlock— "together."

Chatpter 3

JOHN DOES NOT KNOW HOW TO RAISE
a child. He also does not know how to grieve a person—*his wife*—who had passed a year prior without
his knowledge. His comfortable routine is shattered
now as he barely manages to get by. Martha had passed
away in France not long after John had been there. Had
she only travelled there to see him? Is this entirely his
fault?

Laurens sits upon the sofa in the parlour—the
only thing he can do these past few days—and stares
out the bay window with a glassy stare, devoid of any
longing for the future. He is distantly aware that his
mind is only clouded with grief and melancholy after
losing someone so dear to him, even if he had not loved
her the way he wished he could.

Does Frances even know what colour his eyes

are? He wonders absently if she appears more like her mother...or like him. She is only five, turning six in January—the precise day he knows not yet—and he has no image of her. John dry-heaves, nearly losing his constitution upon the thought that he will not recognize his own child when she comes.

"My dear, there is a letter addressed to us both," Hamilton mumbles, startling John from his lost trance.

"Oh?"

Hamilton tosses it onto John's lap as he paces by, crossing his arms behind his back as he approaches the window. John raises a curious brow and picks up the parchment. He watches Alexander's hands twitch and fidget behind his back and frowns in concern.

"We've both been called upon to be delegates in the Continental Congress," Alexander states rather solemnly. "It appears that the essays we've collaborated on advocating the replacement of the Articles of Confederation with a strong Federal Government have paid off, and they wish for us to join next term."

"You seem...forlorn about this?" John replies delicately.

Alexander sighs, his shoulders visibly slumping with his motion. "I must admit that I would have been excited to see this news a week prior."

Before John's birthday.

John places the parchment upon the coffee table. "You should go on with this. I do not mind turning it down, for I've no desire for such a position, anyway."

Alexander turns his head sharply to glare at John. "You will accept this position, John. We are only but a few days from receiving our law degrees. You knew I wanted us to do this—to continue fighting the good fight for our cause."

"I haven't the capabilities as I have before. I could pay my end by opening a law—"

"Enough," Hamilton interrupts. "You may grieve as long as you must, but you will do this with me."

Laurens swallows. "What of my sister and daughter? They shall be arriving any day now."

Hamilton shrugs. "And? Why should that hinder your career? There are multiple men in congress with children. Some have been widowed and perhaps even remarried as well." Alexander saunters towards John and kneels in front of him, placing his hand on his knee. Laurens instantly folds his hand over Hamilton's tenderly. "I know our plans have shifted but we cannot let that stop us. We must keep going onwards. Even if you are close to drowning, John, you must keep swimming."

John nods slowly, caressing Alexander's cheek with calloused fingers and slips his other hand into Hamilton's. Alexander smiles with deep fondness, turning his face to press his lips onto John's palm. John's body ignites like a sparking flame and he subconsciously exhales in content.

Alexander turns his head again after placing a few kisses upon John's palm, his expression warm. "I love you more than anything, you know."

John flushes and smiles endearingly. "Aye, as do I."

Alexander pulls his hand away, tucking it into his inner waistcoat pocket, and grinning like a small boy in a toy store. "I, ahh, have something I wish to tell you. Please do not interrupt, I just" —he skittishly tucks a loose curl behind his ear— "I've wanted to say this for so long but you were quite occupied with..." Alexander sighs and pulls out his closed fist, holding it in front of John and uncurling his fingers to reveal—

"A ring?" John questions with a lifted brow. "What—"

"John, I love you." Alexander visibly swallows, his forehead shimmering as he begins to sweat. "My dearest, John, I have loved you for many years now— you had stolen into my affections, and I would rather you keep them because I have nobody else in the world but you."

John blinks dumbly as the words register in his brain at the pace of a carriage trapped in the mud. "Alexander? What is all this about?"

"Please, allow me to finish," he interrupts again, his voice wobbling with trepidation. "I mean no ill will to Martha as I am sure she was a good girl, but I must admit that I was thrilled when I had read that letter."

John scoffs incredulously but Alexander continues. "I know it be cruel of me, but I had been willing to give it all up for you, however, it pained me to know you were already devoted to another by law."

John opens his mouth to intercept, to correct Alexander over where his devotions lie, but thinks better of it and snaps his mouth shut with his teeth clattering together. "I know the woman traditionally wears the ring—and this is also not legal—but I love you with all my heart, and this ring represents my complete and utter devotion to you. John Laurens, will you grant me the greatest honour and marry me? In spirit, that is?"

John cannot breathe. He opens his mouth to reply but finds the words to be stuck upon his frozen tongue. His vision blurs with oncoming tears and he wordlessly nods. Alexander sighs in relief and carefully pushes the ring onto John's finger beside his right pinky. He stares at it in awe before capturing Alexander's lips with his own.

John stands slowly, pulling Hamilton up with him, and keeping his lips on his lover's skin. "Oui, oui, Alexander. A thousand times over—yes," he whispers into Alexander's lips.

Alexander smiles giddily and holds John's right hand, bringing it to his lips to press a tender kiss upon the ring. "Damn laws to Hell. I take thee, John Laurens, to have and to hold, for richer or poor, in sickness and in health, till death do us part, so help me god."

John bursts into a strange laughter that sounds awfully akin to a sob as he embraces Hamilton. "And I take thee, Alexander Hamilton, to have and to hold, for richer or poor, in sickness and in health, till death do us part, so help me god." John punctuates his eloped vows with a searing kiss, his lungs burning for breath that he refuses to take within his moment of pure elation.

As they part from their embrace, Hamilton lifts a suggestive brow at John, looking up at him through his lashes. "My dear, shall we consummate our marriage?"

Despite himself, Laurens flushes deeply. He allows his passions to capture his soul and drown the grief and worries if only for a short while. He basks in Hamilton's charm and follows him up the staircase with a wide grin. He leans in to press a kiss behind Hamilton's ear, holding his hand on the railing as they ascend the steps eagerly. As he lifts his head away, Alexander catches it in time before he may smack it against the low beam.

"I would not wish for you to injure yourself, my love," Alexander says in a sultry tone, causing John to rumble with giggles.

"Go on then," John whispers, nudging Alexander forward so he may raise his head properly. "I would greatly prefer it if we would move faster."

"Oh, you're rather impatient." Alexander chuckles lightly as he saunters around the railing and walks backwards towards their bedroom door. The windowed doors at the end of the hallway leading to the front upstairs balcony haloes Hamilton's silhouette with an ethereal glow. "I think I will take my sweet, leisurely time with you, mon cher."

John pushes any lingering melancholic thoughts outside the door as he captures Alexander in his arms. Laurens pushes him into their room, slamming the door shut with his foot, and pinning him to it and nipping at his neck eagerly. "We will have to see who bears champion, mon amour..." Laurens growls as he begins removing Hamilton's cravat. Alexander chuckles, holding onto John and settling his head against the door.

They drown in each other's passions by navigating the windward passage before laying together in blissful tranquillity. Their fingers explore each other's skin as they adoringly gaze into each other's eyes. The setting sun leaves their room in a tranquil orange glow, the shadows upon their faces accentuating their sharp edges and glistening sweat. Alexander tenderly holds onto John as if he be a lifeline, keeping him from drifting away into the stormy seas.

They do not speak as they lie together, only listening to their laboured breathing calming down from their exhilarating high. John frowns as the silence begins to loom over him, allowing his melancholy to sneak into the forefront of his mind again. He curls over and lays his head upon Alexander's chest, tracing patterns upon his skin with his index finger and staring at the ring as a way to distract his wandering thoughts from ruining this moment.

"I can hear you thinking," Hamilton mutters drearily.

John snorts amusedly but does not respond, continuing with his patterns, looping his fingers through Hamilton's curly chest hair. Alexander gently holds his wrist, causing the motions to halt. "Have I made an error with my judgement?" His voice is meek as he speaks.

"What do you mean?" John lifts his head to look down into Alexander's eyes.

"Was this a mistake?" Alexander whispers with trepidation.

John lifts a brow. "Us?"

Alexander shrugs and looks away. "I fear you only accepted my proclamation because..."

"...because?" John adds slowly, urging for an answer.

"...because" —he shivers with a sharp intake of breath— "I had taken advantage of your vulnerability whilst you were grieving her passing."

John leans down and tilts Alexander's chin so that they be facing each other. "I carry no doubts on my affections for you, Alexander. I would always say yes to spending my life with you." He pauses and chews his bottom lip in contemplation. "Unless you were having doubts—"

"Of course not!" Hamilton intercepts sharply. "I would not have saved up for that ring if I had doubts!"

John stares at the object in question. "How much did you—"

"For you, my love, everything is priceless," Alexander replies delicately.

John frowns. "Alexander, if you spent—"

"Stop this," Hamilton snaps heatedly. "Please. Can we just lay here?"

John sits up entirely now, leaning against the headboard of the bed. "You were the one who brought up this discussion."

Alexander huffs indignantly. "You were drifting away. I was only worried you were regretting all of this."

John gesticulates to the room around them that

slowly darkens with the setting sun. "Look around us. I have been by your side for five years. I moved in with you. Why the hell should I have any doubts now?"

"Because your daughter is coming here any day now!" Laurens stares in shock at Hamilton's outburst; Hamilton scoffs, rolling his eyes. "Oh don't act so surprised. I have seen you sulking for many days since receiving that letter. You've gone cold and distant, lost in your own mind. You want to leave so you can do what's best for her."

John shakes his head. "Alexander, you forget yourself."

"Are we doomed to be hopeless?" Hamilton murmurs in defeat. "You always go off somewhere in your mind when something goes astray—as if the world is about to implode on itself."

John exhales deeply through his nose, casting his gaze away to cool his growing temper. "What is this? Why propose to me when you have fears of my child getting in the way?"

"I never said that—"

"You didn't have to," John bites back. "Were you hoping I would abandon her?"

Alexander's frown melts into a scowl. "You are a goddamn fool, Jack." He crawls over John and kneels over his lap, causing the other man to blink in bewilderment. "I wish for you and your daughter to stay with me. She is a part of you and I will cherish everything that comes with you." Hamilton sighs as he loops his arms around John's neck. "My only fears were of you leaving. Perhaps the proposal only a week after you had discovered Martha's passing was in poor taste, but I meant every word. I want to spend the rest of my life with you. My sentiments have never been a secret to you."

John bursts into an enamoured grin. He holds Alexander's lower back and pulls him in for a chaste kiss. Hamilton sighs dreamily, lacing his fingers through John's hair to tenderly massage his scalp. Laurens breaks the kiss and raises a brow at his lover; nay, his *husband*. "You truly mean this?"

"Aye," Hamilton replies. "She can sleep in the room down the hallway. We have plenty of space."

"This will not be easy, Alexander. This is a child we speak of. A nearly six-year-old girl who will need constant attention," John elucidates carefully.

Alexander tilts his head with a sheepish grin. "There are two of us and one of her. How hard could this possibly be?"

***

John's fingers tremble as he fumbles with the buttons on his silver waistcoat. She was kind enough to send a messenger boy last evening to notify John and Alexander of their arrival in New York and that she and Frances will come to their home the next morn.

Now it is the morning of their impending arrival and John cannot close these damn buttons on his waistcoat.

"Relax, my dear," Hamilton coos gently as he swiftly takes control of the button situation. John immediately submits to him and puffs out through his nose as his arms helplessly flop to his sides in defeat. "You mustn't *inquiéter beaucoup* on your appearance, John. You are as dashingly handsome as ever."

John rolls his eyes, unable to hide the tiniest smile slipping past his mask of irritation. "You charm me, sir."

"Do I?" Alexander smoothes the waistcoat down and steps back to look at his handiwork. "I only speak the truth, monsieur Laurens."

John turns to grab his coat and put it on with ease. He raises a taunt brow at Alexander as he pulls the ruffles of his sleeves out of the coat cuffs. "Ah, oui. Tu chantes seulement de telles éloges pour que je joue de ta cornemuse, monsieur Hamilton."

Alexander's freckled complexion darkens into a deep shade of crimson and he clears his throat hastily as it appears to have gone dry. John smirks deviously and completes his task of fixing his ruffled sleeves as if he had not said such provocative things.

Alexander nervously wipes invisible dust from his coat and avoids John's gaze. He sighs deeply and looks up at Laurens sweetly. "Come, let us eat before they arrive."

John makes a face of discomfort at the prospect. "Nay, sir. I do not believe I can hold anything down. My stomach feels as if it is bursting at the seams."

Alexander rests his hands on his trembling shoulders and John sighs in relief, not realizing he had been shaking until his dear boy holds him so tenderly. "I am certain she will absolutely adore you, John. There is nothing to worry about—"

A light knocking from the front door startles them and John begins panting nervously. "Breathe, my dear," Hamilton soothes. "I will answer the door. You follow at your own pace." He pulls John's hands to his lips and kisses them sweetly. "I am with you. You are not alone. Remember this."

This is the very reason why John is terrified but forces a smile and nod at Hamilton's attempt at calming his nerves. He watches Hamilton leave and checks his pocket watch. *Nine-forty-three* in the morning, it reads.

Laurens startles at the sound of the front door opening. He hears Hamilton's voice ring up the stairs as he says, "hello," in a kindly manner.

"Ah, you must be Mr. Hamilton," Patsy says politely.

Laurens nervously retreats from the bedroom and makes his languid descent upon the stairwell, chewing his lip as his heart beats heavily in his chest. He sees Hamilton's feet and two skirts outside of the door; he pauses before the low hanging beam.

"Enchanté," Hamilton replies, charming as ever. John hears him kiss her hand. "And you must be little miss Frances Laurens."

"It be a pleasure to meet you, sir," a youthful feminine voice replies with stilted politeness. John nearly collapses down the stairs at the sound of her voice; so soft and gentle like a small bell, and yet her tone has a slight rasp to it, as if coarse from years of use. She sounds almost like Alexander—

"The pleasure is all mine, petite fleur," Hamilton replies smoothly. Frances giggles softly before clearing her throat. John swiftly ducks his head below the wood beam to finish his descent.

He freezes upon reaching the bottom step when Frances gasps, her crystal blue eyes locking onto his own and he somehow knows she is his daughter. A wave of nausea overcomes John and something else— something rather inherently pleasant that he cannot place. His hand gripping the post carries his weight as he stumbles away from the staircase. John approaches her, his eyes unmoving from her small frame.

They all stand in silence as John examines her; her hair is curlier than Alexander's, cascading in shiny gold ringlets and pooling over her shoulders. Her face be pale like his own and her nose be dusted with freckles like himself. She looks so very much like John that he nearly chokes on a sob fighting its way to the back of his throat. Her arched brow and pursed lips reminds him plainly of her mother, full of intelligence and wit and John could weep at how utterly terrifying this small girl appears to be. She does not appear to be happy to see him; in fact, she looks quizzical, as if to say, 'Really? This is it?'

"Father?" She inquires with a small voice, filled with a forlorn longing and that rasp that reminds him shockingly of Alexander's tone.

"Aye," John replies hoarsely, clearing his throat awkwardly as it gravels deeply. "My god, have you grown."

Frances shyly glances up at Patsy who smiles encouragingly at her. She reaches into her skirt pocket and pulls out a locket with a gold chain, inspecting its contents closely whilst chewing her bottom lip in deep concentration before looking back at John. He cannot resist the pained expression controlling his features as she studies him and whatever is in the locket.

"This painting of you is really quite bad," she declares with a set tone.

John explodes into a confounded fit of boisterous laughter.

Alexander chuckles along. "Aye, let me guess, that be a miniature Peale had made?"

John rolls his eyes fondly and shakes his head. "Well, what else was I to do? I was not going to paint myself!"

"You could have done better," Hamilton replies seriously and John scoffs, attempting to hide his flush.

He turns to Patsy and she immediately smiles, all teeth on display, and her arms already outstretched for an embrace. "Patsy, how I missed you so," John mumbles into her shoulder and she nearly tumbles him over in her abrasively lovable hug.

"It's been far too long, Jack," she mumbles into his chest before sighing with content.

They part ways and Hamilton immediately invites them inside since the draft be giving them a chill. They leave their luggage by the front door as John placidly smiles, giving a rather bland tour of the home with Hamilton trailing behind, silently smiling with a deep fondness that John has never quite seen in his eyes until now.

As they approach the second level, John ducking

his head as they ascend the stairs, Patsy immediately furrows her brows at the doors. "Oh dear, it seems there only be three rooms."

John lifts a bewildered brow as he wonders how that could possibly be an issue when—

Oh no.

"You can take my room," John says quickly, his eyes flaring panically towards Alexander. "I can sleep on the sofa until we figure it out." Why did he not consider that his sister would be staying with them after their arrival?

"I've already emptied the drawers for you, Miss Laurens," Hamilton steps in, swift as ever with his silver tongue. "I had spare drawers in my own room that I do not mind sharing with our dear John."

"Are you certain this be alright?" Patsy questions with an arched brow. "I do not intend to impose upon your—"

"All is well. I will have to figure out my sleeping arrangements within the following days as I had forgotten how many rooms we had available," John replies quickly, his eyes nervously flitting towards Alexander.

Frances nervously tugs on Patsy's skirts and she turns to face the small child. "Aunt Patsy, are we living here?"

Patsy looks towards John and he slowly kneels

down to face his daughter eye-to-eye. "Yes, you will be staying with me from now on. If that's alright?"

She flickers her gaze to Hamilton and back to John. Her hands bundle up tightly in her skirts. "Will Mr. Hamilton be staying as well?"

John never considered that she would be weary around him but he supposes he was a fool to not consider this. He and Alexander are strangers to her, after all. "Aye, this be his home. He was kind enough to let us stay with him for now."

She nods carefully then turns quickly, entering the first bedroom by the stairs. "Can this be my room?" She asks brightly and John chuckles fondly as he stands up again.

"Of course," Hamilton replies earnestly. "I'll retrieve your luggage. John, you can show your sister to your room," he adds before descending the stairs.

John proceeds into the only other room on this floor with a sense of dissembled familiarity, moving as if he had done this many times before; his cheeks burn as he forces a smile. He had never entered the other two rooms before today which sounds insane to him as the thought crosses his mind. It sports a deep crimson wallpaper and a wood-framed bed for two with sheer drapes hanging around the perimeter—much like the bed in his and Alexander's room—and pale blue linens.

"Oh, there is a balcony in the back as well?" Patsy

gapes in awe. "I thought there was only one at the front of the house?" She opens the double doors— matching the ones at the end of the upstairs hallway by his and Alexander's room—and the two explore the wide balcony that loops around the back of the home.

He was narrowly aware of the back balcony but never appreciated the sheer beauty of it until today. They find Frances at the very end and John stares in awe at the doors leading to her room. He feels rather sheepish for not appreciating this grand outdoor space until now.

"Aunt Patsy, look at that tree!" Frances points eagerly at the large oak in the back garden. "Much like the one I would climb back home—I mean," she coughs, "in London."

Gravity drags his bodily organs down the two stories they stand on, and he swiftly steps forward to place a protective hand on her shoulder. "You must stay away from it, Frances. Do you understand me?"

She shyly looks up at him, her excitement all but vanishing as she nods solemnly. "Yes, sir."

He wearily looks down over the railing and ushers her towards her room. "In fact, you shall never stand on this balcony without any of us present. Do you understand?"

Patsy's face contorts into an unreadable expression as Frances crumbles miserably. "Yes, sir."

John sighs as they enter Frances' room; the bed with a state-of-the-art metal frame far too large for her small stature, however, the bright yellow wallpaper seems to suit her youthful glow. He kneels in front of her and places a gentle hand on her shoulder. "You do not need to call me sir."

"Yes" —she bites her lip and catches herself— "father."

John's lips curl into a sufficiently awkward grimace as she looks up at him with weariness. This was a mistake. How could he possibly be responsible for—

"John, may I have a word?" Patsy interrupts his wandering thoughts and he nods curtly. He proffers a strange smile to Frances and she returns the same uncomfortable lifting of lips before turning around to rummage through her suitcase. Her stature is stiff and rigid as she moves around the room, and all he can accomplish is observing her from the doorway.

Useless.

John unpromplty follows Patsy out of the room, carefully closing the door, and they bump into Alexander as he exits the bedroom now belonging to Patsy— most likely having dropped off her luggage.

"You need to relax, Jack. She is not a fragile piece of porcelain." Patsy whispers harshly, not caring Alexander stands beside them with wide eyes.

"Have you been allowing her to climb any nearby tall object this entire time?" John snips back with furrowed brows.

Patsy rolls her eyes. "You clearly do not know anything about your daughter."

"You are correct," John mumbles miserably. "I don't. I've only met her today."

"And I am telling you that you are giving a terrible impression," Patsy growls furiously.

"She is my daughter, Patsy," John snaps. "If I tell her not to do something, I have every right to do so. Do I make myself clear?"

Patsy straightens her posture, her jaw clenched and tense with a twitching muscle—much like what happens to John when he does the same thing. "Crystal," she mutters. "You're right. She requires discipline and you can provide that for her." John's features twist uneasily and she turns towards her bedroom. "I'll be unpacking my belongings whilst you figure out your disorganized sleeping arrangements, brother," she adds with a devious smirk. John flushes as the door closes in his face.

Alexander and John stare at the door for a moment before the copper-haired man turns to John with a sheepish expression. "Well, your family seems wonderful. They're all stubborn like you."

John rolls his eyes and begins marching down the stairs. "Watch yourself, Alex—"

SMACK!

"Christ!" John yells, rubbing his head. He slaps the wood beam furiously and ducks under it before continuing his descent, too embarrassed to complete his thought. He hears three distinct chuckles ringing from upstairs, his temper fermenting into utter fondness over the youthful giggles, in particular.

Chatpter 4

JOHN MISSES THE COTS FROM THE WAR at this moment; mainly, his back misses them. Even though they were firm, at least he did not have to lay in such a particular way so as not to fall off. He glowers at the window, watching the bright moon shining directly into his eyes. He awkwardly shuffles until he lay on his back, lifting his legs over the armrest of the sofa. His legs mayhaps fall numb if he continues this position for long. If only he could lie in a proper bed, but he would rather scrunch his brows and stare at the ceiling than fall into temptation.

John is quite aware that his and Alexander's room is directly above where he currently lies. He thinks of the large comfortable mattress with the soft linen sheets, and the sheer drapes hanging from the bedpost blowing in the breeze from the open windows.

He thinks of curling up beside Alexander and resting his head upon his bare chest, imagining Hamilton's soft lips pressing tenderly into his forehead and trailing down, down, down until—he abruptly seizes the thought as he closes his eyes in discomfort.

John twists over to his side again, adjusting his breeches, and curls the cotton blanket more securely over himself as he folds his legs upon the sofa, back to staring out the large bay window.

Laurens sighs in relief as he discovers he had been piss-proud whilst fantasizing over Alexander, but it may not become a false reaction if he continues to let his mind wander again. He cannot risk such thoughts with his sister and daughter nearby.

John twists uncomfortably again as his arm goes numb and he grunts, finally sitting up and rubbing his face tiredly. He abandons any prospect of sleep and instead decides to wander into the kitchen. He shivers from the draft and his toes curl uncomfortably as he walks with socked feet upon the stone floor. He grabs a cup and dunks it into the bucket of water sitting upon the counter. John sips the water and twists his lips at the murky taste before resuming. He gasps with the final gulp and places the cup on the counter before collapsing into the chair, leaning tiredly on the small table.

Sleep begs to consume his consciousness but that damned sofa refuses to allow any sort of comfort.

His mind wanders up the stairs again and he furiously shakes the thought out of his head. John meanders down the narrow corridor, bumping his side into the post of the railing with a hiss.

He gazes longingly up the stairs, but the sight of Frances' bedroom door keeps him from falling into temptation and ascending the stairs. Laurens shuffles into the parlour again and sits upon the sofa grouchily. What would stop him from sneaking upstairs to simply sleep and quickly retreat down the stairs before anyone awakens?

John lays on his side, keeping his back to the window this time, and curling himself uncomfortably under the scratchy spare blanket. He closes his eyes and refuses to open them until sunlight seeps into the room.

***

Laurens rolls over on the uncomfortable cot and stares at Hamilton as he scribbles away, engrossed in his writings. His russet curls glow like fire with the candlelight and his deep violet eyes stay focused upon the page afore him. The lone candlelight perfectly shapes his silhouette and John sits up carefully. "Alexander?"

Hamilton hums but shows no other indication he has heard Laurens.

"There is something I should tell you."

Hamilton pauses then, placing the quill down to lift a curious brow at Laurens. "Could it wait until morning?"

Laurens swallows. "Nay, sir. I've already waited far too long to say this."

Hamilton stands now, his expression concerned. "What is it, John?"

John thinks of his nightmare from the past few weeks that has haunted his sleep continuously. He considers his consequences again, causing his hesitation. He fumbles with his fingers and stares at his hands, unable to meet Alexander's eyes. "There is something I've not told a soul since my return to America. It be something I am rather un-proud of."

Hamilton sits on the cot by Laurens' feet and places a firm hand on his shin under the thin blanket. "Whatever could it be? Surely you haven't done anything so terrible?"

John chews his bottom lip, still unable to meet Alexander's eyes. "The worst thing is that I kept this from you for a year, my dear boy. I care deeply for you and would rather you hear it from me, even if you despise my presence afterwards."

"You're scaring me, John," Alexander whispers. "Spit it out already."

"I am married," John replies hastily, all within one breath and speaking far too fast.

Laurens watches Alexander's hand on his leg slacken before removing it to rest upon his own lap. "Oh."

John sighs and rubs his face. "I also have a child."

Hamilton stands at this, his relaxed posture stiffening with clenching fists. He closes his eyes and exhales sharply through his nose. "I see."

"Please accept my sincerest apologies for not sharing this with you sooner," John begs with a hollow voice.

Hamilton shifts within the shadows of the room, his form contorting into a strange shape. John falls, reaching out desperately, but Alexander does not anchor him into reality as he sinks deeper into the inky black abyss.

"No matter how much you wish it, you will never tell me the truth," Alexander's voice hisses sinisterly within his ear.

"I tried to tell you!" John gasps desperately. "I swear I did!"

"You lied," the voice echoes in his opposite ear,

the tone and inflection shifting eerily into his own. "You refused to tell him and look where it got you!"

A light shines through John's vision and he sees nothing but an enraged Hamilton shoving him away and a letter starting with a simple phrase; '*Cold in my professions and warm in my friendships, I wish my Dear Laurens, it might be in my power, by action rather than words, to convince you that I love you...*'

***

John gasps a sharp intake of breath as he startles awake rather violently, flinging himself off of the sofa amidst his struggle with his limbs twisted between the cotton blanket. He lands on the hardwood floor with a loud THUD and groans in discomfort as he sluggishly realizes he had only been dreaming.

"Good morning, linen-thumper," an all-too-familiar feminine voice chimes from the hallway. John grunts in response and removes the blanket from his face to crane his neck, glaring at the up-side-down image of his sister smiling at him, utterly amused with the view.

"Good morning you errant clay-brained measle," John grumbles with a dry voice laced with exhaustion.

Patsy only laughs mockingly at him, rolling her eyes and sauntering down the hallway. "I see you have not grown up in the slightest since we last spoke, Jack-ass!"

John flushes when Alexander steps down the stairs in that moment with an arched brow and delighted grin. "Jack-ass, eh?"

"Drop it," John warns grumpily as he rolls over to push himself off of the floor, grunting like an old man and rubbing his right shoulder tenderly.

"I can't believe I've never thought of calling you that!" Alexander muses with a devilish grin and John whips the throw-pillow at his head. Alexander chuckles profusely, easily dodging the pillow by swiping his arm to deflect it from reaching his face. "Although, I must admit, your insult for her was rather unique, but quite rusty if I do say so myself."

John glowers at him as he trudges by, rubbing his face and promptly ignoring him as he enters the kitchen.

"In all seriousness, we could always take turns using my bed," Hamilton suggests casually as he brushes past Laurens. "Since you no longer have one." His eyes briefly flicker to Patsy as she obliviously reads the morning paper.

"All is well and good, Hamilton. There's no need to burden your back on my account," John replies lightly. Alexander thankfully drops the matter.

Hamilton and Laurens ease into preparing porridge for breakfast as Patsy sits at the small table with a peculiar expression. She looks around, as if expecting someone else to enter but nobody ever does; that is until Frances enters.

Unlike John and Alexander who are only partially dressed—both having fallen asleep in their shirt and breeches from yesterday—Patsy and Frances are prepared for the day and they ogle perplexedly at the two men who seem to be utterly comfortable and unfazed at their improper state. John smiles endearingly as Patsy whispers into Frances' ear to explain that men are strange beings. John gives her a scandalized look that causes her and Frances to giggle; his chest swells warmly at the sight.

"Laurens, would you mind…" Alexander trails off as he realizes his mistake, turning around and flushing as all three Laurens' in the kitchen look at him expectantly. "My mistake. I am used to living with only one Laurens that my tired mind seemed to forget you are all Laurens." Frances giggles briefly but quickly coughs it away shyly.

"What do you need?" John inquires as he wipes his hands with a nearby cloth.

"Set the table? Breakfast should be ready soon," Alexander replies with a sweet smile.

John nods and retreats from the kitchen. He

looks over his shoulder amusedly as the small girl follows him expectantly, her hands fisting into her skirts
as she trails behind him into the dining room.

"Would you like to place the mats upon the table
while I set the utensils?" John instructs patiently and
she nods with bright eyes. He grabs the pile of place-
mats and carefully puts them into her skinny arms,
smiling fondly as she wobbles awkwardly towards the
table.

The mats seem far too heavy for her but she
manages to place them on the table with a huff before
taking the individual mats and placing them in front
of the seats. She is quite meticulous with her actions,
being sure to make them straight and tidy; flicking a
crumb off of one to clear its surface. John follows her by
placing four wooden spoons at four chairs, the two end
chairs being left unused.

"It is quite strange to see you doing such meagre
tasks, Jack," Patsy says from the corridor, leaning on
the frame separating the dining room from the hallway.
"I would've assumed you would have servants for such
things."

John stares at Patsy, a pang of guilt jolting his
boiling blood. "We cannot afford servants."

"Correction, *he* cannot afford servants. I am certain father would lend you some if you asked," Patsy
retaliates dryly.

John huffs through his nose and looks at the table to straighten a spoon as a distraction for his hands. "I refuse to ask such a thing of him. We do not require the extra services. We've been functioning perfectly fine without one." He flickers his gaze to the floor. "I would also rather not, what with the cause we be fighting for."

Patsy rolls her eyes as she takes a seat. "Right. Your black plan."

John flares up at her, leaning heavily on the table. "Nay, sister. Abolishing slavery altogether."

Frances flickers her gaze anxiously between the two adults, shifting uncomfortably as the conversation grows heated. "Sit, Frances. Remember your manners," Patsy instructs coldly, causing the small girl to stand up straight and seat herself, keeping her posture pristine. John watches the scene with a churning stomach.

"You could always ask father to send a paid servant here if you are so adamant on that," Patsy says with practiced elegance.

"And I already told you that I do not require one," John rebuttals firmly, lifting a challenging brow.

She arches her right brow, examining her brother with puzzlement. "You've changed, John. What happened to my pampered big brother who refused to buckle his own shoes as a child?"

"Breakfast is served!" Hamilton announces brightly, entering the dining room with a tray carrying four bowls of porridge and tea, utterly unaware of the tense conversation.

John smiles and leans over to grab a bowl after the tray is settled upon the table, placing it in front of Frances tenderly. As he continues placing bowls in front of the taken seats, Hamilton pours cups of tea for everyone. Patsy watches the two in astonishment as they move fluidly between each other before sitting down in their seats.

Patsy raises a hand to her brother and he takes it effortlessly, turning to grab Hamilton's left hand with his right one. The ring burns into his flesh as their hands join.

Hamilton and Frances awkwardly exchange a nervous glance before reaching out and holding hands before they all bow their heads in silent prayer. John peeks an eye at Hamilton and frowns at him, seeing how he stares blankly at his porridge and shows no sign of sending a prayer. John closes his eyes and adds a prayer for Alexander before they release their hands and begin to eat their food.

They eat in silence but John takes instant notice of Frances' features twisting in disgust after she takes her first bite. He raises an inquiring brow and lowers his spoon to scoop more porridge. "Frances, is something the matter?"

She looks up at her aunt before looking at her father with a crooked frown. "This food is really quite bad."

"Frances!" Patsy and John hiss simultaneously with red faces.

"Mind your manners! Mr. Hamilton made this for us to eat!" Patsy states with furrowed brows and a stern glare.

The man in question rumbles delightfully beside John, chuckling profusely and causing everyone else at the table to gape at him as his laughing intensifies, causing him to snort. Frances joins his contagious fit of giggling.

"Aye, you are correct, petite fleur. This food tastes like shit."

"Language!" John yelps with wide eyes, his head snapping in Hamilton's direction. Frances seems to be even more amused by this and giggles harder. Patsy covers her mouth with bright eyes, failing to hide her own amusement.

"I know just the thing to sweeten this bitter porridge," Hamilton declares as he places his spoon down and stands up. "Mrs. Rosmund has an extravagant garden with fruits and herbs. I am certain she has something to fix this up."

"Hamilton, we shouldn't bother her," John says. "We can all eat our food as it is." He gives Frances a pointed look as he says this and she ducks her head shamefully.

"She loves to be bothered. She is the kindest lady I've met," Hamilton bounces back brightly. "Besides, I am certain she would love to meet your dear sister and daughter." He offers Patsy a wink and she scoffs, rolling her eyes at his playful charm.

"Aunt Patsy, may I go with Mr. Hamilton?" Frances asks eagerly, nearly hopping out of her chair at the mere prospect of having an excuse to not eat her porridge. John makes a face as he eats another mouthful, realizing that they are accurate with their critiques on the bitter taste.

"Ask your father," Patsy replies swiftly, turning to look at him expectantly.

John blinks vacantly at the three people all looking at him with varying meanings behind their expectant looks. He smiles and shrugs, placing his spoon down to stand up. "I don't see why not. If she is busy, though—"

Frances sprints out of the room excitedly, not waiting to hear the end of it, and Hamilton chuckles lightly as he and Laurens trail behind her. Patsy sighs in defeat and follows them out the front door with a huffed, "wait for me!"

Hamilton reaches their neighbour's door immediately after Frances and knocks on the wooden frame.
John finally manages to take true notice of his and
Alexander's state of dress right as Mrs. Rosmund opens
the door; he flushes sheepishly as she gawks in surprise
at the group of people on her porch.

"Sorry to bother you, Mrs. Rosmund," John
blurts out anxiously. He shifts nervously from one foot
to the other, trying to not look down at his socked feet,
bare of any proper shoes.

Her surprised expression melts into utter fondness as she smiles warmly at the two girls. "You and
Mr. Hamilton are always welcome to bother me."

Hamilton smiles cheekily at John before looking
back at their neighbour. "I made terrible porridge this
morning and these lovely ladies deserve a better meal.
Would you happen to have anything that could spice it
up?"

She taps her left cheek with feigned consideration and John smiles. "I suppose I can provide something for you."

"What's happened to your face?" Frances asks
abruptly, causing John to flush in embarrassment again.
She truly is like Alexander where she simply states
what is on her mind, not worrying about the repercussions. Either she is brilliant or Alexander acts like a
child.

"Frances, don't be rude!" John says sternly, causing her to shrink and nod obediently.

Mrs. Rosmund only smiles and kneels down to reach Frances' eyes. "It be a rather long story. The short version, dear, is to be careful around fire. It can scar your skin."

Frances nods with understanding. "Ah, Uncle Harry told me the same thing! He also has a scar like you. He'd said that my father got very mad when his face was burned by a crazy man!"

John flushes shamefully and rubs his reddened face; Hamilton's right brow quirks but he says nothing. Mrs. Rosmund nods politely, smiling with great patience at the little girl. "Is that so? That sounds like quite the story." She tilts her head. "What be your name, dear?" A smooth transition.

"I am Frances Laurens, but my friends call me Fanny."

Mrs. Rosmund chuckles warmly. "Well, Fanny, it be a pleasure to meet you. I am Hester Rosmund, but my friends call me Ettie." Frances smiles and shakes her hand with enthusiasm, greatly amusing the four adults.

"Nice to meet you, Ettie!"

John had not known Mrs. Rosmund's Christian name before now, let alone a nickname, but Frances had somehow eased it out of her immediately, even after pointing out the scar on her face.

Mrs. Rosmund looks up at John and tilts her head. "I had not known you were a father, Mr. Laurens."

He smiles sheepishly. "Aye. She and Martha arrived two nights previous from England."

Mrs. Rosmund stands and offers a hand to Patsy. "Are you Mrs. Laurens, then?"

John and Patsy choke on their own breath and sputter awkwardly as they frantically shake their heads. "Gods, no! I am John's younger sister, Martha!"

Mrs. Rosmund's features twist uncomfortably. "Oh! My apologies! I shouldn't have assumed..."

"It's quite alright," Patsy reassures with a polite handshake. "His wife was also called Martha Laurens. T'is a simple mistake, really. You may call me Patsy. How do you do?"

"I was having a very quiet morning until you fine people showed up," Mrs. Rosumnd replies politely. "Now, about that porridge, I have just the right ingredients for you. Please, come in! Make yourselves at home!"

Mrs. Rosmund never mentions how Patsy brought up his wife in past tense and John is eternally grateful for it.

***

For the next few days, they have breakfast with Mrs. Rosmund. Laurens absently wonders why Hamilton insisted they continue this. The kind old woman seems to enjoy their company every morning, taking an instant liking to Frances. Who wouldn't? Even John finds himself utterly fond of the young girl, silently begging for her approval, and he has only known her for under a week thus far.

Perhaps that be why Hamilton insists on breakfast with Mrs. Rosmund? After the young girl bluntly stated his cooking was terrible, he had been weary to cook for her, seeming nearly as desperate for her approval as John. He smiles at the thought, finding it rather endearing that Hamilton also be fighting for the young girl's affection like John.

"Why are you smiling, father?" Frances asks innocently as they stride down the bustling streets of New York City. John makes a silent note to school his features around the bluntly honest little girl. She is far too perceptive for someone her age.

"I'm excited to receive my hat." A simple half-truth will have to suffice.

She looks slightly unconvinced but smiles. How can she already tell when he is hiding something? "What is so exciting about a hat?"

"T'is not just any hat," Hamilton says conspiringly, his arms crossed neatly behind his back. He tilts his chin down to look directly at her as they walk. "T'is a hat done by Hercules Mulligan, the best tailor New York City has to offer!"

Her eyes brighten at the mention of his name. "Hercules, like the Greek God?"

Hamilton winks playfully and she giggles. John looks at Patsy with an inquiring brow lifting slightly. "Greek God, hm?"

Patsy shrugs, chewing the skin off her bottom lip to hide a smile. "What can I say? She loves to read."

John cannot say he was so well-versed in Greek Mythology at such an age.

John: 0

Frances: 1,000

"Your hat was made by a god?" Frances asks brightly.

John chuckles. "Nay. But, he was an American spy during the war."

"Ooh," Frances breathes with wide eyes.

"When did you have it commissioned?" Patsy

asks conversationally.

"In late September not long after I arrived. I am finally able to receive it a little over a month later, just in time for winter."

Frances frowns, unimpressed. "That is a long time to make a hat."

"Well, Mr. Mulligan has much clientele to appease," Hamilton replies to the small girl swiftly. "And he needed more fabric to make a hat big enough to fit your father's unusually large head," Hamilton adds with a wink.

Laurens smacks his arm and Hamilton bursts into boisterous laughter when Frances giggles at their antics.

Alexander: 100

John: 0

They enter the tailor shop and Mr. Mulligan turns at the sound of the bell ringing. He smiles widely at the sight of them, a loose pin nearly falling from his lips as he pinches the fabric of the coat on the man standing on the platform in front of him. "Ahh, Hamilton!" He sticks the pin that has fallen from his mouth into the fabric. "And Mr. Laurens, t'is wonderful to see you again. I wager you would like to pick up your hat?"

"Aye, if it be no trouble," John replies casually as he browses lazily at the array of clothing items on display.

"If you give me but five minutes, sir, I can grab it from the back," Mr. Mulligan mumbles offhandedly as he continues attending to the man and his coat.

Laurens waves him off patiently and meanders around the store, smiling at Frances as she ganders dreamily at the dresses hanging up.

"Oh, look at this!" Frances grabs a pastel violet dress that be far too large for her small frame. "Isn't it pretty, father?"

John tries to not panic at the fact that she be asking his opinion of something so casually. He clears his throat. "Aye, t'is."

She looks up at him with wide, doe-like eyes. "Can I have a dress like this one, father? Please?"

John's chest implodes and he smiles like a fool. "Of course." He looks over at Mr. Mulligan as the man removes the coat from the customer. "May I add a dress on my tab?"

Mr. Mulligan smiles as he carefully folds the coat on the counter. "Aye, of course, sir. I will require proper measurements and fabric choices before you make your leave."

Frances bounces excitedly. "Can I stand on the platform?"

The tailor chuckles warmly. "Absolutely, little miss."

The other man shakes hands with Mr. Mulligan before making his leave. Patsy lifts a curious brow at John. "A dress?"

"There is no expense I may withhold from my beloved," John replies smoothly. Frances bounds up to the platform and Mr. Mulligan chuckles warmly.

"Mr. Mulligan, is it true you were a spy?" Frances asks giddily.

He flickers his gaze to Laurens and Hamilton who only smile with great amusement. "Ah, yes, I was." He lightly tugs the dress so it lays flat against her chest, making her smile. "I believe I am a better tailor though, so my spying days are over."

Frances nods, disappointed. Laurens cannot understand how she can make people reveal things about themselves that they would otherwise hide. There truly is something special about the air around her as she looks at the world with whimsical eyes. Mr. Mulligan chuckles warmly before turning to Laurens, saving him from his wandering mind.

"I'll retrieve your hat from the back, sir." The tailor retreats into the back door whilst the three adults admire Frances from behind, smiling at her reflection as she twirls in front of the mirror with the dress still pressed against her chest.

"Do you like it, Mr. Hamilton?"

He puts his hands in his coat pockets and nods. "Aye, petite fleur. The violet makes your eyes shine."

She smiles bashfully and tucks her head shyly away, examining her reflection carefully. John notices Patsy watching Hamilton with an unreadable expression as the man's attention is focused entirely on the child in front of him. Crow's feet form at the corners of Alexander's eyes as he grins at Frances with his own indistinguishable expression; somewhere between pride and joy. John's heart skips a beat at the sight.

Mr. Mulligan returns with a hat in hand and passes the hat to John. He tries it on and Frances smiles at his reflection behind herself in the mirror.

"How do I look?" John inquires with a little wave of his hands, outstretching them invitingly.

"You look really quite good," Frances replies.

"I couldn't agree more," Alexander adds brightly. John smiles and adjusts his hat to fit more comfortably upon his head. He does not miss the strange look Patsy gives him and Alexander from his peripheral; it causes his stomach to flip and sink with deep shame.

Mr. Mulligan brings the measuring tape to

Frances and kneels beside her to measure her height. "Would you like your dress to look like this one?" He asks whilst scribbling her measurements down on a notepad. She nods vigorously and the kind tailor smiles amusedly.

She does not fuss when he takes her measurements and she even picks the fabrics with great enthusiasm. Mr. Mulligan and Patsy casually chat about the types of fabrics and Hamilton helps Frances pick out the precise shade of violet she wishes for. Laurens says yes to everything she picks, of course, even if Hamilton frowns at the price slowly climbing up.

How could he possibly say no to her desires? He is willing to sleep on a small sofa, eat breakfast with his neighbour, and buy any lavish things to prove his worth. Alexander does not speak upon the matter even as his expression twists at John's compliance to spoil his daughter with a pastel violet dress she does not need.

And seeing her bright smile makes every minuscule sacrifice worth the expense.

Frances: 1,000

Alexander: 100

John: 1

Chatpter 5

NOVEMBER HAD BEEN A RATHER
uneventful month besides the earth-terrorizing
introduction to fatherhood and Patsy's suffocating
presence overlooking everything John and Alexander so
much as breathes on. The absolutely unbearable part is
how seemingly unbothered Alexander is of her.

Every morning at breakfast with Mrs. Rosmund —*Ettie, as Frances calls her*— Hamilton brings up
the charm. In the evenings, he teaches Frances how to
write in French, helps Patsy prepare supper, and cleans
the laundry.

John's fingers have begun twitching from his
deep longing to touch Alexander anytime he is
nearby, but Patsy's carefully watchful gaze keeps him
from doing anything. Ever since their trip to Mr.
Mulligan's shop, Patsy has kept a close eye on John and

Alexander, her silent eyes squinting with a dull recognition and John says nothing. Surely she does not know about them? The last time he had shared a kiss with —let alone touched— Hamilton was the morning of their arrival. The longing gazes at school or in the study at night proves that the deprivation also affects his dear boy.

John's back is currently regretful for refusing Alexander's offer to take turns using the bed since he was so adamant to not share it with him. He cannot expect Alexander to sacrifice his comfort some nights because of John's stubbornness in preserving their secret. Frances is far too perceptive and Patsy stays awake as long as he does.

Patsy is seemingly always awake. Always watching but never saying anything.

They currently stay awake beyond reasonable hours in their study on a late November night, studying for their upcoming bar exams when Hamilton makes a rather abrupt suggestion. "What if we purchased a cot to shove into the corner of our study?"

Laurens looks up from his writings, squinting to re-adjust his sight in the dark candle-lit room. "Pardon?"

"Either we get a cot or you take my damn deal to trade places every other night. You refuse to share and yet you have been rubbing at your shoulder like that for weeks." John lowers his hand that was idly massaging his right shoulder. Hamilton's tone is not one of irritation or concern, but rather of bland observation. "The sofa is clearly ruining your back."

John hums gruffly and returns to his work. "I would argue that the war ruined my back."

Alexander snorts dryly, feigning amusement. "I don't know why you cannot simply sneak into our room when they're both deeply asleep."

"You know why we cannot risk sharing a bed," John hisses, gripping the quill with a white-knuckled fist. "If she were to discover us—"

"She won't," he retaliates quickly, keeping his voice low. "Dammit John, I am taking this as seriously as you are. Do you think I don't miss you? Your touch..." His eyes flicker to John's lips. "Your kiss?"

"Drop this," John whispers oppressively. "We cannot share. This be the end of our discussion."

"Then why must you not at the very least accept my offer to trade—"

"I cannot expect you to sleep on your sofa because my family infiltrated your home," John interrupts sharply, his voice rising slightly with irritation. He does not look up from his work, even if he can sense Alexander's blazing gaze upon him.

"What's yours is mine and mine is yours,

remember?" He replies deliberately, his fingers drumming a strange pattern upon his desk. "That ring"—John absently fiddles with the ring on his right hand— "represents our eternal vows, bounded by our souls and beyond any law that man could write upon a fucking piece of parchment."

John stares at him with piercing eyes but Alexander does not falter.

"Stop acting like your family living here is a goddamn burden to me when it is not, John."

Laurens suspires, resting his head in his palms that are propped up by his elbows upon the whiskey-toned desk. "You only agreed to have Frances reside with us, not my sister. Do not pretend that her presence doesn't frustrate you."

Hamilton exhales through his nose and shrugs. "Fine. I will admit your sister's presence was...unexpected, but we compromise. That is what partners do. We shall make it work, right?"

Laurens returns his gaze quickly at his words—a direct reference to the letter he wrote to Hamilton nearly three years ago, now. The very one that had abruptly ended his engagement to—

"Aye," John replies gruffly, his eyes flickering to his writings and pursing his lips.

Even with Alexander being exceedingly willing

to compromise, John finds himself realizing he had only been projecting his own discomfort onto Alexander. If only Alexander said he refused to keep Patsy here, it would have been easier for him to get rid of her without feeling guilty.

But goddamn, does he miss holding Alexander whenever he desires. Their first month in New York was truly a dream and he was harshly awoken with cold water when his daughter and sister appeared upon their doorstep.

John occasionally ponders over whether he could have more alone time with Alexander if Patsy was no longer looming over his shoulder; a constant reminder to him of his responsibilities as the eldest Laurens off-spring—to stay in line and not fall into the stubbornly patient temptation of a man so close by—that he must focus on his work—to simply being a proper father.

You win some, you lose some.

As perceptive as Frances may be, she is still young enough that John could spend nights with Alexander and she would never become aware. His only true blockage is his overbearing younger sister.

Whilst he writes silently across from Alexander, he decides to shove the guilt of his longing for his dear boy aside; he will thank Patsy for her help and send her back home to South Carolina.

***

The very next day, they go over to Mrs. Rosmund's home. She had invited them over for Thanksgiving dinner since all of the other Laurens' are still across the sea. This retroactively changes everything, thus ruining John's hopes of removing his controlling younger sister's lingering presence.

With bountiful laughter and constant conversation all day as they cook together with their kindly old neighbour, eventually, Patsy lets it slip that John's back is rather stiff as she teases him for sleeping on the sofa like a lost dog. Mrs. Rosmund does not take this news lightly; he is honestly surprised nobody had mentioned it around her until now.

"I beg your pardon?" She queries with a worrisome expression. "Sleeping on the sofa, you say?"

John scowls at his sister, flushing deeply as he proffers a sheepishly crooked smile to the short old woman. "Aye... we only have three bedrooms and I had to offer my room to Patsy..."

Mrs. Rosmund tuts him with a frown and stern shake of her head. "Oh, that simply won't do, Mr. Laurens." She turns to Patsy. "My dear, you are more than welcome to claim one of my guest rooms. I live alone, you see, and have two spare rooms that lay vacant."

Patsy shakes her head, blushing as she quickly catches on to John's distress. "Oh, I couldn't stay here. I do not wish to intrude upon you, ma'am."

Mrs. Rosmund glares blankly, her lips in a thin line, unimpressed with such a response. "You stand in my home now because I invited you over for Thanksgiving. You visit me for breakfast every morning. If Mr. Laurens has no bed to sleep in, the least I can do is offer one of my empty rooms." She scoffs and wipes her hands on her apron. "I wish you would have told me sooner."

Patsy looks at John and shrugs. "Thank you, but we won't be staying here much longer anyway, right?"

John wipes his hands on a cloth with a raised brow. "What?"

"We were returning to South Carolina when you finished law school, weren't we? I am certain father would wish for us to stay in Mepkin. You'll end up inheriting it anyway."

The disgruntled expression on Alexander's face causes John to panic. "I never said we were moving back to South Carolina..." He chases the first excuse he could grab that is not 'I cannot leave my husband' as that would simply be a horrendous response. "Hamilton and I were called upon to serve in congress." *Smooth.* "And afterward, we planned to open a law firm together in New York."

Patsy blinks languidly. "I thought you would have wanted to return home? I promised Frances that she could see Mepkin."

The small girl in question watches the argument unfold with wide, glossy eyes.

"Why would you give such empty promises to my daughter?" John snaps frustratingly.

"The spare room is still available," Mrs. Rosmund swoops in, physically stepping between the bickering siblings with a calm expression. "Free of charge."

"No," John says. "I will compensate for my sister living in one of your rooms."

"But, t'is a gift—"

"You can simply add it to mine and Mr. Hamilton's rent bill every month," he cuts in. "I refuse to not pay for this."

Mrs. Rosmund sighs resolutely and nods. "Very well, then." She turns to Patsy brightly. "We can move you in as soon as possible so your poor brother may save his back. How on earth did he even fit on that small sofa with his height?"

"The answer is he didn't," Hamilton pipes in cheekily. "He mostly met his fate with the hardwood floor." Laurens smacks him with the cloth, making Frances giggle.

John would give himself a point for making Frances laugh if his plans to rid himself of his sister had not fallen into the mud. *'On the bright side,'* he muses silently, *'at least she will no longer sleep in the house any longer.'*

You win some, you lose some.

***

"We can call our firm *Laurens and Hamilton Esquire!*" Alexander boasts proudly, waving his hands in a wide gesture, vividly envisioning a large sign with their names on it.

"We had only just received our results for the bar exam," John chuckles amusedly. "We haven't even made it home yet, Alexander. You're already thinking ahead of yourself."

"I am always thinking ahead, Jack," Hamilton muses brightly. "Be proud, my dear Laurens. We did it!"

John sighs with relief, looking at his degree with pride. "Aye, thank the Lord. I barely passed, I believe. It was difficult to spend most of my time studying while still in war."

"And yet you did it." Hamilton frowns. "Don't undervalue your hard efforts. You and I just did the unthinkable together."

John smiles easily at Alexander and shakes his head. "Also, why put my name first? Why not *Hamilton and Laurens Esquire*?"

Alexander shrugs; however, John still catches the way his lips curl downward and his jovial eyes dimmer. "Your name is more notable."

John frowns, near scowling at this. "I see."

"T'is only a business move, my dear." Hamilton shrugs again as if this does not hinder him. "Just because I am aware of how society functions does not mean I underrate my own efforts. I know my name means nothing..." he pauses, grinning deviously with a nudge on Laurens' side "...yet."

"Just you wait. Your name will be more important than mine in no time, I am certain," John says with a prideful grin.

Alexander, despite himself, blushes; he ducks his head downward to admire his law degree. "They'll know us both. You will be remembered for you, John, and not your father. We will be an unstoppable force in American Congress."

John blinks and looks up at a developmental building to avoid the sudden onslaught of tears threatening to spill at the kind compliment. He sniffles and puts a hand in his pocket to avoid rubbing his face out of nervous habit. "Speaking of, we will have to specify our focus on our plan to present to Congress.

They will expect us to offer a useful objective for the future of our country."

Alexander hops giddily in his step, greatly accepting the subject change. "Aye! We'll have to pack soon as well. Where do you suppose the two of us will stay?"

Damn. John never even considered such a thing. He had been far too preoccupied with passing the bar exam that travelling to Philadelphia had somehow slipped from his mind.

"We cannot leave Frances behind," he mumbles the thought aloud. "I've only just got her in my life."

"Of course." Alexander raises a curious brow. "Doesn't your father have a large enough home in Philadelphia we can stay in? I believe if my memory serves me correctly, that was where you stayed during your, ah..." He pauses. "Your imprisonment?"

John hums noncommittally as he carefully tucks his and Alexander's degrees into his satchel as the crowds around them thicken. He shivers, covering the bag with his cloak again to withhold his dwindling heat.

"Well, perhaps then we could stay there and have plenty of space for all of us," Alexander suggests as they turn around a sharp corner.

Laurens thinks about his father across the sea in

Europe. He'd rather not stay in that house again, but he also finds it to be the best option for them at the moment. It's not like the house is being of use otherwise; the estate currently lies empty until occupants may fill its vacancy once more. John bumps into a young lady, jaggedly tearing him away from his thoughts, and he apologizes before turning his attention to Alexander again. He hears the group of young socialites giggle behind them as they continue their trek towards their unique dwelling.

Alexander nudges him playfully and waggles his eyebrows. "Careful, John. Don't go stealing some poor girl's heart before you leave for Philly."

Laurens scoffs and rolls his eyes. "I've no idea what you're speaking of."

Hamilton laughs and Laurens awkwardly bends over as Hamilton grabs his shoulder, pointing at a group of ladies across the street. They slow their stride as Laurens looks over at them; the three ladies blush and smile, looking at each other conspiringly whilst stealing glances at the two men.

"Do not forget that you are exceedingly handsome amongst these common men, my dear," Hamilton whispers hotly into his ear. Laurens tries to smile at the ladies so he may ignore what Hamilton's voice does to him. The sound of his voice is like flint whilst the words that fill the tone is the fire that follows, and it burns him from the inside out. He prays that his rosy cheeks will be excused as a cause of the cold weather.

"They're also looking at you, Hamilton," he replies gruffly, casually pulling himself from his grasp.

"What can I say? We make an attractive pair." He winks and Laurens speeds up his stride again.

***

Frances plays with her dolls on the floor in front of the fireplace when they return home. Patsy and Mrs. Rosmund look up from their sewing as the two men remove their cloaks and hats on the hooks by the door. Patsy watches them expectantly as they enter the parlour through the open corridor passageway.

"Well?" Patsy asks eagerly. "Did you receive it?"

John smiles and pulls out his and Alexander's degrees to show them off. The room fills with jovial cheers from Patsy and Mrs. Rosmund as they stand to congratulate the two men. Mrs. Rosmund kisses Alexander's forehead and he melts with fondness over the kind older woman. She dotes upon the dust on his coat with maternal energy and he sheepishly grins as she whispers her best wishes to his upcoming career. Meanwhile, Patsy kisses her brother's cheek and holds his degree with a wide grin.

"Look at this! I am so proud of you, Jack!" She beams with enthusiasm. "Father will also be proud," she adds whilst returning his degree.

His smile drops and he sighs, tucking it away into the satchel again. He hums in acknowledgement but says nothing more. A small tugging on his breeches steals his attention, and he looks down to see Frances hugging his leg. His chest bursts with something indescribable at the sight. He kneels and pulls the tiny girl into a gentle hug, a sudden tear trailing down his cheek.

"Con-gratilons, father," she mumbles.

"T'is pronounced as congratulations, Fanny, not—"

"Thank you, sweetheart," John intercepts Patsy as he pulls back from the embrace, wiping his eyes.

"Why are you crying?" Frances asks; her brows furrow with concern.

"I am just...very happy," he replies in a low tone.

"We should celebrate!" Alexander declares. "We can have a grand feast within the next few days!"

"I hope you're not cooking it," Frances deadpans.

"Frances!" John, Patsy, and Mrs. Rosmund all yelp simultaneously in horror.

Hamilton cannot help himself; he begins to

cackle boisterously.

***

As December dawns upon them, so does the snow. Hamilton and Laurens work hard, properly preparing for their departure to Philadelphia before the week is out. After they have eaten a grand meal—made by the collective efforts of Mrs. Rosmund, Patsy, and Hamilton—packing consumes their lives. Patsy slowly moves into Mrs. Rosmund's home, occupying the room perpendicular to the one she had been staying within John and Alexander's home since their layout is a direct mirror reflection of Mrs. Rosmund's.

John wonders why Frances refuses to pack her things valiantly, giving an enormous fuss whenever she is instructed to do so. It seems the moment after they finished their meal and told her to start packing, she had been extremely difficult, always trying to find an excuse to avoid the task altogether. Today is no different as she mentions the lavender dress John had commissioned for her a fortnight ago with Mr. Mulligan.

"I highly doubt it will be ready before we leave, sweetheart," John tries to explain delicately. Frances stomps her foot and crosses her arms.

"I want my dress!"

"We can have it shipped to Philadelphia when it be ready."

"I want it now!" Frances yells furiously.

John sighs exhaustively and leans against the wall, rubbing his face. "We can go to Mr. Mulligan and instruct him on where to send the dress when it be—"

"I want my dress now! I want it now, father!" she whines fractiously, her youthful tone irritating his eardrums. His soul drags through a thorny field as she throws her suitcase onto the floor and begins tossing her clothing about in an enormous mess.

John watches her with bewildered stupor as it truly dawns on him that he does not know how to control a child's tantrum. His siblings had been far more well-behaved than her. Even Frances had been an absolute angel until now. What changed?

When she throws her doll at the wall, screaming bloody murder, John finally steps closer to her. "That is enough, Frances. If you do not behave yourself this instant, you will be punished!" She shrinks away from him but keeps her expression stern. "Pick up your clothes and your dolly."

"No."

John nearly growls in frustration. "Frances Eleanor, pick up your belongings this instant or you will not be receiving the dress at all."

"I hate you!" she yells before stomping out onto the balcony.

John gawks in befuddlement as she sits with her legs criss-crossed on the balcony floor, glaring at him through the doorway.

"Frances, why are you being so difficult?"

The small girl shrugs but her expression holds firm; she shivers in the brisk air.

"Come inside, now. T'is freezing out there." She harrumphs, not budging. Stubborn girl.

"Frances..." John sighs and slowly sits on the floor, leaning against her bed and keeping his eyes on his daughter. "What's the matter, sweetheart? You know Mr. Mulligan needs to take time on the dress."

Frances' lips wobble as she looks away.

"I cannot help if you do not tell me what's on your mind," he pries gently.

"Please don't send me away!" she bursts out, her voice hiccuping as tears begin to spill. "I promise to do better."

John stares with dismay at her crumpled form. "Pardon?"

"I don't want you to leave me again."

"What?" He balks, waylaid by her adumbration. "Frances, we're to be moving *together*." She regards him quizzically; he exhales deeply through his nose. "My dear, whatever gave you the impression that I was sending you away?"

"I don't know." Her voice garbles and her tone is so youthful, it breaks his heart. "I thought you didn't want me anymore. I tried to be good for you, father. I really did."

John struggles to wrap his head around her statement and discovers that he is unable to form a coherent response. Had she only been courteous out of some strange obligation to appease him? It's no wonder they had such a stiff beginning.

"I miss mama," she concedes under her breath, turning her head away with red-rimmed eyes. "I don't wanna lose you, too."

That is a deeply profound thought for someone so young to dwell upon, but John cannot argue against the merits of it. Truth be told, he had left her and his wife with no intention of returning to them when he had initially sailed across the sea. He had realized at some point during his time as an aide-de-camp how terrible that notion was, but he cannot deny that was his aim at the beginning of the war.

He subsequently decides upon his response. "I am here now." She gazes at him with dried tears staining her rosy cheeks. "You are coming with me wherever I go because I confess that I'd rather not lose you, either."

Frances peeks at him through her lashes, thick and dampened from her tears. She shivers involuntarily before relenting, crawling through the doorway and collapsing into his lap. She wraps her arms around his neck, secure and tight. "Promise?" She sounds so broken and uncertain that it punctures his heart like a needle in fabric.

He returns the embrace with fervour, burying his face into her pile of golden curls. "I promise."

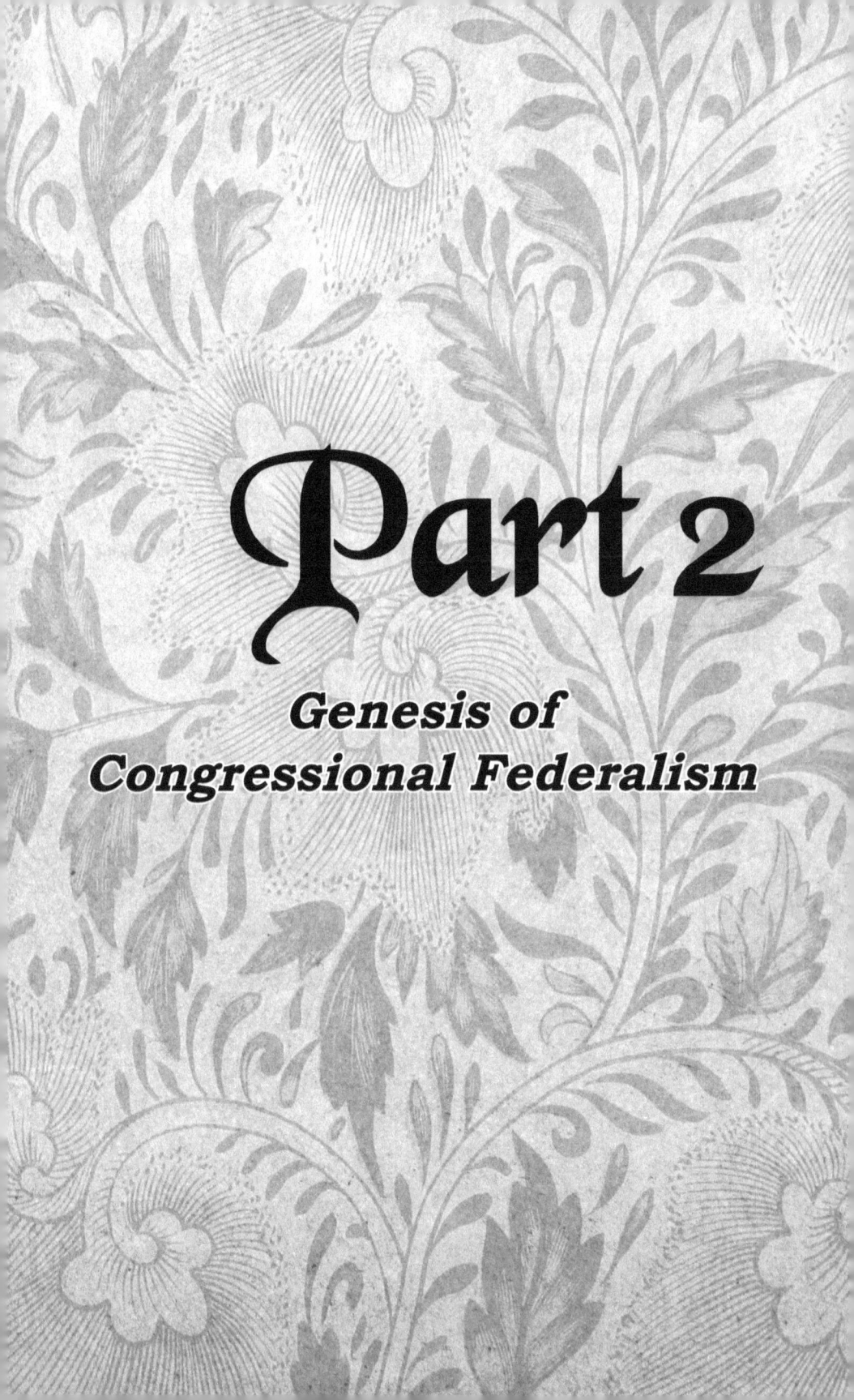

Part 2

Genesis of Congressional Federalism

January 8, 1783

Philadelphia, Pennsylvania

My Dear Uncle

We have finally settled into Papa's Philadelphia home, and I was ultimately able to sit down and write to you since it had already been far too long since my previous letter. Even as domestick as my life may now be, I had still suffocated great hardships with my newfound fatherhood, lawyership, &cetra. I appreciate your birthday wishes to me that I received in October, and I understand now why you also had not heard from my wife—she had passed a year and two months ago *(Patsy says it was yellow fever in early Autumn of 1781)* and I do not know if the guilt regarding my knowledge of this not coming to my attention until Patsy's letter on my birthday will ever depart from my sorrowful soul.

Speaking of your dear niece, Patsy is now permanently residing with my neighbour, Mrs. Rosmund—a kind old woman who reminds me so very much of my mother—and my sister currently works as a seamstress for a Mr. Mulligan in New York City. She was quite adamant about paying her own expenses rather than using my money that comes directly from our father.

And ma petite Frances & I had finally come to some semblance of a mutual understanding recently, and I hope to be a proper father to her—Mr. Hamilton has also taken a liking to her, calling her his ' petite fleur '—and was kind enough to welcome her into ~~our~~ his home for these past few months.

Before we had ventured to ~~Philyd~~ Philadelphia, Patsy insisted on travelling with us initially, but she only laughed me out of ~~my~~ Mr. Hamilton's New York home when I insisted on using this time to grow with Frances on our own—she had persisted that I would fail to control my own child without her presence as a ' buffer between us '—whatever the hell that entails. I consider this notion to be highly offensive and I vowed to not write to her for any assistance out of pure stubborn will against her lack of faith in my ability to be a proper father for my own ~~fucking~~ child.

Mr. Hamilton and I passed our bar exams and now are expected to serve in congress. I hope I may do you proud, My Dear Uncle, and I hope you are well-abled to visit soon. If not, I will have to put time aside to see you, myself. ~~Every day I live on with my dearest family is a cherished separation between myself and that god-forsaken war. I cannot sleep most nights, many of my dreams entailing a gruesome display of~~

My shoulder has healed considerably, yet it still tires now as I reach the end of this letter. I must bid you adieu and I hope to hear from you soon.

Do not forget to write to yr. most affectionate ~~son~~
nephew,

*John Lauren*s

PS. It has come to my attention that my daughter's birthday is on the 11th of January and Patsy decided that now was the best time to inform me on this—a few days before the date—and she had treated this as an afterthought at the end of a letter! ' Oh, by the way, dear brother, do not forget your daughter's birthday! ' To supply more wood to the flames erupting around me, Mr. Hamilton's birthday happens to fall upon that very same date. This coincidence must surely be some profoundly ineffable jest from God, Himself, as I am left to play this Jeu de follie. I send my best regards and beg of you to pray for me as I struggle to appease both my daughter and dearest friend on the very same ~~goddamn~~ day!

Chatpter 6

Philadelphia, Pennsylvania
Friday, January 10, 1783

THE SUN'S RAYS SHINE THROUGH THE
frosted windows of the study in the Philadelphia
mansion. John kneels in front of the safe inside his
father's study that he and Alexander have taken over
for their work. He opens it and shuffles through the
three-hundred dollars, adding forty-five in his purse
for his errands and writing down his withdrawal in the
accounting book. He seals the safe up and hurries down
the stairs.

"In a rush to be somewhere?" Hamilton asks with
a warm chuckle from the parlour as Laurens drapes his
cloak over his shoulders.

"I have a few errands to run before supper," John

explains as he finishes tying his cloak strings. "I will return for supper."

Alexander places his travel writing desk down to stand and approach John. "Would you like me to wait until your return to start preparing supper?"

"No, you may start without me," John replies quickly as he puts on his leather boots. "Keep a close eye on Frances while I am out?"

"Of course," Alexander replies with a curt nod.

As John stands up to leave, he catches sight of Alexander's lips, lingering for a moment too long before hurrying out of the estate.

***

John stares vacantly through the display case, his eyebrows furrowing at the jewelry shimmering in the sunlight beaming through the shop window. He blinks and readjusts himself when the shopkeeper comes through the back door carrying a small box.

"You are in luck, sir. I still had this floral necklace in stock. I hope it will do?" The jeweller asks as he places the box upon the counter and opens it, revealing a silver chain necklace with a lavender flower pendant dangling from the chain.

John smiles and nods, looking at the man. "It's perfect. How much do I owe you?"

The man considers him for a moment, drumming his fingers upon the wooden counter thoughtfully. "One-hundred should suffice."

John scoffs incredulously. "That much for such a small piece of jewelry?"

"Either you give me that or you don't get the necklace."

John glowers at the man as he shoves his hand into his pocket to procure his purse. The man gives a slimy grin as John hands him the desired amount, grateful to have added the extra money to his purse earlier.

"I hope she enjoys the necklace, sir."

John nods with a terse jaw and grabs the little box, putting it into his pocket with his purse. He briskly retreats from the store and strides down the bustling streets of Philadelphia, rubbing his hands together aggressively to keep warm in the harshly cold January afternoon. Snow lightly falls and he nearly slips on a frozen puddle as he makes a sudden turn down a side street.

He goes through the list of items in his head required for tomorrow as he continues to walk, unwilling to slow down even as he slips again.

A gift for Frances, check.

A gift for Alexander, check.

A hired chef for the day to make grand meals, check.

A cake for—

Goddamn! John frantically ponders over the cake. He had not considered such a delicate detail; he will require two cakes, perhaps? Would purchasing one cake for two people be the wrong thing?

John has also failed to mention to either Frances or Alexander that their birthdays fall upon the very same day. Why he chose not to disclose this information to either of them, he will never know. He wanted to surprise them, he remembers. But he worries that he will get this entirely wrong.

As his father's home can be viewed in the threshold, he slips yet again and falls on his bosom with a disgruntled groan. He struggles to ignore the soreness in his rear and the damp patch on his breeches as he attempts to stand up with a low grunt. His attempts, of course, fail miserably and he falls down again.

"Fuck!"

"Are you alright, sir?"

John snaps his head around to gape bashfully at the young woman approaching him from the street on his right.

"I swear I am typically far more coordinated than this," he blurts exasperatingly.

She smiles with reserved amusement. "Is that so?"

He returns the expression. "Aye. Do I appear to be a liar, ma'am?"

"Miss," she corrects swiftly, offering a hand. "You may call me Miss Valenfort."

John accepts her proffered hand and she helps him stand up, this time staying up and stepping gently away from the black ice. "Mr. Laurens. Thank you for your assistance."

"You're most certainly welcome, Mr. Laurens." She abruptly pulls her hand from his and shyly tucks a strand of her chestnut hair behind her ear.

John shoves his hands in his pockets and nods curtly. "Farewell."

She echoes his phrase politely and they both part ways rather sheepishly. As John nears the property entrance of his father's home, he hears a distant, "wait!" He turns his head to see her smiling at him from across the street. "Will we ever meet again, Mr. Laurens?"

He leans his arm against the brick wall on the edge of the property and smiles. "Mayhaps." He does not linger, turning quickly and retreating down the snowy yard leading to the front door.

Upon entry, he is greeted with jovial laughter echoing through the house and the aroma of stew cooking in the kitchen. He smiles softly, closing the door as quietly as possible, hanging up his cloak and hat before tiptoeing towards the back of the large estate. He peeks through the open kitchen door and leans on the wooden frame, admiring the sight.

Frances stands on a wooden stool with a humorously large apron over her dress and stirs the contents of the pot with a wooden spatula, using both hands. Alexander stands behind her with his arm hovering across her back, not touching, but simply there as a precaution in case she falls. He looks into the pot with a wide grin and adds more spices into it, chuckling as Frances whispers something in his ear.

John's heart thumps offbeat and his cheeks begin to hurt from the constant grin upon his features. Alexander turns his head slightly to put the spice on the large wooden counter behind him and pauses as his eyes interlock with John's.

"Ah, I did not hear you come in. We're making the classic Eleanor Laurens stew, with some helpful advice from our sous chef here." He winks at Frances and she scoffs.

"You're the sous chef, Mr. Hamilton. If not for me, you'd fail miss-ah-bly."

John laughs and Alexander gasps theatrically.

"You wound me, petite fleur!" He turns completely to saunter towards John, patting her head on his way. "And as creative as that pronunciation may be, I believe it is typically said as miserably, dear girl."

"Mis-er-ah-bly?"

"Aye, excellent!" Alexander says proudly. He bumps his hip against John's as he approaches him, grinning widely. "So, have you finished your errands for the day?"

"I have," John replies, unheedingly reaching out to rest his hands upon Alexander's hips. He stops short of touching him when he remembers where they presently stand and reluctantly pulls his hands back to his sides. He turns his attention to Frances briefly to see she is still preoccupied with stirring the soup as valiantly as her thin arms will allow her.

"Well, that's good then, since we could use your help after supper." Alexander steps back and leans against the opposite end of the doorway, crossing his arms and legs casually.

"Whatever do you require me for?"

"Laundry day," Hamilton replies dryly.

John groans, rolling his head back against the frame. He puffs an amused breath through his nose as Frances giggles at him. "Speaking of, I ruined my cloak, coat, and breeches today by slipping on ice."

"Oh really? Are you alright?"

"Aye. A kind woman helped me up when I could not stand on my own." Alexander and Frances laugh at this revelation and John grumbles, retreating from the kitchen. "Oh piss off, it was slippery and I am far too accustomed to the South Carolinian heat!"

***

John's arms currently tire as he scrubs his filthy breeches against the waterboard in the washing basin; the flower necklace tucked discreetly into his wardrobe upstairs. He wipes the sweat from his forehead with his rolled-up sleeve before continuing to scrub relentlessly.

His mind wanders as he carries the repetitive and arduous task, mulling over the past week. It has been rather exhausting, to say the least. The two men begin work in Congress on Monday; however, moving from one state to another shockingly requires an entire week of unpacking and settling themselves into their much larger dwelling. Frances had taken to exploring the home with sparkling eyes and nearly falling as she ran around sharp corners, worrying John greatly.

Even as she excitedly explored the large home, John cannot shake off the dusted memories of confine-ment and claustrophobia linked to this house. Alexander had been supportive and accommodating during their transition, staying in the room across the hall for John's peace of mind and protecting Frances' proprietary.

All he can fantasize about in the night is Alexander; his gentle hands and chapped lips caressing his scarred skin, easing his tensions and bringing him to euphoria.

Darkness envelops the skies as he finishes with his breeches, squeezing them out and passing them off to Frances who eagerly hangs them up on the clothesline behind them.

"Shall we call it for the eve?" Alexander suggests with folded arms.

"Please? I am far beyond fatigued."

"Your father is a dramatic man," Alexander muses lightly to the small girl snapping the final clip on the breeches hanging upon the clothesline. "He was a spoiled and pampered little boy, not very accustomed to washing his own clothing."

"You bite your tongue, sir!" John says with no ill intent, his tired smile enveloping his features. They seem to fall into a dream-like trance as they stare at each other with soft smiles. Alexander appears tranquil and cozy as he leans against the wall, his eyes wandering over John's entire body, setting the blonde man's skin ablaze with the trail of those deep violet eyes.

There's something unspoken between them as they simply admire the view of one another, noticing fading scars and fresh wrinkles appearing around tired eyes.

Frances yawns as she steps down from the stool, snapping the two men from their daze. "I'm very sleepy."

John clears his throat and stands abruptly, unrolling his sleeves and buttoning the cuffs to distract his wandering mind. He silently curses himself for allowing such a vulnerable moment to overtake him whence his soon-to-be six-year-old daughter stands only a metre away.

"You know the drill, sweetheart. Upstairs to your room and I will meet you when you are dressed in your nightclothes," he whispers, resting his palm upon her shoulder and leaning down to press a quick peck upon the crown of her head.

She looks up at him with wide eyes. "Could you read me a story tonight, father?"

John hesitates, flickering his gaze to Alexander who proffers a gentle quirk of the lips. "I don't believe we have anything you would like me to read to you."

"I have something!" Hamilton proclaims, springing out of the room.

Frances and John exchange peculiar looks before he leads her out of the washing room. They slowly venture up the stairs and Frances enters her room whilst John searches for Alexander.

John finds him in the study —in the midst of tucking away The Iliad with skittish fingers— and watches with fond amusement as Alexander continues to search the bookshelf with great vigour. He rubs his chin in a ponder, his body illuminated with a lit oil lamp upon his desk behind him, setting his auburn locks ablaze in the low light.

"What could you possibly own that Frances would enjoy?"

Alexander ignores him as he squints at each book before letting out a breathy, "ah-ha! There you are!" The book he pulls out causes John to take pause.

Gulliver's Travels. Such a simple book, one that John had nearly forgotten about until his eyes lay upon it in Alexander's hands. Memories of stolen kisses in a barn rush through the forefront of John's mind and his breath catches in his throat as Alexander looks over at him with a heavy gaze.

"This book is probably my favourite. I am certain she will love it," Alexander says whilst handing John the book. He opens it to the front page and brushes his fingers across the short note.

'To my dearest, Alexander. I am enthralled to have known you this past year and I pray to know you for many more.

Yr. most affectionate, John Laurens. 1778.'

He examines Alexander's eyes. "You kept it?"

"Why wouldn't I?" Alexander replies incredulously.

John looks back at the book. "Writing a note on the inside cover was probably a mistake."

"Perhaps, but we have always been rather affectionate in front of others," he says, shrugging indifferently.

John lingers on the year written after his note upon the inside cover. "God, has it truly been five years since I bought this for you?"

"Time flies when you're with the ones you love," Hamilton murmurs, looping his arms around John's neck. Laurens leans down against his will; his heart is full again now that Hamilton is touching him after three months of careful separation.

"Alex..." John ducks his head away, nervously observing the door.

"It only be us here," Alexander whispers, turning John's face to interlock their gazes. "No more watchful eyes lingering within our presence. Only you and I..."

John places a gentle hand on Alexander's hip and pulls him closer. He bends down and tilts his head, nearly about to press his lips against—

"Father? Where are you?" Frances calls from the hallway, startling the two men. John swipes Alexander's arms away from him mere moments before she bursts through the doorway. John tries to ignore the distraught look upon his lover's face as he forces a placid smile towards his daughter.

"There you are!" She giggles brightly.

"Mr. Hamilton found a book for me to read to you," John declares, waving said object as he approaches her.

"Will you join us for storytime, Mr. Hamilton?" she asks sweetly, bunching her hands shyly into her nightgown.

John looks at Alexander expectantly. He sighs with a warm smile, showing no sign of upset from moments ago, putting on an eerily solid mask for the small girl. "Of course, if that's what you wish, petite fleur."

She smiles toothily and Alexander grabs the oil lamp before the trio retreats from the study. She runs giddily into her room as they trail behind her. Frances struggles to climb the large bed, her left leg dangling off the edge until finally rolling onto her back. John tucks her into the sheets and lays along the side, leaning his back against the headboard. Alexander lingers in the doorway, leaning casually against the wall and watching them fondly.

She looks at the cover and chews her lip with

concentration. "Gull-eh-vur's trav-ells?"

"Good girl," John enthuses.

She smiles proudly. "What's the story about?"

"A man who travels across the sea, if memory serves correctly?" John looks to Alexander for his input and the man nods. "We will have to read it slowly since it is too long for one night."

"I can listen to all of it tonight! I swear!"

"Well, if that be the case, I should sit down," Hamilton says whilst pacing to the chair on the opposite side of the room.

"Sit closer so you can see better, Mr. Hamilton!" Frances insists, patting the other side of her bed invitingly.

Hamilton does not say anything; he swallows, staring at her with his fingers barely grazing the back of the wooden chair. Alexander cautiously approaches the bed and Frances wiggles closer to John to allow more room; an endearing motion as the bed is quite large enough for the three of them. His eyes sparkle with something John cannot trace as he hesitantly sits on the bed, resting his back against the headboard and not saying a word.

John opens the book to the introduction and holds it out so his two companions may see the contents of the book. He begins to read and is terribly awkward at the start, but slowly eases into it. Occasionally, Frances will ask what a certain word means and will attempt to say it until she gets it correct. John manages to produce chuckles from Frances and Alexander with his character voices and even begins adding a performative element behind the emotions of each line of dialogue, making the story as immersive as possible.

He does not recognize himself getting lost in the story until a hand lightly taps the corner of the book to capture his attention. John looks over to find Frances fast asleep before he has completed chapter two and smiles warmly at the sight of her curled up against himself.

Alexander gently presses his finger to his lips before carefully slipping off the bed. John places the book upon the bedside table and carefully untucks himself from his daughter. He straightens her sheets and snuggles her under the blankets before leaning to press a kiss to her forehead. He slides his socked feet across the floor to retreat as quietly as possible. Alexander leads them out of the room with the oil lamp in hand.

The two split off to their respective rooms, but John hesitates at his door. The heavy anchor that sinks whenever he separates from Hamilton tugs at his heart and causes him to face the back of his retreating form.

"Alex?" He halts, turning around to acknowledge Laurens; their faces lit by the lone oil lamp in Hamilton's hand. "I do not believe I thanked you for being so patient with Frances these past months. You have been nothing short of incredible."

"There be no thanks required, mon amour." He chuckles warmly. "She is a marvellous little one. Vastly intelligent and far too witty for one so very youthful."

"Aye..." John grips the doorframe, flickering his gaze to Frances' room down the hall. "I also wish to thank you for your patience with me. I did not intend to distance myself from you but that was precisely what I did and it was unfair to you."

Hamilton hums thoughtfully and John looks at him again. "Well, your reasoning for doing so was valid so I cannot hold it against you." He sighs. "But thank you. Your actions did not truly require forgiveness but I admit that it pained me so to be apart from you."

"Believe me when I say that I understand you deeply. I suppose you were right when we spoke earlier," John whispers. "We finally do not have a watchful eye lingering upon us here..." his voice drops an octave. "And Frances is currently asleep." He swallows, resisting the urge to rub his neck habitually. "Would you stay with me tonight?"

Alexander's expression shifts subtly in the candlelight; a simple quirk of his lips. "It would be my pleasure, Jack."

John reaches out to grab Alexander's hand, excitement causing his heart to flutter, and deliberately leads him into his room.

Alexander closes the door behind him before discarding the oil lamp on the bedside table. His fingers linger on the handle as John approaches from behind and gently loops his arms securely around Alexander's abdomen; Laurens nestles into his neck and Hamilton eagerly tilts his head to give him better access. Laurens presses his lips upon the salty smooth skin there, smiling when the action elicits a low moan from his lover.

John nibbles on the skin and licks it before dragging his lips lower, grazing his feather-light fingers up Alexander's arm to nudge the fabric away from the nape of his neck. Hamilton sighs dreamily and leans back into Laurens, twisting until their chests are pressed securely against each other. He grazes his fingers along John's biceps and follows the trail to his cheeks, setting John's skin in his path aflame.

John tucks a loose curl out of Alex's face before leaning down to capture his lips with his own. They move in tandem, staying as quiet as humanly capable amidst their searing passion. Hands explore familiar curves and edges, untying cravats and unbuttoning waistcoats languidly.

John nudges Alexander to the large bed, watching him sprawl and bounce with his landing. His husband in spirit watches with hooded lids as John carefully unbuttons his sleeve cuffs; Hamilton's eyes are dark with a magnificent blend of affection and lust.

"You need to hurry, my beloved."

"Patience is a virtue, Alex."

He scoffs, hooking a leg around John's waist to pull him closer to the bed. "I am far from virtuous right now." John flushes and fumbles clumsily with his second sleeve button. "You fly beyond fate's control and leave me utterly at your mercy."

John grunts impatiently and pulls his shirt over his head, tearing it carelessly from the confines of his hand and promptly ignoring the clatter of the sleeve button impacting the floor. He tosses the white cotton shirt away and leans over Alexander to steal a kiss.

It be far less chaste than their kiss moments ago as they hungrily nip at their plump red flesh and consume each other's breath. Alexander's passion sinks into John's skin with desperate fingers scratching his exposed back for purchase.

Alexander gasps as if he is nearly drowning in a merciless sea with high winds knocking him defenceless, and he lays his head back in pure ecstasy. "Please," he whimpers.

"Tell me whatever you desire, my dear boy," John whispers hotly into his ear, smirking proudly whence his lover squirms relentlessly and yerks his hips upward in search for John's. "I am at your mercy tonight."

"Touch me, John," he begs breathlessly. "Touch me for every time you wished you could these past months and take me to the stars."

John lifts Alexander's hips and pushes him completely onto the bed so that he may climb on top of him entirely. With a low growl, he ghosts his fingers along Alexander's shivering body until reaching the waistband of his breeches. His own hips buck wantonly at the mere sight of the tented fabric below him. Laurens suavely untucks his dear boy's shirt and relinquishes the melodic moans emanating from the man below him. Hamilton's back arches, allowing smooth access to remove his shirt with graceful fluidity and tosses it away.

"John." The name is spoken like a subconscious prayer as it slips past Alexander's lips; he twists his head over in delight and opens his eyes to watch John. His pupils are dilated and his eyelids flutter with ardour as John runs his fingers down the chest of his lover.

Hamilton giggles abruptly as Laurens reaches a sensitive spot on his sides and he shushes him with a gentle kiss upon his glossy lips. Hamilton hooks his arms around John's neck and pulls him closer, causing him to collapse onto him rather clumsily. They erupt into soft chuckles as they adjust themselves until they are kneeling in front of each other upon the bed.

John pulls his stockings off and watches hungrily as Alexander does the very same. They ball up their stockings and toss them carelessly over the edge of the bed before advancing on each other.

"I need you," Alexander declares breathlessly as John overcrowds him yet again, caging his head between his arms as Hamilton's russet hair lands upon the pillow. John laces his fingers into the flaming hair and pulls out the ribbon, allowing the soft strands to halo his lover's face.

Alexander runs his fingers along John's arms until they capture his soft locks of honey hair, partially untying the queue and tugging him down to press a languid kiss upon his lips. John thinks of every fantasy he craved during their forced celibacy and releases the final chains confining his heart with fervency.

He needlessly unlaces Hamilton's breeches and tugs them down, no longer able to pretend he has patience. Alexander lifts his hips to aid in the removal of his breeches and small clothes in one fell swoop. John carelessly tosses the garments over his shoulder, uncaring where they land as he dives down to press hot kisses on Alexander's exposed hip.

His fiery-haired lover wiggles and moans softly with each press of John's lips and every gentle caress. John pulls back to admire the view of his beloved as he begins unbuttoning his own breeches.

"Look at you," John says breathlessly, smiling with great fondness over his sweetheart. "So beautiful and vulnerable as you lay impatiently beneath me."

Alexander responds with a low-pitched whine; he chews his bottom lip as his hooded gaze follows the leisure removal of John's breeches and small clothes. After all clothing has been discarded, Alexander grabs John's bicep with the fragility of someone carrying fine porcelain.

"Joue-moi comme une symphonie, mon chéri," Alexander whispers huskily as he spreads his legs invitingly.

John groans, bowing his head to lick a stripe up Alexander's neck. He wiggles his fingers up the opposing side of his neck and taps his dear boy's lips. Alexander eagerly takes his fingers in his mouth and sucks obediently, keeping their lust-blown eyes latched with one another. John pulls his fingers away and kisses Alexander sweetly, being gentle with his ministrations. Hamilton relaxes with him and his grunts morph into breathless panting as he rolls his hips for more friction that is currently unattainable.

"John!" he pleas desperately, shoving his head into the pillow. "I need more!"

"Hush, darlin'," John coos serenely into his ear. "As much as I enjoy making you sing for me, we must be discreet."

Alexander is far beyond modest as he growls and grips John's loose queue to tug on it. John is unable to repress the low moan that escapes past his lips as his head jolts backwards, the icy sensation of the pull rolling down his entire spine. Alexander leans up to press his lips to his earlobe. "I challenge you to also remain quiet with me during our game of backgammon."

John manages to make not a sound as he pushes Alexander down and rolls his hips against him. Hamilton slaps a hand over his mouth as his moan comes out louder than expected. He arches his back as John aligns himself and takes him with great delicacy.

"Fuck," Alexander whispers into his palm as John rocks into him at an excruciatingly slow pace.

"I missed you," John confesses into his lover's neck, his hips picking up speed. "I longed for you every single night as I lay alone with nothing but my vivid imagination of you" —Alexander cries out into his hand as John hits that sweet spot— "I cannot get enough of you."

"Oui," Alexander moans, burying his head into the pillow with vigor. "S'il te plaît, Jack! J'ai besoin de plus!"

"Pour toi mon amour, I will do anything."

John moves faster and throws his head back in ecstasy as his entire body tingles with euphoria. His blood pumps heavily as his heartbeat picks up its pace with his movements. His arms shudder as the muscles grow tired but he pushes further, chasing the coil in his lower regions as it approaches its snapping point.

Alexander mumbles French and English obscenities into the pillow as well as a repetitive string of, "yes, yes, yes!" with each thrust, encouraging John to maintain his rigorous pace.

"Foutre! John, don't stop!"

John barely manages to form a response, his entire body trembling with adrenaline. "Mmm— merde! —M'close..."

"I need" —John begins stroking Alexander in tandem with his thrusts. "Yes" —Alexander arches and claws at John's back— "yes! John!" he drags the word as his muscles spasm with his exhilarating release. The sight of his seed spilling upon his stomach triggers John's coil to snap; he shudders intensely as he collapses onto Alexander, muffling his blissful groan in the juncture of his neck and shoulder. John's hips stutter and twitch before he practically melts into Alexander's glistening skin.

They pant heavily as they come down from their elysian high. John pulls away with a grunt and rolls off of Alexander to lay on his back, staring vacantly at the ceiling for a moment before gaining his bearings and rolling off the mattress.

John grabs a rag from the washbasin and chuckles warmly as Alexander watches him with sleepy interest. "You like what you see?" John inquires as he leans over to clean a sated and spent Alexander with great care.

"You are so beautiful," Alex mumbles with an adoring grin. "So good to me, so gentle..." Laurens places a chaste kiss upon Hamilton's lips before pulling away to toss the rag in the unlit fireplace. He lays on the mattress, tucking them under the sheets and snuggling closer to his dear boy. His body hums with delight; even his stiff shoulder rejuvenates as he lingers within the tranquillic moment.

"I most certainly missed this," Alexander admits with a breathy laugh. He curls up against John and wraps his arms around him, running his fingers through the soft hair upon his chest. "It's been so long since you've taken me as such."

"Aye," John hums whilst wrapping his buried arm to securely hold him closer. He nuzzles his nose into Alexander's sweat-coated hair and breathes in his scent. "Tu sais que je t'aime beaucoup?"

"Oui, et moi aussi, mon bien-aimé," Hamilton replies sleepily. "Merci...for staying with me tonight."

"I regret my decision to not do this sooner." Hamilton snorts with good faith at Laurens. "I had forgotten how you can so effortlessly relax all stress within me."

Hamilton tilts his head up to gaze into John's eyes; the thin outer rim of his pupils exposing the colours of his soul. "I will gladly bear the role of your burden remover if it involves more frequency of our nightly activities."

"Nightly?"

"Why not?" Hamilton muses with a shrug. "It will be no different than the war."

John considers him carefully before relenting; he is not certain whether his conclusion be made out of cautious logic or due to his post-coital state. "Alright, Mr. Hamilton. I'll see to it that we continue these discreet nightly endeavours. For our health, of course."

"Aye, of course," Alexander chuckles. "For the greater good of our manhood," he adds, winking cheekily.

"I take it back. That was terrible, even for you," John jests with feigned irritation.

"Oh, piss off. It rhymed!" Alexander quips, causing John to rumble into a low chuckle. Alexander smiles and snuggles closer upon John's chest, sighing with content.

Alexander yawns theatrically. "Bonne nuit, mon cher."

"Good night, Alex," John whispers before leaning over to blow away the flame of the oil lamp and succumbing to his drooping eyelids.

Within the inky void of John's mind, he ponders over the checklist for his family's collective birthdays tomorrow. He considers their setup and is rather content as he lay with his husband wrapped securely over him. With the daytime belonging to Frances and America and the night belonging to Alexander, John finds he is grateful for this new chapter of their lives.

What once was a prison for John has been demolished into a blissful paradise; nothing can surely hinder their family anymore...right?

Chatpter 7

JOHN BLINKS DREARILY AND SQUINTS AT the shadows of the dark room, his mind hazy from sleep. He attempts to sit up but finds himself locked in place, unable to wriggle, twitch, or even speak. John breathes quickly through his nose as his heart rate picks up; he can't move. Why can he not move? A sinking weight upon his chest pushes him deeper into the mattress and he squeezes his eyes shut, silently praying for this occurrence to pass.

"You left me," a hauntingly familiar voice whispers into his ear. He has not heard her voice in years. "You left me for dead and planned on leaving our child alone in this world."

John tries to reply but his jaw is sealed tightly shut, defenceless in his frozen state between wakefulness and slumber. He manages to whimper through the back of his throat but is eminently left unheard in his pleas. A large, slimy snake slides down his chest; he grunts as his fingers refuse to wiggle. John's heartbeat picks up its pace as the snake coils around his entire body, slowly suffocating him.

"John," his deceased wife hisses through the snake tongue. "How could you abandon your family for your sinful desires?"

A sudden dim light to his right causes him to blink owlishly at the creature over him.

"John, you don't deserve to breathe," it snarls with venom leaking into his blood. He tries to squirm and scream but nothing comes of it; only paralyzed fear.

"You will pay for your—"

"John, breathe with me. You are going to be alright," his dear boy's voice instructs calmly, interrupting the sinister voice. John listens to his lovers' breathing and follows him, even though he is unable to see him. "Good. That's good. Breathe with me. It will pass. I won't leave you."

The serpent-like beast above him slowly fades away like fog in the wind as Alexander's beautiful face comes into greater focus. Hamilton rubs Laurens' chest soothingly, smiling patiently at him. "I am right here, John. You will be alright." John finally manages to twitch his fingers and Alexander rubs his arms encouragingly. "That's it. Almost there."

John breathes slow and deep as he takes his time forcibly twitching his limbs. The more he can move, the clearer the room around him becomes, and he sighs with relief when he finally manages to caress his hand up Alexander's arm.

"Alex," he finally croaks and the man in question leans down to place a gentle kiss upon his cheek before pulling away.

"You're safe now. Your body was still paralyzed with sleep. That is all."

"It felt so real," John whispers hoarsely. "I felt her—I felt the serpent squeezing me."

"Well, I scared the beast away," Alexander replies with a warm smile.

"I am damned," John sobs, covering his mouth as he realizes his rise in volume. "It was the serpent of temptation from Eden with my wife's voice. I was—"

"It was only a dream," Alexander coos soothingly. "Sometimes dreams can spill into the world when we wake."

John sits up slowly and rubs his face. "But she is dead—that is quite real—and it's my fault."

Alexander holds his right shoulder and squeezes it, massaging the tense muscle. "It wasn't your fault she died, John. You didn't know."

"I should have been there for her. I should have been there for both of them," John cries. "What good am I worth if I cannot protect them."

"You do not give yourself enough credit for what you're worth," Hamilton replies soothingly. "You cannot undo what has already occurred, my dear. That be an impossible burden to carry. The best you can do is this" —he gestures vaguely to the room— "coming home from the war, taking good care of your daughter, and continuing the good fight for America's inception. That is enough."

John wipes a stray tear away, refusing to allow himself this weakness. "I'm sorry."

"Why the fuck are you apologizing to me when you have not done any wrongdoings?"

John looks out the window, seeing the purple skies crawl into pink as dawn breaks past the horizon. "I already destroyed your birthday with my melancholy and the sun has barely begun to rise."

Alexander squints, confused. "My birthday...?" He looks outside for a brief moment before gasping at John. "Wait, what day is it?"

John raises a confused brow. "January eleventh. It's Saturday."

Alexander blinks owlishly before snorting

amusedly. "Bloody hell, I lost track of the days again. I had completely forgotten."

"How does one simply forget their own birthday?" John asks incredulously.

Alexander shrugs nonchalantly and places a kiss on John's shoulder. "Well, you are rather distracting. After a night like that, I am bound to forget anything."

John flushes deeply and notices their nakedness, remembering the previous night's events. He covers his face when Alexander smiles playfully at his reddening skin. "You blush, sir!"

"I do not!"

Hamilton rubs small circles into John's back and pecks his ear with a low chuckle. "I can see the flush on your skin enveloping your chest, dear."

"Oh, hush. Don't mock me." John peaks through his fingers, utterly embarrassed.

"I would never mock you," Alexander whispers in a gravelly voice. He gently pries Laurens' hands away from his face and grins. "You are magnificent when you blush. Truly the most alluring man I have ever seen."

John rolls his eyes and falls on his back, letting out an exasperated breath. Alexander crawls on top of him and smirks deviously when John's flush darkens. "I see you are distracting me, sir."

"Am I?" Alexander gawks with faux bafflement.

John sighs, rubbing his sore head and casting his gaze to the wall opposite the bed. Alexander's amusement simmers away and he lightly nudges John's chin so that they may gaze at one another again.

"If you are still haunted by your past demons, John, know that I will be here to chase them away for you." Hamilton places a chaste kiss upon Laurens' lips, sighing in content as John reciprocates. "Happy birthday to me," Alexander whispers to himself between kisses, grinning like a lovesick fool as John spoils him with kisses on every freckle upon his cheeks and down to his shoulders. Hamilton begins to giggle fruitfully as Laurens trails his fingers up his sides.

"You know, I believe this will be your first proper birthday we will spend together since the beginning of the war," Laurens muses as he wraps his arms securely around the blissful man on his lap.

"Oh, yes. You're correct," Hamilton replies. "Seventy-eight was my first and last birthday with you until now since we had been parted around that time every other year between."

John frowns as he chases his thought. "You were twenty-one that year, I believe?"

"Mhmm." Alexander nuzzles his nose against the nape of John's neck and smiles when John sharply intakes a sudden gasp of pleasure. "And today I am twenty-six."

John chuckles to himself as he realizes Alexander and Frances are a perfect twenty years apart from each other; an even number.

"What's so amusing? The fact that I am twenty-six?"

"Nay, not amusing but rather ironic in nature," John replies without thinking. "I was only thinking how you and Frances are precisely twenty years apart. She turns six today."

John does not realize his error until Alexander pulls himself away, frowning in bewilderment. "Pardon?"

Damn.

John silently peps himself into not panicking as he nervously chews his bottom lip. "Right, I've been meaning to tell you. Patsy informed me—in an off-handed letter I might add—that Frances was born on January eleventh. What are the odds of that?"

Alexander climbs off of John entirely, his bewildered expression morphing into one of rage. "Why have you waited until now to tell me this?"

Laurens blinks with wide eyes, blindly reaching out to grab Hamilton's hand. "I wanted to surprise you both and did not wish to risk either of you figuring out what I may have planned—"

Hamilton pulls his hand away sharply. "What the hell, John? That is no excuse!"

Laurens frowns. "You're upset."

"Aye, John, I fucking am!" Hamilton throws the blanket off and slides off the bed to start pacing about the room, not necessarily in search of anything, until nearly tripping over one of their loose articles of clothing. He bends over and drapes the shirt over himself before pacing again.

"I'm sorry. I seem to have made a terrible choice," John says wearily. "I did not believe you would be so upset about this. I did not choose her birth date, let alone become aware of it until a few days previous."

"It not be that," Hamilton replies with a dismissive wave of his hand. He stops, pivots, and paces in the other direction. "If I had known, I would have retrieved a gift for her!"

Laurens gapes in surprise at this admission. "Why would you want to gift her something? I already covered that."

Alexander stops, glowering at him. "I wanted to—" he cuts himself short, flushes, and folds his arms as he turns away to sulk out the window.

Alexander glances at John over his shoulder, his eyes sparkling in the fresh sunlight beginning to shine its rays through the window. John does not need to hear his response as his eyes say it all. John slowly slips out of bed and approaches Alexander, unwilling to break eye contact. His lover looks away, gazing beyond the horizon as John embraces him from behind.

"I am truly sorry—for everything," John says. "This morning has been a complete disaster, but I promise to make it up to you." Alexander sighs and leans his back against John's chest. "I'd only wished to give you both a wondrous surprise and I had failed..."

"You did not fail." Alexander turns around, straining his neck to meet John's eyes. "You are a damn fool, but you have not failed. The day has only begun. It's like I said earlier. You cannot change what has already happened. I hope you know not to surprise me with vital information like the date of your daughter's birthday again?"

"Aye. Never again will I keep anything as sensitive as such from you again."

"Nothing, John. You keep nothing from me, and in return, I do the same." Alexander lifts John's right hand and places a firm kiss upon the ring. "Even though we're not married by any law, we must act the part if we shared our vows in spirit."

Laurens nods solemnly and lowers his head shamefully. Hamilton holds his face up slightly so that their eyes may meet yet again. "I love you, John. Do not forget that we are partners."

"Marriage isn't exactly a partnership," John replies with a slanted frown.

"Our marriage is not traditional, so we can decide our own rules," Alexander states defiantly. "And I say it be a partnership."

John smiles and leans down to rest his head against his dear boy's. "Alright."

Hamilton sighs with satisfaction. "Now, what did you have in that beautiful mind of yours for our shared birthday?"

John smiles into Alexander's hair. "You'll see soon enough."

***

John tries desperately to reassure himself everything is fine when, after getting dressed, a young messenger boy comes to the door to alert him that the cook he hired has fallen ill and will not be able to attend for his services today. John smiles and thanks the boy before closing the door and dropping his polite façade to panic.

He glances up the stairs when Alexander trots down the steps, buttoning up his sleeve cuffs with casualty. He pauses when he sees John's face.

"What? What is it? What's wrong?"

John forces the same smile he gave the messenger boy. "Nothing at all. Everything is going according to plan. All we have to do is prepare breakfast and wake up Frances."

Alexander raises a suspicious brow but nods slowly. "Were you originally going to cook by yourself? That would have been a disaster."

John laughs. "Ah, yes. That is why there is no need to worry. I have you to help me." Alexander frowns at the near-hysterical tone of John's voice.

"I never said I was worried." Alexander finishes buttoning his sleeve and steps entirely off the staircase. "Are you worried?"

"No! I'm not!" John says as he quickly paces towards the kitchen.

"Slow down, John. You're panicking."

"I am not!" John replies as he comes to a halt. Hamilton bumps into him and grunts with the rough collision. "My apologies," John yelps anxiously, spinning around and placing his hands on Alexander's shoulders. "Are you alright?"

"John, I'm fine," he reassures with a relaxed smile. Hamilton cups John's jaw and strokes his thumb across his cheek tenderly. "You do not need to panic, my dear. We will give her a marvellous birthday."

Laurens nods feebly. "Right, yes."

"You are utterly adorable, you know."

John flushes and turns sharply on his heel to enter the kitchen, Alexander chuckling warmly to himself as he follows.

They use the ingredients John had purchased for this particular day and they prepare the food themselves. They chop up the fruits and put them into bowls before slicing the bread and toasting it in the stone oven. John keeps a keen eye on the bread as Alexander prepares the coffee.

"I have this under control, dear. You wake her up," Hamilton instructs.

John nods obediently and retreats towards the corridor. He turns around one last time and does not miss the way Alexander uncomfortably massages his rear as he reaches for the kettle.

Laurens hesitates in the doorway, frowning. "I've hurt you."

Alexander startles, looking over at John with a sheepish expression. "I thought you left the room."

"Was I too rough with you last night?" John asks gingerly, guilt rising through his chest.

Alexander waves him off. "Don't start with me now. It was the best damn night I've had in a while.

162

Perhaps we could have used a more reliable lubricant but I'll be fine." John raises a brow and Alexander shoos him with a wave of his hands. "I said I'm fine, you fool. Go wake up our daughter."

John freezes at this admission as he watches Alexander return to his task at hand, seemingly unaware of what he had said.

John's head buzzes with a numbing pressure as he turns himself around and begins his trek down the hallway and up the stairs in a dream-like haze. Hamilton considers her to be of his own kinship. Was this a conscious choice of words or was it an accidental slip of the tongue? Regardless, he considers Frances to be his own child. John nearly collapses in front of Frances' door but holds himself up by leaning against the wall. He nearly bursts into tears as a wave of emotions courses through his veins and shakes him to the core.

Our daughter.

John sniffles and sighs before proceeding onwards, storing that thought away to unpack on another day. He opens the door and smiles instinctually at the sight of her sprawled across her bed with her sheets bundled at the edge, snoring softly with drool leaking from her parted lips. Her hair is a mess and her limbs are scattered in a very uncomfortable display, her left arm being entirely submerged under her weight and her hand peeking out behind her.

John carefully approaches her and gently untangles her limbs. She sniffles and groans before rubbing her eyes. "Good morning," he whispers soothingly as she dramatically scrunches her eyes in displeasure. She reaches blindly for something and John chuckles fondly as he watches her hand search for her blankets that are down by her feet. "It's time to wake up, sweetheart."

"No," she moans, dragging the word with great theatrics.

John hums fondly. "Frances, breakfast is almost ready. You have to get dressed."

"Five more minutes," she mumbles sleepily.

"I'm afraid I've already let you sleep in far later than usual, my sweet girl," John coos gently, leaning over to wipe the drool from her chin with his thumb. He smiles as he lightly shakes her. "Today is a big day after all. Girls who turn six don't fight with their fathers when the morning comes."

Her eyes snap open at this and she smiles widely at him. "You remembered?"

John's smile falls crooked, but he still manages to hold it. "Mhmm. Happy birthday, sweetheart."

Frances sits up so quickly, John is unable to pull his head backwards in time to avoid the harsh smack of their skulls. He wobbles back, grunting and rubbing his head as she flops back onto her pillow, biting her trembling lip as she rubs her sore head.

John begins chuckling and she smiles up at him, mirroring his bright demeanour and laughter. "C'mon, Mr. Hamilton is waiting for us in the kitchen with our breakfast. Let's have you dressed to your best."

She hops giddily out of bed with barely any trait of sleepiness from a minute ago and eagerly bounds towards the wardrobe.

***

Breakfast goes by in a far greater fashion than what John had initially planned. Frances only teases Alexander about the food once which is truly a miracle given her nature. John wonders if she consciously chooses to tease him , if only to hear the rigorous laughter he responds with every time.

The pair of men clean up the mess whilst Frances hops giddily as she looks out the kitchen window. "It's snowing!"

John gazes up through the glass and hums in acknowledgment. "Aye, t'is."

"Can we play outside?"

"We can walk to the park soon, but first we

should finish up here," John replies patiently.

She folds her arms and juts out her lip. "But it's my birthday!"

Alexander snorts out a chortle and John elbows him in the side. "Give us fifteen more minutes, sweetheart. We will clean faster, though, if you help us," he adds pointedly.

"Nobody should have to do chores on their birthday!" she whines.

"Alexander is cleaning," John replies offhandedly.

She scrunches her face in confusion. "So?"

Alexander frowns at John until he realizes his slip of the tongue. "It's also Alexander's birthday, today."

Frances looks at Alexander with wide eyes. "Oh, it is?"

Hamilton smiles. "Aye. Although, I am far older than you, today."

Frances raises a brow. "How old?"

John chuckles as Alexander faces her completely, placing his hands on his hips defiantly. "Twenty-six."

"That's really old."

"Ha!" John bursts into boisterous laughter as Alexander pouts indignantly.

He scoffs. "Your father is older!"

"Oh, don't drag me into this mess!"

Frances giggles. "How old are you, daddy?"

John's breath hitches with great affection. She had never called him such before. For so long they had been stuck under the spell of stiff formalities that the casual nature of calling him an endearing term nearly has him toppling over. "I'm twenty-eight."

Frances makes a twisted face at this admission and John bellows out a hearty laugh. "Woah, you're *both* old!"

"Ouch," Alexander replies, mockingly gripping his chest. "You're one to speak. Six is far older than five in dog years, ma petite fleur."

"Dog years?"

"Aye, in dog years, you would be older than us!"

Frances' face melts into horror as she pats her cheeks. "Oh no, *I'm* old!" Alexander nearly falls over as he bends over the countertop to laugh vigorously at the dramatic sight of Frances acting like a little old lady.

"Alright, that is quite enough of that," John chuckles warmly. "We should finish this task if our birthday girl and boy wish to do other things today that do not involve cleaning our breakfast dishes, hmm?"

Frances shakes her head and Alexander wipes a tear away. "No, I wanna play outside!"

"Frances" —she takes off, giggling as she runs through the estate— "wait!"

Alexander continues chuckling again as they chase her to the front door. John's eyes widen as she opens the door and runs outside in nothing but her shoes and dress. "Frances! Get back inside! We're not dressed properly for the weather!"

Just as they approach the door, John's face is pelted with a snowball.

"You'll have to catch me, old man!" She taunts from a few metres away before giggling brightly.

Alexander proffers a devilish grin and he bounds outside, packing a ball of snow in his palms before whipping it at her in retaliation, causing her to squeal with joy. John shoots an incredulous glare at him.

"Alex!"

"Oh, come now, John. It's only good fun—" he is cut short when a snowball hits his face. John snorts amusedly as Alexander wipes his reddened cheeks and turns his attention towards the little girl sticking her tongue at him from the front garden. "You will find no success in cheating!"

"I can't cheat if there be no rules, Mr. Hamilton!"

Alexander smiles with defiance as he quickly scoops up a large pile of snow. "No rules, you say?"

"Wait!" She giggles and shrieks as he chases her through the snowy garden with his humorously large pile of snow. John bursts into bubbling laughter as Alexander slips and falls on his rear, dropping the snow onto himself.

"You mock me, sir?" Hamilton yells across the garden at the amused Laurens doubling over on the porch.

"No, not at all. For you have made a mockery of yourself, sir!" John replies cheekily. John struggles to catch his breath as he leans against the brick wall, wiping tears from his eyes. He startles when his face is abruptly pelted with a clump of snow.

His skin hurts from the icy-wet sensation and he glares in shock at Alexander as he cackles from his place. John quickly realizes it was not he who had thrown the snow at his face, but his daughter who has an eerily incredible aim. "You hit me with your snow, miss?"

Frances giggles and shakes her head innocently. John grins wickedly with his teeth bared as he bends over to scoop up snow in his hands. She squeals in delight as he arches his arm backward and throws the ball of snow directly at her retreating back. Hamilton stands up and pounces on John, throwing a sloppy snowball at his chest that bursts and melts into his waistcoat. John shivers as his clothes dampen but he ignores the cold as he enthusiastically builds another snowball to throw back at Alexander who dodges it swiftly.

"You think you can hit me, sir?" Alexander boasts pridefully as he swings a snowball at John's arm that be exposed from his rolled-up sleeves. "I am the—"

Alexander's speech cuts short when he is hit in the shoulder with a snowball from his right.

"Excellent aim, sweetheart!" John cheers and Frances grins widely.

"Frances, I thought we were on the same team?" Alexander whines with jovial mirth as he builds another snowball. "It's *our* birthday, not *his*!"

"True, sir!" She beams up at him. "Sorry, dad!" Frances whips a snowball at John and he gasps in horror as another one from Hamilton hits him in the face. Alexander and Frances cheer in victory together before they are cut short by John lifting Alexander from behind. He yelps and Frances giggles rigorously as John plops a pile of snow onto Alexander's head, dampening his auburn curls.

"Put me down, John!" Hamilton yelps between chuckles as John holds him up against his chest.

He laughs into Alexander's shoulder. "No... Not

unless you surrender."

"Never!" Alexander's voice echoes down the streets. "Fanny, avenge me!"

"I'll save you, Mr. Hamilton!" Frances declares with great determination. She grabs a pile of snow and shoves it into John's side before locking her arms around his legs. He wobbles and falls over with wide eyes, grunting painfully as he and Alexander fall onto the snowy ground together. Frances' giggles are infectious as they lay in a pile upon the ground, completely covered head to toe in melting snow.

"I hope I'm not interrupting." An amused feminine voice interrupts their activity from the edge of the property. John snaps his head in the direction of the entryway between the two stone walls bordering the estate and gapes at the woman smiling with delight.

"Miss Valenfort?"

She chuckles respectfully behind her gloved hand as she watches the three of them struggle to stand up. "Hello, Mr. Laurens. I could not help but hear the ruckus emanating from your property and had no choice but to investigate."

He smiles with rosy cheeks, flailing his arms as he awkwardly attempts to pat away the snow from his breeches. "How strange that we keep meeting this way?"

"Aye, sir. You seem to always find your way in the snow whenever we meet," she replies with a knowing smile.

John startles when he hears someone clearing their throat beside him. Hamilton looks between the two with an arched brow whilst Frances tucks herself behind the two of them shyly.

"Oh, this is Miss Valenfort. She was the kind woman who helped me stand from the ice yesterday."

He turns his head to the young woman. "This is my friend Mr. Hamilton, and my daughter, Frances."

"How do you do," she says, politely ducking her head in greeting.

"Enchanté, mademoiselle," Hamilton replies in a sultry tone. John snorts as he gives him a once-over; he is covered head-to-toe in wet snow and his cheeks are rosy and damp.

"Have you noticed, sirs, that you are not properly dressed for the weather?"

John and Alexander examine each other sheepishly. "Aye," John says lamely. "But you see, we had no time to change as this was rather spontaneous."

"I do love a little spontaneousness," she replies with a challenging grin, her brow lifting with defiance. Her voice is laced with something John cannot quite place as she keeps her eyes locked on his. "May I join, perhaps? To even out the playing field?"

"Girls against boys?" Frances calls out, hopping on her feet; the cold seems to completely un-bother her somehow, but John is already chilled to the bone.

"I don't know. We should probably go inside and warm up. I don't want you getting sick."

"Ah, a few more minutes won't hurt," she replies with a glint in her eyes.

Before he can respond, Alexander bends over and throws a snowball at the young woman and she yelps gleefully before pulling up her skirts to run into the garden, accepting it as an invitation. John sighs but relents with a grin.

They split off, the two men against Miss Valenfort and Frances. They laugh jovially as they throw snowballs at each other, time seeming to escape them. They manage to have Miss Valenfort covered entirely with snow like the rest of them in no time. John's hands have gone numb when they are interrupted by a man clearing his throat loudly.

"What the hell is this?" The hauntingly familiar voice sends new—different—chills down John's spine. He gapes in distress at the sight of his father stand-ing at the entryway between the stone walls; a young black woman stands wearily behind him with luggage packed under her arms.

"Father," John says breathlessly, his ears beginning to buzz painfully. "I thought you were in Europe."

"I was," Henry says gruffly, his face contorting into one of pure displeasure as his eyes scan across the snow-covered people in his garden. "Did you not receive my letter informing you that I was returning to the colonies?"

"It's America now, Father. The war was won."

"Ah, yes, of course." Henry waves his hand dismissively. "You're distracting me from the point at hand, here. What the hell are you doing, Jack? Have you noticed you are not dressed properly?" He flares his nostrils at the sight of Frances. "And god forbid, your child will freeze to death!"

John flickers his gaze to Frances who stands with her head hung shamefully. Miss Valenfort stands with pristine posture and a worried expression as she carefully examines the scene before her.

"My apologies, miss. I have not introduced myself," Henry says, veering the conversation quickly. "Henry Laurens."

"Margaret Valenfort," she replies politely, giving a curtsy and accepting his hand.

"Ah, you wouldn't happen to be of the William Valenfort family? Just down the road?"

"Aye, sir. I am the eldest," she replies wearily.

"Does your father know where you are?" He queries with an arched brow. "It is rather improper of you to be here with one—nay" —he glares at Hamilton— "*two* grown men, unchaperoned."

She flushes deeply and John steps in. "T'is not her fault, father. We were only just—"

"Why the hell aren't you taking your daughter inside to warm her by the fire?" Henry snaps furiously. "I'll deal with you later. Go take proper care of your daughter you damn fool."

John's face burns with shame and he bites his cheek, nodding stiffly and turning his attention to Frances. "Come now, Frances," he says sharply and she quickly scurries to his side to follow him inside without uttering a peep.

"Sir, if I must say, I was the one who prolonged this game. Your son was very adamant about taking her inside." John hears her say as he enters the home. He barely registers Hamilton following behind them, closing the front door upon their entry.

The three of them migrate to the fireplace in the parlour and John begins dumping logs from the andrion into the hearth whilst Alexander lights the flint and places it at the base underneath the logs. John sits beside Frances on the cushioned bench as she shivers violently, curling into him as they wait for the fire to properly start.

"I'll retrieve dry clothes for us to change into," Hamilton mumbles drearily. He goes unheard from John who stares blankly into the small flames sluggishly burning the wood before him. He securely holds Frances against his chest as the warmth slowly builds. Even as his skin slowly warms, his heart freezes into ice as it ultimately dawns upon him that his father is here.

His mind wanders through a murky void as his body goes through the motions of changing into clean clothes and sitting by the fire again. John stares at the flames but cannot seem to return to himself as he shuffles through every excuse he can make for why they are here and what they are even hoping to accomplish.

Hamilton places a firm hand on his shoulder after an endless amount of time and John blinks painfully as the weight of his own flesh anchors him down; he flinches away from the burning hand. "John? Answer me—why is your father here?"

"I don't know," he retaliates, rubbing his forehead stressfully. "Where is he now?"

"He's still outside speaking with Miss Valenfort," Hamilton whispers as he leans over to peek out the front window. "He seems to be calm whilst speaking to her but there's no way of knowing his temperament once he enters the building."

"Coming here was a mistake," John croaks out defeatedly.

"Whatever do you mean? We start our work with Congress on Monday, John. We had nowhere else to stay," Hamilton replies, sitting beside him on the cushioned bench that perimeters the overwhelmingly wide fireplace. "I'd have thought he would return to South Carolina rather than coming to Philadelphia."

"He must have known that I would be here. Why else would he come?" John says meekly, his eyes unmoving from the dancing flames licking the logs.

"I highly doubt he would purposely intrude upon your life. You're a grown man," Hamilton replies in a conspiring volume. He briefly leans over to look out the window again before shifting closer, reaching his arms out to proximate himself with the heat.

John laughs dryly with no trace of humour left in his soul. "Nay, sir. You clearly know nothing of my father if you think that he would leave me to" —the front door opens and John stands abruptly at attention— "father."

"Jack," Henry grumbles in response. Hamilton and Frances also stand beside him and step away from the fireplace. "I had sent Miss Valenfort home."

"I hope she returns safely," John replies, moving his hands behind his back and straightening his posture.

Henry hums before becoming distracted by the woman struggling to carry the luggage. "You may stop to introduce yourself."

John's stomach twists with bile threatening to spill from his tight throat as she puts the bags down to curtsy with her head bowed. "How do you do."

"I am well, thank you," John replies with a small smile. "What be your name?"

"Diana, sir. Diana Kingsly."

John nods respectfully. "It be a pleasure to make your acquaintance, Diana." He flickers his eyes towards Henry, narrowing them slightly.

Henry huffs out a scoff. "Relax, son. She is a paid servant. I knew you would irritate me upon the matter, otherwise."

"So, you knew I was here, then?"

"Aye, son. Did you not receive the letter I sent in late October?" John shakes his head. "Hmm, perhaps it miscarried. Regardless, I heard of the good news through mutual colleagues in London that you were considered to join the Continental Congress in January and I made leave to stay in Philadelphia with you and my granddaughter." He gives Hamilton a disapproving glance. "I hadn't realized you invited your friend to stay as well?"

"Yes, right." John awkwardly gestures between the two. "You remember Mr. Hamilton? We were both aides-de-camp to General Washington."

"I remember," Henry says deliberately, his eyes unmoving from Hamilton.

"Well, he and I are both expected to be in Congress starting Monday, so I had invited him to stay with us since it would be more convenient, what with all the work we will have to do..."

Henry nods slowly, his dark eyes leaving an insolent trail upon Hamilton before he forces a placid grin. "Seems reasonable. Welcome to our home, sir. I hope you are comfortable with your stay so far?"

Hamilton's face tints with a crimson hue but he keeps his demeanour cordial. "Of course, Mr. Laurens. Thank you for opening up your guest room to me. John and I have great plans for America and we will surely make good use of the study—if that be alright with you, sir?"

Henry's smile seems to loosen somewhat, allowing his mask to slip for a mere moment before hardening his expression and forcing a false grin again. "Yes. If you two require anything at all, do not hesitate to ask. I was President once, after all."

John resists the urge to scowl and scoff in annoyance; opting instead to chew on his inner cheek and narrow his eyes. He could strangle his impudent father. Henry turns to Frances and his smile softens considerably as he kneels. "And do not think I had forgotten you, my dear granddaughter. Come give your grandpa a hug."

Frances grins and gallops to him before leaping into his embrace. He bellows a deep, hearty chuckle as he nearly topples over. John watches his entire demeanour change with perplexity. "I missed you, grandpa!"

"I missed you, too," he replies earnestly. "And don't think I forgot your birthday! If I am correct, you turn six today?"

"Yes sir!"

He pats her head before standing up with a grunt and cracking bones. "My, how much you've grown since I last saw you. Have you been good?"

"Mhmm! Did you get me a present?"

"Of course, but it will have to wait until Diana finishes unpacking my luggage." He turns and gives her a pointed look; she quickly begins collecting the bags, seeming to snap from a daze that had her locked in place for so long. "Speaking of, will you be sure to leave my cigar box on the mantle in my room?"

"Sir, you did not bring it with you. Remember your condition?"

"Oh, that's right—remind me to buy a new set, then—"

"Condition?" John interjects curiously. "What

condition?"

"It's nothing to worry about," Henry replies, waving him off.

Diana huffs in a shockingly maternal way. "Now sir, it's not nothin'. The doctor said you shouldn't smoke with a heart condition like yours—"

"What?" John gawks in bewilderment.

"I said it's nothing," Henry grumbles. "Diana, take my bags to my room. You're paid to serve, not to be my nurse."

"Yes, sir. Sorry, sir," she replies hastily before climbing the stairs with the luggage.

"What is a heart con-dik-ton?" Frances asks with wide eyes.

Henry grunts impatiently, shooting a glare towards John. "Do you educate your child? Why can't she speak correctly?"

"She's six," John replies, deadpan.

"Daddy and Mr. Hamilton have me read and write in both English and French!" Frances declares proudly. John bites his lip in embarrassment as Henry stares down at her vacantly. "I can count to ten in French! Listen —un, deux, trois, quatre—"

"Alright, that is quite enough. I believe you, Fran." Henry rubs his forehead tiredly. "Did you not hire a tutor for her, Jack?"

John feels his resolve depleting further as this conversation bellows on. Why won't the floorboards open up and swallow him to Hell at this moment? Why must he wait for damnation through this torture? "I was to set that up, father. We had finally settled ourselves yesterday, you see, and today we were celebrating her birthday."

"Tomorrow, then, we will search for a suitable tutor. I know of a few in town that might be of interest," Henry replies off-handedly. Frances whips her head back and forth between the two with incertitude. "We will discuss your foolish snow-game behaviour later on after I am settled. Until then, keep her warm for god's sake."

"Yes sir," John states firmly.

Henry nods curtly and nudges Frances towards the parlour. "You keep warm with your father. The last thing we want is for you to fall ill on your birthday from his negligence."

"Okay," she replies with a solemn nod before obediently marching towards the fireplace, incorrectly muttering the word negligence under her breath.

"I'll be in my room if you need me to coddle you some more, Jack," Henry adds with a disgraced scoff before retreating up the stairs.

John catches Hamilton wearily glancing at him in his peripheral, but he simply ignores his worried glance by closing his eyes and breathing deeply through his nose.

"John—"

"Don't," he grumbles, turning around to join Frances on the fireplace bench. "Just...don't."

Hamilton sighs deeply as the door upstairs closes. "He was wrong to call you negligent—that is neh-gleh-jent, petite fleur," he adds quickly and she nods gratefully, muttering the word properly under her breath. "You are doing your best, John—"

"It's not enough!" John hisses grimly. "You wouldn't understand the responsibilities required of me. You do not have a fortune, or younger siblings, or a child."

Alexander's eyes flutter once, twice, then visibly alters his posture as mental barriers build around his entire demeanour, shielding away any of his authentic emotions. "That may be a veracious claim but my sentiments still stand. There is no need to rectify your behaviour, John. Your father is—"

"Stop," John interjects cruelly. "Please, stop." He looks up at him. "You have no place to make any claims based upon what my father may—"

"You listen to the man who can only criticise

your behaviour but not the one who sees your valiant efforts? No, *fuck* that and *fuck you*, sir!" Alexander whispers, his voice hitching up as he seethes down at John. Frances blinks owlishly at the two of them, her teeth clattering as her jaw tenses with the stressful mood filling the air around them. "I am already   humiliated enough as it is. I don't need you adding to the flames your father ignited."

"I'm sorry he came unannounced and looked down upon you like—"

"It's his house," Alexander replies with folded arms. He subconsciously huddles closer to the fire and shivers. "We cannot act as if he be the one intruding when it is technically I who be the intruder upon your family."

John rubs his head with disposition. "Can we discuss this later? My head is squeezing with tension."

"As is mine."

"So you'll drop it, then?"

Alexander scoffs and Frances smacks the cushion, stealing their attention and shifting their expressions from rage to concern. "Stop it! Stop fighting!"

John's heart sinks with disdain. "Frances. I'm sorry, sweetheart."

"Don't be negligent with each other!" she grumbles furiously. John's face twists with discomfort at the meaning behind her words. Even though she still does not fully comprehend the proper use of such a word, her statement still be clear:

John nods. "I promise I won't."

"You swear?"

"Aye," John replies with watery eyes. "I swear."

"And you, Mr. Hamilton?" she asks with a raised brow. "You swear, aussi?"

"Oui," he croaks. "I swear upon my mother's grave."

John and Frances shoot him mirrored gazes of empathy. She nods once and turns towards the fire with a glassy-eyed stare, seeming to sink further away.

"Okay," she mumbles, content.

Chatpter 8

FIRE AND ICE CONSUME HIS BONES AND flesh, forcing him to go frigid upon command, and yet burning whenever he catches Hamilton's eye. John carries himself in a haze for the rest of the day, trying to appease his father by indulging in his tale of his time in Europe. A very soft blackness frames his vision as his body continues against his will, nodding along and drinking with his father in the parlour.

Diana cooks a grandiose dinner for the household and serves it after the strike of noon upon the clock; its chimes sinking John deeper into his own murky mindscape. Frances and Alexander fall into a respective haze of their own, eating with apt politeness. Frances almost is unrecognizable as a child whilst she eats with near-perfect posture and grimly neutral features that mirror her father's.

John barely pays any mind to the nostalgic ramblings of his father's time in Congress, only nodding or shaking his head and humming when prompted for a response. Alexander's face remains cordial and polite, a practiced mask of a poor man famished for acceptance from upperclassmen like Henry Laurens. John would rather cease to exist than witness such an expression on his lover's face for another moment. Somehow his body has gone numb, but deep within his mind, he watches with screams of agony, begging for this all to end.

"What plans do you have in mind?" Henry inquires with an arched brow, raising his wine glass to his lips.

"We still have much to discuss upon the matter, but we desire to propose a unique design for the government," Alexander replies swiftly.

John watches the red liquid slip past his father's dry lips; some of it partially backwashes into the cup before he places it on the table. "What fresh ideas have you in mind, sir?"

Alexander glances at John briefly and his heart pounds at the intensity behind his gaze. "We would like to propose a strong central democracy."

Henry scoffs. "There be no such a thing, sir."

"Not yet," Alexander replies with a confident edge to his tone. The smile he proffers could make anyone attack and swoon him simultaneously.

"You have a mighty ambition for capturing the sun, sir," Henry says slowly. "You may not have an opportunity to appeal such a plan at this time. You two most likely will only vote upon other people's ideas. Not the other way around." Alexander's jaw twitches as he punctures the meat with his fork. "For now, you may only be present for approving or disapproving pleas and bills. When I asked what your plans were, I had not expected such a ludicrous response."

Alexander hums and John does everything he can to not strangle his father. He places his fork down abruptly, causing it to clatter upon impact with his plate. "As Mr. Hamilton said, sir, we still have to discuss our plans amongst each other long before we could propose it to Congress," John begins with white-nuckled fists. "We only share with you our inevitable goals with Congress as you have asked. Until we actually start work, however, there is not much else for us to say at this time but that. So get off your high horse instead of ridiculing me and my partner for having the drive to make America a prosperous place to live for our children."

The table is silent as Henry glares at John. "Do not speak to me in such a tone in my own house, boy!" John flinches at the risen volume of his father's booming voice. "Your input was highly inappropriate and unnecessary for such a matter!"

"Sir," Diana cuts through the tension swiftly. "Watch your temper. You recall what the doctor said about your blood pressure?"

Henry guffaws as he grabs his glass cup. "Mind not, Diana. I will be fine."

Diana gives him a hard look and John blinks in surprise when his father visibly slackens his stiff posture. He mutters inaudibly to her before taking a sip of his wine. She nods and retreats from the room at once.

"I'm sorry, Jack. You were correct; I had been the one who inquired upon your plans." John stares in bewilderment at the man before him. He does not know if he should fear Diana or thank her for whatever spell his father is under. "I only worry over your ambitious attitudes. All I intend to share is my own wisdom from my presidency," he grumbles with a sigh. "Do not expect to have your ideas listened to. You will discover that my response might be the most charitable compared to the others."

John's temper simmers, deciding to catch the fishing line his father throws at him to cease this discussion. "Thank you for sharing your wisdom, sir," John replies in a strained tone. Everyone continues to silently eat, daring not to bring light upon the subject matter again.

***

The afternoon is a boring affair for Frances and a stressful game for John and Alexander. They keep their distance from one another like they had in New York, and during dire times in the war. Alexander seems less patient than before, taking any opportunity he can to glare at Henry Laurens whenever he turns his back on him. The rather petty action would amuse John if he wasn't stressed out of his mind.

After supper is served in the evening, Frances asks for a bedtime story and John eagerly retreats up the stairs to read to her whilst Hamilton plays the part of an enthusiastic guest for Henry.

John leaves her to ready herself for bed and re-treats into his bedchambers to catch his breath. He steadily approaches his wardrobe to rest his head against the cool wood, closing his eyes and breathing deliberately until his palpitating heartbeat composes itself. He wills his mind to go blank as he leans against the wardrobe—

"If I have to hear one more story about your father's presidency," —John startles fiercely— "I may go insane," Alexander grumbles as he softly closes the door.

"Alex—"

"Don't misunderstand me, for I mean no ill intent towards your father," Alexander adds, keeping his voice low. "But that man is very...intrusive."

"Alex, what the hell are you doing here?" John steps away from the wardrobe and hurries towards the door. "Did my father see you—"

"Of course not, I'm not asinine!" Alexander retaliates with an arched brow. He grabs John's arm, halting him from opening the door. "He went on a stroll into the gardens and I took the opportunity to talk with you briefly. What are we to do with him living with us like this? I am aware this is his home, but I thought we would be alone here, Jack."

"I know, I know," —John leans against the door, sighing exasperatingly— "I swear I had not received any letter that he mentioned sending. If I had known, I'd suggest living somewhere else."

"All we can do now is make a plan," Alexander replies, folding his arms over his chest. "What do you suppose we shall do?"

"For now, we should keep our distance from each other," John says with a frown. "No spontaneous meetups in private like this. At least not for a while."

"Alright." Alexander paces towards the window. "If I had known the night previous would be our last time together for the unforeseeable future, I would have taken my time with you."

Despite his yearning to control his composure, John flushes deeply; he clears his throat and gazes at the oil lamp hypnotically. "Aye. This was not what I had planned for yours and Frances' birthday."

"Speaking of," —Alexander turns around, leaning against the windowsill— "What did you acquire for her as a gift?"

"Oh," John staggers towards the wardrobe and opens it. "I'd nearly forgotten her gift. My mind was preoccupied with distracting my father from my sins."

Alexander snorts. "And how is that going for you, sir?"

John grunts in acknowledgement as he pulls out the necklace and holds it out to show Alexander. The other man steps forward conspicuously to get a closer look, nodding with approval.

"How much did that cost?"

John doesn't reply right away, chewing his bottom lip as he slips it into his pocket. "Nothing you need to worry about, darlin'. I can inform her it be from us both since I thought of you when I picked it out. You always call her little flower."

Alexander shakes his head incredulously. "Nonsense, I couldn't possibly—"

"Relax. T'is fine." John smiles, subconsciously lifting his hand to brush a stray curl behind Alexander's ear. "I promise to let you get your own gift for her from now on if you desire."

Alexander frowns. "You spent a fortune on this necklace, didn't you?"

"I did not!"

"How much, John?" Alexander inquires with an arched brow. "Do not lie to me, sir."

John mutters his response. Alexander leans in with a baffled expression. "What's that? I've not heard you speak clearly—"

"One hundred dollars," John interrupts, his voice firm yet still low.

Alexander's eyes bulge from his sockets as he gasps in pure bewilderment. "Jesus Christ, John! You could pay a year's rent twice over with that kind of money!"

"Please, you mustn't worry yourself over such trivial details," John replies.

Alexander scoffs before pinching the bridge of his nose. "Trivial details." He scoffs again. "Who the hell carries one hundred goddamned dollars in their purse?"

John shrugs. "I do?"

"Fuck you and your lack of monetary management," Alexander grumbles. "You need to be more conscientious of how you spend your money, you damn fool."

John smiles. "It be not my money, sir, but rather my father's money."

"Still," Alexander replies sharply. "Even though you are from a wealthy family, it's not an endless supply. You have to save it and invest it to earn more."

"Perhaps you should be in charge of my personal accounting," John suggests with a shrug. He steps closer. Alexander swallows. "We are partners, after all. Are we not?"

"Aye," Alexander says huskily—he clears his throat. "We are."

John steps closer, his heart pumping harder as he reaches for Alexander's cravat against his better judgement. "I suppose then, that would mean we share our wealth now, does it not?"

Alexander stares at John's hands untangling the knot of the tie. "We will have to have many secret meetings like this, then. To discuss your terrible spending habits."

Whatever dance they are participating in is rather dangerous, John reckons; he pursues it anyway. "You'll have to persuade me to control myself," John whispers in a sultry tone, his lips brushing against Alexander's ear as he slips the tie off his neck.

Alexander hums, tilting his head and closing his eyes whilst John takes the opportunity to pull the collar aside and press his lips against his pulse point on the juncture of his neck and shoulder. "I'd rather you didn't control yourself just this once, Jack."

John grunts, pushing Alexander into the bedpost before capturing his lips fervently. Alexander reaches up to tug on John's queue, thus pulling his head back and eliciting a low groan. Alexander pulls John down to his level, capturing his lips with great reverence and urgency.

John pulls away to gasp for breath, his nose still brushing against Alexander's. "What are we doing?"

"You started this," Alexander replies with a challenging tone. "Will you finish it or tease me with the preview locked within my mind's eye to wander through when we all lay in our separate beds tonight?"

John near-growls at this and leans down to kiss and lick at Alexander's delectable rosy lips. Alexander responds eagerly, tugging John until spinning them to reverse their positions; pushing John against the bedpost and exploring his body with deft fingers. John melts into the explosive sensations, detoxing himself of all the pent-up anxieties and stress with every touch Alexander leaves upon his skin.

Alexander's fingers trail from his chest all the way down until reaching the buttons of his breeches, fiddling with them as he defiantly nips and licks into John's mouth with longing desire.

"Alex," John groans breathlessly, rolling his head back as he responds by releasing a single button. "Please, I need..." Another button is released and the fly-flap of his breeches fall with gravity.

"I know," Alexander replies in a low, breathy tone against the shell of John's ear. "One last time together before the inevitable cannot surely be wrong, can it?"

John whimpers in response, twisting his head away as his skin flushes, his entire body sparking with a desperate want for more—

Tap Tap Tap.

Alexander leaps away from John as if he had touched fire. "Mr. Laurens? Are you in there?" Diana's muffled voice barely travels through the thick wooden door.

John sheepishly begins re-buttoning his breeches, utterly ashamed of the actions he had initiated with Alexander when he knew better, goddammit— "Yes, my apologies. I will be out momentarily." His voice comes out as a pathetic crackle; he clears it. "Is there something you require me for?"

"I was gonna put your daughter to bed upon your father's orders, but she had told me that she was waiting for you?"

"Aye, that is correct. I tuck her in at night." John tries to not curse his father out as he continues to hastily re-tuck in his loose shirt. "Regarding my daughter from now on, you will not take orders from my father, do you understand me?"

"Yes, sir. Sorry, sir. I'll inform your daughter you will be there shortly. Have a good evening, sir," Diana replies quickly before the sound of her feet shuffling grows distant.

John doesn't even glance at Alexander as he anxiously fixes his hair in the mirror. "You'll see to letting yourself out of my room before I return?" He hears no response but assumes Hamilton nods. "Good night, sir. Until further notice, we will not let ourselves be so reckless like that in this household again."

Hamilton's voice is grating and hoarse as he replies. "Aye..."

John nods curtly and retreats hastily from the suffocating room. He trudges down the hall and into Frances' room, smiling sweetly at her. She already be dozing off in her bed, having waited for a tad too long for her father to come and tuck her in. John sighs, swallowing his growing resentment for his foolish behaviour, and places the necklace on top of Gulliver's Travels that lay upon her nightstand. He presses a chaste kiss on her forehead and blows out the oil lamp to submerge her into blissful darkness.

***

The following week goes on in a dizzying haze of avoiding one another. John tries to ignore the buzzing in his head as he sits in meetings at Congress, glaring at the floor as men argue about trivial details. He and Alexander argue in favour of paying the soldiers their promised commissions, yet other men who have not fought in the war can sit there and argue reasons why not to do the very thing they promised. It forces John to question his loyalties and what he even fought for. He fought for freedom and liberty, not...this.

"What of the fund that the women in the United States of America raised?" Alexander argues gratingly. "Lady Washington herself saw to that charity."

"We have not raised enough quite yet to pay everyone," a man by the name of Doctor David Ramsay replies solemnly. "We need more support."

"Why not consider adding it into our taxations?" John Adams suggests after taking a puff from his smoking pipe. Laurens fiddles with his quill, flipping it through his fingers mindlessly.

"The people will be appalled by such an arduous taxation, it's already high enough that people are angry," another man replies. "We just won a war, sir. Let's not risk starting another."

"We will ignite another damn war either way if we do not pay our men," Laurens snaps, gritting his teeth. He nearly cracks his quill in half before he places it down and takes a deep breath.

Silence.

"There were already mutiny's within our ranks during the war and I would not be surprised to see another uprising against Parliament if this persists, this time being against our own." John stands up and begins to pace, ignoring the sneers from many men. "I was out there, I witnessed the war first hand. These men earned their compensation and we shall give them what they deserve. Instead of discussing whether they deserve it or not, we shall compensate them without another thought. There was no time for rumination in the war they fought for, so why act that way now?"

"If we do not ponder our ideas, we will become savages," Thomas Jefferson replies with a curled lip. "And as you stand there, sir, why have you not offered your own money?" Jefferson inquires with an arched brow, smirking with a prideful ego. "You expect us to give up our money while you whine like a petulant child who did not get what he wanted?"

A few men chuckle and John's face burns with rage and embarrassment.

"One hundred dollars," John abruptly announces to the council with grim features. "I will pledge one hundred of my own dollars to start, then."

Everyone stares in shock as John pulls out his purse and throws the money onto the head table. A few men whisper in surprise as John walks back to his seat beside Alexander, glaring darkly at Jefferson.

Doctor Ramsay walks up to the table and places some of his own money with the pile John began,

offering him a curt nod in solidarity.

Alexander smiles proudly at John, offering a brief wink as he leans back and folds his arms, watching with amusement as other men slowly begin donating money. Jefferson gapes before shifting his features into contempt, humming and sipping his wine as he sneers at Laurens and Hamilton smirking his way.

They all leave the meeting with a plan to ask the people to donate. The men disperse onto the streets of Philadelphia and towards their homes as another day in Congress comes and passes.

"I don't think you understand what you just did in there, Jack," Alexander whispers as they stroll down the street side by side with their arms behind their backs. "You created a good example for the people, showing you are not above them. This might actually work."

"I never thought of myself as above others," John replies. "Sometimes to send a message to people, you have to make the sacrifice yourself, first."

"You are absolutely right," Alexander says with a bright smile. "This is the best meeting we've had since we joined Congress. And the best use of a hundred dollars, I might add."

John, against his better judgements, actually laughs at Alexander's reference to his terrible spending habits. "I was also quite bored of the constant arguing when the answer was so simple," John grumbles.

"Bastards."

"Aye," Alexander replies grimly. "Couldn't have said it better, myself."

"Oi, Mr. Laurens?"

John and Alexander stop in their trek to turn around at the sound of Doctor Ramsay calling out.

"Yes, sir?" John asks as the man catches up with them.

"Doctor David Ramsay of South Carolina, at your service, sir," he says, grabbing John's hand to shake it firmly.

John's eyes light up with recognition. "Oh, yes. You're the one who is documenting the war, correct?"

"Aye!" Ramsay replies lightly. "I had only wanted

to say thank you, sir. They have not faced the enemy like either of us has. They bore us with their talk and lack of action. No time for talking whilst in war."

"You are correct, sir." John smiles as he gestures towards Alexander. "This is my partner, Alexander Hamilton. We had recently graduated from King's College and plan to run a dual Law Firm after our time here."

Ramsay and Hamilton shake hands and nod curtly at one another. "A pleasure to make your acquaintance, Mr. Hamilton. I can appreciate a man who is willing to speak his mind, no matter how harsh it may seem to those pompous assholes."

Alexander snorts out amusedly and tucks his hands in his pockets. "Likewise. Thank you for your generous donation, sir. Once we pay what these men are owed, we can move onto greater issues like our future government system."

"Absolutely," Ramsay responds with a tired nod. "T'is rather exhausting to handle these leftover matters from war but greatly necessary for the future of America."

"You should come by my father's home for supper one of these days, bring the family," John suggests.

"I'd enjoy that greatly, sir. I only have the wife at home who has fallen ill recently, but hopefully we can have little ones running about soon enough," he replies lightly. "You've got a little one yourself, isn't that right, Mr. Laurens?"

"A little girl, Frances Eleanor, who recently turned six," John replies eagerly. He finds his spirits lifting whenever people mention his daughter these days and he has not a clue how to label his strange new feelings towards her.

"Ahh, soon enough she'll be a woman and you'll wonder where the time went," Ramsay says with a polite chuckle.

John's blood runs cold at the prospect. He cannot imagine her growing old enough to marry and bear children. He would rather prefer not to think of such a thing as he had recently introduced her into his life. He also would rather not have to think of her perceptiveness growing sharper alongside her physical growth; it already be hard enough to hide his sins—

"Well, speaking of, John has to make sure she is properly seen to so we should be going. It was good to properly make your acquaintance, sir."

"Likewise, Mr. Hamilton." Ramsay shakes their hands again before tipping his hat in salutation. "Until we meet again, sirs." Ramsay turns to leave but stops as an afterthought catches his attention. "Oh, and best of luck, Mr. Laurens. Regardless of what others may whisper, I see you to be an honourable man, working hard to raise your child on your own."

John frowns in confusion. "Whispers? What whispers do you refer to, sir?"

Ramsay looks akin to a man seeing a ghost as his features go pale. "Oh, I thought you were aware? Philadelphians tend to enjoy their gossip, but that's all it is, sir. Just gossip."

"Don't beat around the bush. What is it they say, sir?"

"Just about infertility and whatever nonsense people can procure as a reasoning to your lack of efforts to re-marry," Ramsay replies with a distractible gesture of the hand. "Same types of whispers anyone like Washington himself has heard, as well. Nothing to worry over. Anyone who truly knows you will recognize you as a man of honour and one who has been dealt a terrible hand from God." Ramsay sighs solemnly. "I know what it be like to lose a wife, myself—especially by illness. It is rather painful to the heart. I respect your decision to wait as I am sure you loved her very much."

John automatically nods, grunting instead of speaking his reply.

"Anyhow, I will not hold you any longer from your paternal duties. Send your family my best regards, sir." He nods before turning swiftly and walking away.

"If only those who question your fertility knew that you managed to accidentally impregnate a woman on the first try," Alexander whispers with a cheeky grin. "In any case, I'd suggest you'd listen to Doctor Ramsay. They're only whispers, after all, and not to be listened to."

"Still, people are already beginning to notice I have yet to re-marry," John replies as they continue their trek to the estate.

"People will always be nosy buggers," Alexander quips back nonchalantly, his eyes gazing at the sights as they stroll by. "As long as we do not allow them to get to us, we will be fine. We knew this would be difficult."

"I don't know if I can handle what they say of me," John mumbles bitterly.

"You think you're the only one they whisper about, Jack?" Alexander replies harshly. "I am still a bachelor—who was engaged to a high-class socialite before I broke it off, I may add. Trust me, if any one of us looks more questionable to these people, it would be I over you. We'll both be fine."

John stares stoically ahead of himself and tenses his jaw. "It's not like there is anything for them to whisper about, anyway," Alexander adds in a low murmur near John's ear as they turn a corner. "We go to work, go home, and repeat. Ramsay was correct in his judgements. There truly is nothing beyond what people are seeing of us anyway. Can't get caught if you don't do anything—isn't that right, Jack?"

John halts in his track and gawks at Alexander as he keeps walking with his shoulders set and jaw raised in clear defiance. Laurens glares at the dusty roads for a moment before he begins to follow Hamilton again, keeping a safe distance from him as thoughts of the previous week play through his head on a loop.

Chatpter 9

A WEEK OF REPETITIOUS ARGUING IN
Congress over trivial matters and walking on eggshells
at the estate leads to another crisis that is comparable
to the infiltration of Patsy; it now being Henry instead
of her. With every pressing matter within his life, he
wonders if he ever truly had command over anything
he acted upon within his twenty-eight years on this
god-forsaken planet.

John, despite all of his repressed frustration,
becomes rather numb towards everything. T'is a
strange mechanism his brain developed as a young boy
when he realized that emotions impede his rationality
in dire times. As John sterlizes his emotions, it
exacerbates his rage—bubbling to a boiling point
behind the façade of placid smiles and firm handshakes.
He could burst at any moment like a musket or cannon,

booming with great destruction, and leaving him with either broken   furniture or bloody red-coated corpses upon a battlefield.

Without a revolution, John grows weary over his reckless inclinations and what they may uncover regarding his daughter. Henry had done the same thing when John was a boy; hiding his grief and lashing out on his remaining children. If not with physical trauma, then with the aura of a deity onlooking John's every decision, moving him around like a pawn in Henry's ongoing game of chess. John was not born the eldest, but has been since his fifth loop around the sun, and he must carry that burden until his final breath.

And now with Frances being Henry's only grandchild as of late, he can sense the passive-aggressive persistence of his father demanding John to be strict and oversee her entire life like a puppet master. Just like his father was to himself.

John desperately wishes to abstain from being anything akin to his father.

So he takes to following Alexander's suggestion of continuing their weekly tradition of family Washing Day—where the trio clean their clothes and John can pretend for a moment that his emotions have not ceased functioning at a healthy capacity.

Frances rolls her sleeves up and begins scrub-bing the shirt against the washboard, panting heavily as she uses her entire body for the motion. John smiles proudly as they work together and pull the clothes out to squeeze the water free. They flip the shirts and scrub again, John only stopping to offer words of advice to Frances regarding her technique so she does not injure her back.

Alexander hangs the clothes on the line in the washing room and smiles at them as he slips a pin from his teeth to snap the clothing to the line. Frances tucks her lavender necklace over her back, refusing to take it off even as it repeatedly slides over her shoulder and hangs over the washing basin again.

"Oh, what's this?" Diana asks curiously as she enters the washing room with Henry's dirty clothes.

"Washing day!" Frances declares brightly as she pulls out the shirt to squeeze the water from it.

Diana gapes at the three of them, placing the basket down by her feet. "Ah, yes. I can see that, now."

"Are those my father's?" John inquires as he finishes wringing out his shirt before passing it to Alexander to hang upon the clothesline.

"Yes sir." Diana nods. "He asked of me to wash them today."

"We can wash them! Add it to our pile!" Frances replies eagerly.

John chuckles warmly and gestures to the small

basket between him and Frances. "You're welcome to join us or leave us to it so you may do some other task if you wish?"

"Perhaps you can sit and rest. You're always working, Miss Diana," Frances suggests as she hops up to pass the shirt to Alexander to hang up.

Diana smiles graciously at the vibrant young girl. "I would very much like to take your suggestion as my bones are feeling weary today."

Alexander gestures to the stool by the window. "You're welcome to sit there if you'd like. I apologize that we do not have another place for you to sit and rest."

Diana thanks him and moves her basket by the near-empty one between the father and daughter before sitting down. "I'll have to return to work soon...since your father don't pay me to sit around all day."

"You've still certainly earned this break," John replies as he begins washing one of Frances' skirts. "We have grown accustomed to doing our own laundry. You're more than welcome to only do my father's laundry since we've already done our own."

"What a good skill to teach your little girl, Mr. Laurens," Diana says with a grin. "I did not take you as the type to do your own laundry, sir."

"Don't let his good looks fool you, Diana. He only

started doing his own laundry after I taught him how," Alexander replies cheekily as he finishes clipping the shirt on the line.

John flicks soapy water at Alexander, chuckling amusedly as he flinches away like a cat; Frances giggles as Alexander retaliates by whipping a wet shirt at John's arm. Diana watches the domestic scene silently with perplexed features, furrowing her brows as Frances rolls onto her back in hysterics whilst the two grown men start battling for dominance; John flicking water and Alex slapping him in the face with the wet shirt. Diana's features melt into a fond smile.

"Alright, enough distractions. We must get back to work if we wish to go to the park," John interrupts between deep breaths as he struggles to resist his laughter.

"Can we play in the snow at the park?" Frances asks with great enthusiasm as she positions herself to begin scrubbing again.

"Jack! Where are you?" Henry's deep bellowing voice echoes through the enormously vacant estate halls and into the washing room, interrupting their activities. John's posture stiffens as he stares at the doorway with wide eyes, watching in trepidation as Henry walks by. The man stops and backs up, turning into the washing room, puzzled. "What the hell are you doing?"

"T'is washing day, grandpapa!" Frances squeals jovially and John flinches with shame as Henry glares at him.

"I don't pay Diana to sit and watch my son and granddaughter wash the laundry," Henry grumbles, his gaze flickering to Diana as she hastily stands at attention and begins hanging wet clothes on the line to make herself busy. Alexander stands still behind the dangling clothes, his wide eyes peeking above the line and flickering anxiously between Henry and John.

Henry turns his attention to John. "Why is she not ready for her lessons?"

John blinks in bewilderment. "What lessons? T'is Friday. Her tutor only comes on Monday to Thursday?"

"I signed up Frances for piano lessons, remember? You were supposed to help her get ready for her session with Mr. Murphy." Henry pulls out his pocket watch and huffs. "And now she will be late since she still not be properly dressed!"

John flushes deeply as he slowly stands. "You never told me you signed her up for piano lessons. I'd thought it was only a suggestion?"

Henry scoffs and tucks his pocket watch in his coat. "I informed you the day before last. Have you paid attention to anything this week, Jack? You've been quite distant since my arrival."

'I wonder why...' John exhales deeply through his nose in frustration as he rubs his head. "My thoughts have been consumed by the funding for the soldiers and other bills presented to Congress."

Henry sighs, shaking his head. "You need a wife, son. You can't raise a child on your own. You're far too distracted."

"I can raise her perfectly fine, father," John snaps. "It be you who continues to make decisions for her without my goddamn consent!"

"Watch your tone with me, boy!" Henry roars. "Without my help, you would be floundering more than ever."

"I am perfectly capable of looking after my own child."

"Are you?" Henry scowls deeply. "You couldn't even look after your own brother when I had asked you!"

John swallows as the memories flow by like a stream, oozing into the crevices of his mind's eye. His stomach twirls and daggers form in his throat as the image of the large oak tree burns into his eyelids. Alexander shares a sheepish exchange with Diana as John's dull ache sluggishly bubbles into a low boil.

"Do not make any more decisions relating to my daughter without properly discussing it with me first,"

John replies dryly, opting to ignore the unscrupulous attack. "May I also add that you never re-married after mother passed? So do not belittle me for not rushing into marriage only two months after discovering my own wife's passing."

Henry gapes with wide eyes as John urgently grabs Frances' arm and tugs her out of the washing room, fuming as he marches past his father who stands frozen, dumbfounded.

"Ow, father! My arm!" Frances whines as John drags her through the labyrinth of hallways.

John releases her immediately and heavily leans against the wall, exhaling in exasperation. "Sorry, sweetheart. Could you go off to dress yourself for your lessons?"

She pouts. "But I had lessons all week! I wanted to go to the park today."

"I know," John replies solemnly. "Perhaps we can go to the park tomorrow."

"What about washing day?" Frances tilts her head in query, meek and skittish as she rubs her hands down her apron.

John glances back, watching his father fuming as he retreats down another corridor to clearly avoid facing John. "Diana can handle it."

"What about Mr. Hamilton?" Frances adds in a low voice.

"Enough of this. Go dress yourself," John orders in a loud, booming voice as he points up the stairwell.

Frances sighs, bowing her head and mumbling a fragile, "yes, sir," before turning away theatrically, stomping the whole way up the staircase.

John presses his back against the wall and closes his eyes, willing himself to simmer his lingering anger.

"What the hell just happened?" Alexander's voice startles John away from the wall.

John peers into the empty dining room; for a house so vast and empty, it seems suffocatingly cramped. The adrenaline from his outburst finally depletes. "I yelled at my father and then at my daughter."

"I noticed that, yes," Alexander responds with folded arms. "Are you alright?"

"No," John grumbles defeatedly. "I'm exhausted and he's only been here for two fucking weeks."

"I haven't seen you this angry since Charles Lee." Alexander raises an inquisitive brow. "Did anything in particular set you off? I mean, you went from content to livid in a microsecond and it was concerning to witness, to say the least."

"He scheduled a piano lesson without telling me."

"Is that really it?" Alexander sternly searches John's eyes and he sulks inward. "What he said... About your brother. That was—"

"Drop it," John hisses. "This is purely related to him doing things for my daughter without my knowledge."

"Henry said he spoke with you about the lessons—"

"Are you going to defend my father for taking over my daughter's well-being?" John flares at Alexander like a rabid animal.

"No, I—"

"He always finds his way into infiltrating my life and starts controlling it like a goddamned puppeteer and I get the painful reminder that I am suspended by his strings every damn time he does it." John paces erratically as his heart pumps harder. "I am her father."

"Aye."

"I should make these decisions for her, not him. If he has suggestions, that is all well, but when he goes behind my back like this—"

"John, you need to calm down," Alexander whispers, holding John's upper arm, thus halting him in his incessant pacing. "You have every right to be upset but do not take it out on me or your daughter. Especially not your daughter."

John sighs, resigned. "You're right." He ducks his head and gazes at Alexander. "I apologize for my outburst."

"Perhaps we should talk," Alexander says, lower. He glances over his shoulder before leaning in conspiringly. "You have been tense all week. As have I. We cannot keep up this ruse of avoiding each other for the sake of propriety when we both know that it damn well be making us miserable."

John pulls away from Alexander, shaking his head. "No, we cannot discuss this now. Not here."

"When, John? Anytime I suggest it you simply run away and then get lost in your mind." Alexander scoffs. "It's like you haven't even been present all week, barely focused on a goddamned thing ever since—"

They both turn sharply at the sound of the front door opening. Henry's voice echoes through the halls as he welcomes Mr. Murphy into his home. Alexander grabs John's arm again and tugs him into the kitchen.

"I cannot keep doing this, John," Alexander whispers the moment the door is closed behind them. "Watching you be nearby but not being unable to even touch you is insufferable."

"We cannot and will not repeat what happened on your birthday," John replies pointedly.

"What is the point of keeping our secret if there be no secret to keep?" Alexander hisses in retaliation.

"Oh, I see now," John guffaws incredulously. "This only be about myself giving more attention to your nose, is that it?"

"Piss off," Alexander snaps heatedly. "It's not just that. You do not speak to me as we used to. We do not spend time together anymore. When was the last time you recall us sitting together whilst you draw on your sketchpad and I read? Or going on a walk and chatting about anything on our minds at the moment? I did not propose to you to have you enter my back doors, sir. I proposed because I love you—but it's hard to allow our relationship to blossom when you fucking ignore me unless it be otherwise absolutley necessary."

"Have you forgotten why I stay away from you?" John replies drearily. "As long as my father's shadow lingers within this household, I will not risk your safety." John delicately holds Alexander's hand. "I stay away because I love you."

"And yet we are both afflicted with a lingering melancholy the longer we stay apart."

John sighs in resignation. "We were aware that this was not going to be an easy road for us."

"Still," —Alexander whimpers as he pushes up against John's body, resting his head upon his chest— "It pains me so to have you be so near...and yet be unattainable."

"What do you propose we do, then?" John inquires softly, wrapping his arms securely around Alexander. "We should not even risk what we do now."

"Can I not embrace you in peace?" Alexander snuggles closer. "My love, why must you deprive us of moments like these? You deserve to take control over your own life and not dictate all of your actions around him."

"I can't lose you," John confesses into Alexander's hair. "And so I cannot risk the possibility of discovery."

"What happened to the John that wrote me that letter?" Alexander replies. "The one describing in eloquent detail how we can write our own story and defy all odds against the very world that condemns us to Hell for simply loving one another?"

'I was a fool to send you that letter. I should have burned it.'

John's muscles lock up at the intrusive thought. He closes his eyes and imagines himself standing before the fire, nearly throwing the sealed letter into the open flames, but ultimately deciding against it.

"That John is still here," he replies instead of

voicing his impulsive thoughts. "In all honesty, that letter was selfish of me to write but I did intend every word."

"It proved to me that you are worth it," Alexander says, pulling back to crane his neck to look into John's eyes. "I know you're scared—I'm scared too. But I do not regret my devotion to you. I am willing to take that risk. Are you?"

John's breath hitches in his throat. They've come this far—why go back now? He makes his intentions clear with the deliberate motion of holding his lover's—husband's— face and pressing their lips together with his promise. *'This is worth it,'* he considers with a smile, deepening the tender kiss. *'He is worth it.'*

***

John's daily schedule proceeds as follows: First, he wakes in the morning, washes briefly with the basin, dresses himself, eats breakfast—stealing a few glances of Alexander across the table—leaving his daughter with the tutor and going off to parliament with Alexander before returning home to settle down with his daughter, reading her another chapter of Gulliver's Travels, and going off to bed with one final longing glance in Alexander's direction.

Tuesday's are John's favourite day of the week purely because his father tends to go out and socialize those evenings while Diana cleans dishes or clothes with Frances.

It is on a Tuesday when John walks around a dark corner and gets tugged into a dark room, his lips being captured with fierce devotion from his secret husband. They never go further than a few kisses and teasing touches, but it seems to be enough to satisfy their growing desire for each other until the next Tuesday can roll around.

As weeks go by with this mellow pattern of events, John finds he has managed to reach a point of relaxation within the repetitive schedule, knowing he has time to balance everything.

Until one day when it all comes spiralling into an unexpected mess.

"We were invited to the Valenfort's estate for a grandiose dinner party this upcoming Tuesday," Henry announces casually as he sips his wine. "You wereinvited as well, Mr. Hamilton."

Alexander looks up from his plate in surprise, his gaze flickering between John and Henry. "How kind of them to consider me."

"I was the one who asked if you could join us, sir," Henry replies as he places the glass down to continue eating. "The Valenfort's have three daughters of marrying age, so I assumed you both would be interested. Especially since you two had acquainted yourselves with the eldest daughter—Miss Margaret."

John pauses, his fork waiting in front of his mouth as images of a kind young woman laughing brightly whilst covered in snow flashes through his mind. He had nearly forgotten her until now. "I do recall her, yes..." John places his fork down and steals a glance at Alexander who keeps his eyes nailed to his plate, his features neutral.

Henry's lips quirk slightly as he cuts his food with great dexterity. "Mr. Valenfort and myself thought it would be in our family's best interests to properly acquaint you two—and I had put in a good word of Mr. Hamilton's honour as well which rather impressed the man as you have also impressed me, sir."

John stares blankly at his father as Alexander thanks him for his shockingly kind words. How can someone simultaneously say something so accepting and yet so utterly terrible?

John continues his evening in a haze, his mind murky since his comfortable pattern has been shattered by his father's insistence for them to attend this dinner party on the one day where Alexander and John can sneakily steal kisses and caresses. His innate schedule is further interrupted whence he is hastily tugged into the upstairs study. Before he can make word of his discontent, the door is latched shut and Hamilton's hot breath is sinking into his pulsing neck.

"What are we to do about the dinner party?" Alexander whispers in a deep tone, the sharp shadows upon his face flickering with the lone candle in his hand that is not gripping John's bicep.

"You gave me a fright," John replies breathily, ducking his head away from the door and closer to Alexander—closer to those rosy chapped lips—

"Do not avoid the issue at hand. What the hell are we supposed to do?" Alexander questions with an arched brow, his lips curling downward.

"We indulge my father for one evening and worry not of the consequences," John responds with a shrug. "I've been to enough of these by now that I have somewhat gained a skill in avoiding the prospect of marrying any of the eligible ladies attending."

"We cannot be aloof," Alexander hisses in retaliation. "Your father went out of his way to invite me. You don't think he is aware of—"

"No," John interrupts without hesitation. "That cannot surely be it. Perhaps he is impressed with your work in Congress?"

"I am doing the same nothing that everyone else is doing. We have been arguing over the same trivial matters since a few weeks prior," Alexander says wearily. "If it not be any suspicion of us, then surely he wishes to rid me of his house. Consider how this appears from my end, John. I am an unmarried, eligible man living with another unmarried, eligible man. If people were to start whispering—"

"Since when have you begun to worry about whispers?" John grumbles.

"Since your father started acting kindly to me," Hamilton snips in retaliation.

Laurens glares. "How is my father acting kind for once something to be worrisome over?"

"Because he has not once shown me such blunt kindness until now, when he sees an excellent opportunity to cut me from your life," he says, deadpan. "I may not know your father as well as you, but I still have perspective—he only does good deeds if it benefits himself or his legacy."

John scoffs, leaning against the wall and folding his arms over his chest. "You're right—you do not know my father as I do. Do not presume to judge his character in such poor taste."

"Why are you defending him?" Hamilton snaps, keeping his voice low enough to still remain quiet in his outrage. "First you complain about him controlling you, then you suddenly defend his controlling behaviour? I do not understand this ice and fire attitude of yours, switching your beliefs when it deems fit to your needs."

Alexander huffs, jutting his chin defiantly. "You're exactly like your father."

John peers at Alexander; a coil within himself snaps. He invades Alexander's space, caging him between his arms against the wall, and ignoring the clatter of the candelabra as it impacts with the ground. "Compare me to my father again and I'll—"

"What? Hurt me?" Alexander cuts in abrasively, holding his ground even as his figure dwarfs John's. "Why threaten me when I only intend to speak nothing but the truth with you?" John slackens his offensive posture, his expression melting into one of immense distress. "Am I the only one trying to keep this relationship afloat?"

"No," John whispers gently, sighing as he steps away, rubbing his face. "We cannot allow ourselves to worry over this. T'is one dinner party. How terrible could it possibly be?"

"Very much so if we do not play the game well," Alexander mumbles with wide-doe-eyes. "Why must you doubt me over your father?"

"I trust you with my life," John affirms as he steps closer, leaning down to level their gazes. "I only counter your worries with my own experiences at dinner parties, and I promise, this party will be so utterly forgettable that you will laugh at the idea of ever worrying yourself over it."

Alexander considers him with furrowed brows before nodding slowly. "Alright, Jack...I'll trust you."

John smiles with relief. "Thank you." He punctuates his sentence with a chaste kiss, his hand tucking behind the back of Alexander's neck to pull him closer and urging him onto his toes to reach. They part with a soft smack of the lips before Alexander leans against the wall again, chewing on his bottom lip and raising a devious brow at his husband.

"John Laurens," he gasps theatrically. "Stealing a kiss when your father's present in the house? You must be feeling bold tonight, sir," Alexander teases lightly with dreamy eyes and kiss-swollen lips. "Not really the actions of a proper southern gentleman..."

John grunts as he crowds Alexander's space again, basking in the passionate energy bursting between the two in the dark room. "I am no longer a courting gentleman, for I bear your ring, and so I may feel bolder within your enticing presence, sir."

Alexander chuckles warmly and shares one last kiss with his dearest beloved before the inevitable retreat from their safe shadow.

Chatpter 10

THE DAYS COUNT DOWN CLOSER TO
their impending Tuesday dinner party and John does
not allow his anxieties to best himself as he had put
great effort into calming Alexander's nerves only a few
nights previous. But as all good things in John's life,
his calm demeanour is slowly chipped away when he
notices something rather...strange.

John closes Frances' door and approaches the
study on his way to his room with a small candle
leading his dark path, like he has every night previous.
As he glances through the cracked open door, he halts
abruptly. Alexander pulls a few dollars from his coat
pocket and slips the money into the binding of The
Iliad before tucking it away into the bookshelf. John
blinks in surprise as Alexander hastily spins around to
face the desk and dips the quill into the open inkpot,

scribbling something in his accounting book before cleaning up.

John sharply retreats down the hallway as Alexander turns towards the door; he does not look back as he quickly strides into his bedroom for the evening. He leans his back against his closed door with a deep exhale, staring blankly into his room with a deep perplexion overtaking his mind. He recalls Alexander holding that very book when he had proffered Gulliver's Travels the night previous to his and Frances' birthday. How long had he been tucking away money into the book's binding?

Where did he even acquire such money?

John frowns, wondering why Alexander has been keeping such a peculiar secret from him. He places the candle beside the washbasin and stares at his reflection, his pale features unable to form a mask to shield his deepest concerns over this matter. Perhaps Alexander is saving up for something—whatever it may be, he knows not. He pours water from the porcelain jug into the bowl and cups his hands into the water to wash his face and his mind of this mysterious matter.

Alexander would tell him about his secret stash of money if it were important...right?

That single thought keeps him up that night as every possibility swarms through his mind like cicadas chirping vociferously, forcing his eyes to bore a hole into the ceiling until sunrise. Why would he hide such a thing from John? They're husbands now—perhaps not by any true law, but by heart and spirit. John openly trusts Alexander with his own money; surely John has a right to know whatever it is he is building that savings fund for. They discuss everything together—so why not this?

John keeps a sharper eye upon Alexander in the following days to come.

John watches Alexander when he eats. He watches him when he argues with men like David Ramsay or John Adams in Congress. He watches him in the evening after tucking his daughter in and stalking by the study, squinting through the crack as Alexander fumbles with The Iliad. As John continues watching from a safe distance, dark clouds build within his mind regarding why Alexander continues to act aloof, refusing to step forward to John and speak upon it himself.

After countless days of spying on his own husband, he has come to a chilling conclusion: Alexander does not want John to be knowledgeable of this secret fund.

'Could this be related to the dinner party?'

"No," John mumbles to himself as he paces through his room. "He must have started this long ago..."

'But when did he start collecting the money?'

"It's hard to say…" John whispers to himself under his breath as he continues to walk himself through his racing thoughts. "He could have started it in New York or even when we moved to Philadelphia?"

'What if he stole from your father?'

John freezes as the thought hits him and shakes his head. "No, no…he would never…why would he…?"

'Why else would he hide it from you?'

"He loves me. He would never betray me like that…"

'But you have. You selfishly convinced him to break off his marriage and then leapt head first into battle when he had begged you to stop—'

"I am acting like a damn fool." John glares at his reflection as his rationality and emotions become the better of him. "I've not betrayed him and he would never steal from my father."

'Perhaps you should check your father's safe and your questions will be answered…'

John stares at his bedroom door as the thought echoes through his mind. He impatiently taps his foot as he glares at the metal latch, refusing to give in to his suspicions. He had never even discussed his father's safe with Alexander so he knows it should still have everything in place…and yet his legs begin to carry him out of his room, down the hall, and into the study.

Alexander is out in the city on this sunny Sunday afternoon to take Frances to the park. John's guilt for feigning an ache in his head quickly fades as his skull pounds with great pressure. He unlocks the safe with trembling fingers and takes a deep breath before turning the latch. He tugs the safe open and drapes his arm over the door, staring intently into the safe. He thinks back to the day he took out extra money for his daughter's gift. He knows he had not opened it since then, and has seen his father avoid the study since he and Alexander took over the space for work.

John notices no jewels are missing and begins carefully counting the money.

Two-hundred-and-ten dollars.

John frowns and recounts the money.

Two-hundred-and-ten dollars.

Forty-five dollars is missing. John's breathing goes laboured as he hastily puts the money back and pulls out forty-five of his own dollars and places it inside the safe so his father does not discover the missing money. John closes the safe and rushes to his bedroom in a panicked frenzy.

Alexander stole from his father. Why would he do that? Did he take it because John told him his money is also Alexander's? But why would he take it secretly? Why would he do that? What is it for?

John breathes deliberately as his heartbeat hammers in his chest. He startles at the sound of the front door opening and the sounds of Alexander and Frances' laughter ringing through the halls. He lays back on the bed and ultimately decides to end his internal suffering once and for all tonight—only two nights before the dreadful dinner party he had nearly forgotten in his haste to spy on his husband. Now he cannot stop.

***

After supper is served, John leaves Frances to play with her dolls in the parlour with Diana in the room, dusting the mantle of the fireplace. John watches Alexander stalk up the stairs from his position on the armchair and counts to one-hundred in his head before following his trail. He plans to simply enter the study and confront Alexander. Should be easy enough to handle.

John hesitates at the door when he realizes Alexander is not in the study at all as he stares into the dark void of a room. He slides his feet across the wooden floors to not make any sounds and peeks around Alexander's bedroom door to find—yes, he be in here.

John furrows his brows with his back pressed against the wall, craning his neck to watch Alexander hastily tucking some money into a mysterious letter before grabbing the wax spoon to seal it. As it dries, Alexander stares at nothing in particular whilst drumming his fingers along the desk, seeming to ponder something profoundly. He abruptly stands and John pulls back into the nearest room, keeping the door open a creak as he listens to the shuffling feet next door.

John watches him stalk down the stairs and waits twenty seconds before entering Alexander's bed chambers, his curiosity at its peak. He frowns upon entry when he notices the letter is missing. He does not recall Alexander holding onto it when he left. Perhaps he tucked it away in his pocket when John was hiding?

"What the hell am I doing?" John mutters to himself in disbelief. He leans against the desk and sighs, rubbing his face with his palm. He hears the front door downstairs open and close and he ducks to watch Alexander through the window, walking with a lantern and a cloak into the foggy streets of the evening.

'Stay put. Leave it be. You are acting irrationally.'

John grunts indignantly as he pops up and practically jogs down the stairs, taking the steps two at a time, and takes long strides towards his cloak by the door.

"You're leaving as well, Mr. Laurens?" Diana asks from the parlour.

John doesn't look at her as he ties the string of his cloak around his shoulders and begins lighting one of the hanging lanterns nearby. "I'll be back soon. I just remembered that I had an errand to take care of."

"What is it with you two and running errands after eight in the evening?" Diana inquires in a light tone. A nosy one, she is. John scoffs and shoots her an incredulous look after lighting the lantern. Her hands are resting on her hips and she smirks at him with an arched brow. "I won't pester you about your where-abouts. All I wish to know is whether or not I should say anything to your father."

"I'd rather you did not relay every little thing I did to my father," John grumbles in retaliation.

"Noted, sir. I'll keep an eye on Miss Laurens and put her to bed if you so wish."

John softens at this and nods amicably. "Aye. Thank you. I apologize if I have been short-tempered with you—I don't want to be late."

She waves him off with a chuckle and a, "shoo, then!" before John manages to escape the bounds of the estate, hurrying down the foggy streets in the direction Hamilton disappeared off to.

Laurens must surely be losing his mind if he has resorted to following his secret husband through the dark streets of Philadelphia. *Talk to him like a normal person, you imbecile.*

That is what he intends, right? To meet up with

the man after following him in secret and discuss the stolen money with him?

'Was it even stolen? Or are you following a delusion?'

John halts and hides behind a parked carriage as he watches Hamilton reach the post office. The bloody place should be closed by now. Who the hell sends a letter at this hour? John snorts in mild amusement. Alexander does, apparently.

John blinks in surprise when Alexander places the lantern on the ground, pulls the letter out and stares at it. His face appears grim; his lips curled downward and his eyes narrowed. He looks at the letter as if its very existence had offended him. Alexander slowly taps the letter against his left palm whilst he stares down at the slot beside the post office's door.

He seems to contemplate sending the letter at all while he nearly slides the parchment through the slit before pulling it back at least three times, grunting loudly enough for his discomforting tone to echo down the quiet street. Laurens decides to make himself known, standing up and clearing his throat as he stalks across the street, loud enough to startle Alexander.

"John?" He discreetly tucks the letter in his coat pocket as he leans over to pick up the lantern and aim it towards John, squinting to get a clearer view of him. "What brings you here at this hour?"

"I am here to ask you that very thing, Alex," he

replies coolly. He stops a few metres away, keeping his features neutral. "Why not send that in the morning?"

Alexander sighs and pulls out the object in question. "It is hard to explain."

John shrugs. "It can't be too difficult for you of all people to explain yourself, Hamilton. I'd rather like to know, sir."

"Everything I do is not your concern, Laurens," he replies harshly. "I'll return soon. Leave me be."

John's demeanour shifts loosely as Alexander stands stiff and shielded like a caged animal. "Alex—"

"I said leave me be—"

"Where did you acquire the funds you had tucked into that letter?" John snaps, his grip on the lantern handle tightening enough to make his bones crack.

Alexander's frown deepens into a scornful scowl. "Do you spy on me now, sir?"

"Just put my mind at peace and tell me you did not steal from my father," John replies quickly, his eyes closing and his breathing laboured.

Alexander scoffs, the sound moulding into cynical laughter. "You think I stole from your father? Who do you think I am, John?"

"I don't know what to think when you act so secretive about such a simple letter." John pinches the bridge of his nose. "What is the money for? Where did you—"

"I had it saved—stashed away in safekeeping, you bastard," Alexander retaliates with a snarl. "And as for the contents of the letter, well" —he angrily steps closer to smack the parchment against John's chest, who manages to grab it before it falls— "why don't you read it then if it piques your interest so fucking much..."

John's stomach twists and sinks deeper as he places the lantern down to peel off the wax seal and opens the letter. He pulls out the twenty dollars and frowns at the words:

***

Father,

I had not received any response correlating to my previous letter last, so all I can assume is that it had unfortunately miscarried or you were simply too preoccupied to write back—I had been assiduous in my work these past months and have managed to supply you with more funds this time. Congress has invited me to work with them and soon after I will open a law firm with a dear friend of mine that I wrote of earlier—Mr. Laurens, if you so recall?

I have not much to say at this time so I must bid

you adieu, father, but know that I will continue to do you proud and carry our name high upon the ranks in America.

I send my best regards, yr. son

A.Hamilton

***

John lowers the letter and gapes at Alexander with a hollow chest. His voice is deep and croaky as he whispers, "my sincerest apologies..."

Alexander blinks and sniffles as tears leak from his eyes, leaving a glittery trail upon his freckled cheeks. He wipes them and huffs with irritation. "Fuck you, John."

"I had not known—"

"No, you assumed that I stole from your father—and for what, exactly? What did you possibly think I was doing with that money, hmm?"

John slumps in defeat. "I know not what I assumed. I had only come here to find out."

"Are you satisfied, Jack?" Alexander asks with folded arms over his chest, his voice frail. "You had the pleasure of witnessing a pathetic display of a poor bastard trying to win the affection of his estranged father."

"This does not please me," John clarifies as he tucks the money into the letter. "What I don't comprehend is why you assume such cruel things of me."

Alexander raises a brow. "I beg your pardon, sir?"

John presses the wax seal between his finger and thumb, his jaw tensing as his emotions skyrocket into oblivion. "Do you truly believe that I would look down upon you for this?" John glances around to be certain they are still alone. He steps closer and lowers his voice before continuing. "I love you, Alex. I wish you wouldn't hide from me. I desire to support you wherever I can and it is impossible to expect me to not worry when you keep secrets like this from me. I thought we promised to share everything with each other, my dear boy."

Alexander sniffles and nods solemnly. "I'm sorry. I didn't want you to think—"

"Shh," John coos gently, leaning in to wipe Alexander's tears before placing his hand on his shoulder. "I would never think less of you for anything. And I know you would not make the same horrid judgement for me, right?"

"Right," Alexander confirms as he miserably wipes his face. "Why did you assume I stole from your father, though?"

"What else am I to think when you keep a secret from me? My mind had assumed the worst since we share everything with each other—yet even so, I knew in my heart you wouldn't do such a thing, which is why I had come here to ask you." John pulls Alexander into a tight embrace, squeezing further as Alexander clings onto the back of his waistcoat. "You are allowed to have your struggles that I cannot possibly help with, but please!" —he pulls back to look into Hamilton's eyes— "don't hide from me. Let me support you, even if you think it won't work. You'd be surprised at what I am capable of. And regarding my father's money, I would not give a damn if you took some if you needed it. Please, all I ask of you is to not hide from me."

Alexander nods and sniffles one last time, proffering a sweet smile. John returns the letter and Alexander frowns at it. "I don't know why I keep trying to earn his love. I continue to make a fool of myself by sending these."

John puts his hands in his pockets and smiles. "If there is one thing I've learned from you, Alex, it be that real love is not a conditional thing. You cannot earn someone's love—it is boundless by any law. It is unspoken, raw, disastrous, and out of our control. Your father is the bastard fool for not loving someone as magnificent as you. I am so honoured to work with you and if he cannot see your worth, then he is the one with the error to fix, not you."

Alexander pauses in bewilderment. "Jack..."

"Send the letter. Don't send the letter. I do not mind. No matter what you choose to do, whether you send more letters or none ever again, know that I will stand by your side every step of the way. Sending letters to your father does not make you a fool, for even I still stand by my own father—regardless of how much he infuriates me, so."

Alexander looks around at the empty streets and sighs frustratingly, his voice lowering considerably. "Why must you speak such wonderful declarations when I cannot kiss you?"

John smiles knowingly. "Because I do not expect anything in return. I say such things whenever I wish because you deserve to hear it."

Alexander sighs gingerly, his eyes closing as he rests his head against John's chest. Laurens chuckles warmly at his demeanour, yet keeps a keen eye on the foggy streets. Alexander stands there for a moment, his forehead pressed against John's chest as he grips the letter against his own.

"This is the last time," he mutters, stepping away to approach the postal slot beside the door. "And then I'm done with him."

"Whatever you wish," John whispers.

Alexander quickly re-seals the letter before sliding it through the slot.

A lone and rather chilling thought lingers: *there was still missing money from the safe...where could it have gone?*

Chatpter 11

JOHN COMPLETES TYING THE CRAVAT around his neck and gives himself a once-over in the mirror. He nods in approval and puts on his crimson coat with floral embroidery, matching his waistcoat. He pulls the ruffled ends of his sleeves through the coat cuffs and puts Alexander's ring on his right-hand finger beside the pinky. He stares at it, trying to ignore the looming thought that money is still missing from the safe.

Alexander said he did not take it, so he has no reason not to trust him. John considers how he had so easily lied to Alexander in the past, but Alexander is not like him—he values honesty most of all, so why would he outright deny taking money from the safe if he had done it? He would have nothing to gain from that.

A knocking on his open door steals his mind's attention, reverting to the world around him. John watches Alexander's eyes examine his entire physique from the doorway, his skin tingling with the phantom sensation.

"You look dashing tonight, sir," Hamilton says with a raised brow and a charming grin.

Laurens considers Alexander's dark blue coat made by Mr. Mulligan and smiles at him. "As do you, sir."

"You should see Frances. She looks beautiful in Mulligan's purple dress," Alexander adds excitedly, waving at John, urging him to follow. "You did not spare any expense with this one."

They make their way down the hallway and hesitate at Frances' bedroom door, watching as Diana finishes touching up her golden curls. Her pastel purple dress flows down to the floor, the silky fabric shining smoothly in the low candlelight. The material appears soft and bright, and Frances' floral necklace matches it impeccably.

"Daddy, look! Diana did my hair!" Frances beams with a toothy grin. "Isn't it pretty?"

John's heart lurches painfully. He sees so much of Patsy in her features; in the way she smiles crooked-ly and bashfully twists her hands into the fabric of her skirts. , twisting her torso side-to-side as she awaits his response. "Yes you are, sweetheart. Very pretty."

Frances' grin somehow widens further and she looks into the mirror again. "I'm so glad I finally get to wear my new dress!"

"You'll have to be on your best behaviour tonight at the party, alright?" John reminds her as he enters the room to grab the white ribbon from the vanity. "These dinner parties mean a lot to grandpa." Diana smiles modestly and steps back as John ties the bow into her hair.

"Okay, daddy. I promise," Frances replies, wiping down her skirts anxiously. "Will there be any children there?"

"I believe the Valenforts have many children and a few of them might be near your age, but I am not certain," John answers as he steps back, tucking his hands in his pockets. Frances admires her reflection, running her fingers through the ribbon and straightens her necklace.

"I hope you enjoy your night off, Miss Diana," Frances says, watching Diana through the reflection.

"Ah, yes. Thank you, little miss," Diana replies with a warm chuckle. "I hope you have a wonderful time at the party."

"Mr. Hamilton? Jack—Fanny?" Are you ready?" Henry calls from the bottom of the grandiose staircase.

"It's nearly time for us to leave!"

"Coming!" Frances replies excitedly, lifting her skirts to zip out of the room past Alexander and John.

"Woah, careful, petite fleur! We don't want you getting hurt, sweetheart," Alexander says quickly as he stops her at the top of the staircase in haste. "Hold onto the railing and walk carefully, Fanny."

"Sorry, papa," Frances mumbles before doing as she is told. Hamilton tenses, staring dumbfoundedly at Frances as she retreats down the stairs. John blinks in astonishment, his heart summersaults as her words settle into his mind.

"Did she just—" Alexander cuts himself off in disbelief as he continues to look down the stairwell. He grabs his chest and blinks quickly as his eyes visibly become glossy. "T'was likely a jest because I had been ordering her around," Alexander adds abruptly. He sniffles and assumes his stiff posture.

"Aye, must be what it was," John replies, still staring at Alexander in surprise. He slots whatever had occurred in the back of his mind as they follow Frances down the stairs.

John helps Frances put on her cloak by the front door and Diana waits at the bottom of the stairwell, holding Henry's hat as he puts on his gloves and ties his cloak over his shoulders. She hands him his hat and the four of them retreat from the house, into the cool March evening. They walk down the street, John walking beside his father whilst Alexander and Frances walk alongside each other in front of them.

As Frances skips beside Alexander, making him smile and chuckle, Henry leans closer to John. "He takes well with children. T'is a shame he has none of his own as of yet—this dinner party should hopefully change that since there are a few eligible ladies in the family."

John grunts in acknowledgement, keeping his eyes on Alexander as he laughs warmly at Frances' bigger than life smiles and jests thrown his way. Papa is such a simple word, yet Frances had subconsciously reserved it for Hamilton. Whether it be a jest or a slip of the tongue, it changes John's entire perception of their relationship.

In truth, John never wished to father a child and he believed himself to be doomed with his inflection towards men—but Frances and Alexander, as the forces against nature that they be, have simply erased his previous way of thinking by merely existing in his life. Before, John would die for anything; his country and his honour. Now, his only desire is to live...for them.

The strange family unit turns around the corner, revealing the large Valenfort estate. They slowly follow behind a few other guests to enter the enormous dwelling; John's heartbeat palpitates with every step he takes. Their cloaks are taken by servants—John tries to not grit his teeth at the thought that they might not be paid—and they meet up with Lady and Lord Valenfort.

"Ahh, Henry Laurens. Glad you could make it!" the older man muses brightly, shaking Henry's hand with poised enthusiasm. He turns his attention to John and grips his hand tightly; John returns the same amount of firmness in his handshake, his faux smile shining with great charisma. "And this must be your son? John, was it?"

"T'is a pleasure to finally make your acquaintance, sir," John replies, attempting to shield how tense he is.

"William Valenfort," the man's grip tightens and John swallows. "I would have preferred you meeting me before canoodling with my daughter..."

"Bill!" his wife gasps with a nervous smile, furiously waving her parchment fan to distract her fidgety hands. "Don't be rude."

John's face simultaneously freezes and burns, paling and then morphing into a deep crimson to match his coat. William's features loosen and he slaps John's shoulder. "All is behind us, sir. I must confess, however, that I have never found a man who impressed my daughter quite like you—"

"Father, that is quite enough!" Margaret Valenfort intercepts quickly, hurrying towards them with her skirts bunched up in her fists. A few young women she had been standing with are clearly attempting to hide their giggles whilst she hastily joins the party at the entrance. She smiles bashfully at John as he recovers from William's firm handshake. "Mr. Laurens, I hope you fare well?"

He nods feebly as Frances hops on her feet. "How do you do, Miss Valenfort?"

John glances over his shoulder, already dizzy, and watches Hamilton introduce himself to the Valenforts.

"I am well, Frances. How do you do?" Margaret inquires sweetly.

"I'm fine. Do you like my dress? It's new!" Frances asks, twirling around to show off the flowing material.

"T'is very beautiful, little one," Margaret replies earnestly, her smile growing. "Did your father buy it for you?"

"Mhmm!" Frances hums, nodding excitedly. "T'was made by a spy, Miss Valenfort!"

The young woman giggles, covering her lips to stay discreet. "How miraculous! Also, you may call me Peggy, if you wish, since that is what my friends call me," Margaret adds with a smirk.

"My friends call me Fanny," the buzzing little girl replies with a toothy grin.

"—Isn't that right, John?" John swivels around, barely able to keep up with all of the conversations happening within the doorway.

John hums curiously and Henry chuckles with deep gerth. "I was telling Bill that you and Mr. Hamilton currently work in Congress and plan to open a law firm in York City."

"Ah," John nods sheepishly. "That is correct."

"York City, you say? My Peggy's always wanted to go there—" he abruptly stops, staring at Margaret and squinting. John turns around to see her abruptly straighten her posture, forcing a smile.

Alexander snorts amusedly before clearing his throat. "Well, I am rather parched," he says, averting the subject. "Wouldn't you agree, Mr. Laurens?"

"Yes," Henry and John reply simultaneously.

"Oh, Fanny, if you come with me, I can take you to meet the twins! They're about your age," Margaret says, looking at John for approval. "If that is alright with your father?"

"Of course. Have a wonderful time sweetheart. Remember what I said?"

Frances nods. "Be on my best bee-have-er?"

"Bee-hay-vior," John replies and she nods, repeating his pronunciation. "Good girl."

Margaret and Frances disappear into the crowd and John dizzyingly wades through the endless rooms and corridors in the Valenfort Mansion alongside his father and Alexander. His cheeks begin to hurt from strained smiles as the night carries on; he guzzles three glasses of champagne and eventually separates from his family to speak with one of the many Valenfort sisters.

John bobs his head, humming in feigned interest as he reaches out and grabs a new champagne glass from a servant walking by and replacing it with his empty flute on the platter. He takes a generous sip as Eleanor —or was it Alice?— rambles on about...something he cannot recall.

John drinks again, tilting away to scan the area. He smiles when he sees Frances run by with two other children, all of them giggling before immediately being told to slow down and behave from Mrs. Valenfort. John's eye catches sight of Alexander and lingers, watching him speaking with one of the other older Valenfort sisters that could be Alice —or Eleanor— with a charming grin.

"Penny, there you are!" Margaret's voice interrupts the young woman speaking to John. He stares sheepishly at the two sisters. "Mother was looking for you!"

"What for?" Penny —fucking hell, how many sisters are there?— replies with a raised brow.

"Oh, I don't know. Why don't you ask her?" Margaret answers sharply. Penny sighs indignantly and shuffles away.

"I am so terribly sorry about my younger sister, Penelope. I hope she wasn't a bother?" Margaret asks with elegance and grace, though her trembling fingers cause John to wonder what could have her on edge.

"Oh, no. She was not a bother in the slightest," John replies with a friendly grin. "It seems you continue to rescue me, Miss Valenfort—"

"Please, call me Peggy. We're beyond the formalities by this point, sir," she cuts in with a sly smirk.

"Aye, you have saved my bosom from an icy ground and we have thrown snow at one another which invalidates any formalities beyond this point," he quips back, causing her to giggle into her hand with pink cheeks. "Please, call me John."

Her smile timidly widens as she nods slowly. "Alright, John. Does this entail removing all formalities? Because I would very much wish for you to ask me to dance."

John flickers his eyes towards Alexander as he dances with one of the sisters. He finishes his glass of champagne and places it on a nearby table. "I am a gentleman and would very much wish to start fresh with you, Miss Peggy. Would you care to dance?"

She beams and John realizes that he is drunk as he nearly stumbles in his spot. "It would be my pleasure."

Despite his inebriated state, he dances the Minuet flawlessly, convincing himself that he only glanced at Alexander one....two times within the duration of the dance. He finishes off with a gentle kiss upon the back of her hand.

"Why Peggy?" he asks as they pull away from the dance floor.

She gives him a strange look and snorts amusedly. "I beg your pardon?"

"Why the name Peggy? How do you get that from Margaret? I never under-understood that," John adds, slurring a bit over his words.

"I don't know. Does it bother you, sir?" she asks with a grin.

"Hmm," he taps his chin, smiling at her. "I feel Maggie makes far more sense than Peggy —or Greta."

She laughs boisterously, causing a few heads to turn her way. She coughs nervously, trying to subside her laughter. "You are quite the jester, aren't you, John?"

"I only speak the truth, Greta," he replies, deadpan.

She snorts and covers her face, her cheeks burning a bright red. "If you ever call me Greta again, I may have to cease from existing."

"What about Maggie, then?"

She considers him as she whips out her fan and waves it quickly, attempting to compose herself. "This conversation is rather improper, sir."

"I thought we were beyond formalities?" John replies with a raised brow.

She hums and smiles contentedly. "Maggie works fine for me. But I must call you something other than John as that is far too boring for my tastes."

John lights up with a devious grin. "Oh?"

"Aye, sir. I will have to call you Johnny, instead," Maggie replies.

"Absolutely not. I would hope John is fine for your tastes, no matter how plain it may be," John replies, scrunching his face in playful disgust. She giggles.

She gives an exasperated sigh and John holds back a grin as she plays along with whatever game they are playing. "Fine," she drones, dragging the word as if it carries all the weight of the universe. "I suppose the name John will have to do. So long as I may call you that whenever I please and you may continue to call me Maggie."

He feigns consideration before nodding. "Alright,

Maggie. You have a deal then." John proffers a hand and she stares at it before shaking it firmly. She giggles as they release their hands.

John glances over and notices Alexander turning his head away at that moment, his lips no longer carrying that light charm. He appears rather grim and stiff. Serves him right for playing such a charming charade with the ladies. John shakes his head —his thoughts are becoming senseless— and he politely excuses himself to breathe in some fresh air, escaping the confining heat and bustling noise from inside.

The crickets in the moonlit garden immediately puts John at ease; he leans against the railing of the back porch, staring up at the night sky. His experiences tonight are one large blur of events that frankly transpired far too quickly for him to get any real chance to stand alone with his thoughts. As much as he constantly would seek out Alexander's flaming curls, he found his inner thoughts to be very quiet all evening.

"I thought I'd never get a moment alone with you this evening." Alexander's raspy voice startles John from his peaceful stargazing; he turns towards him with a sheepish expression. "You were not lying about your high society social skills. You actually seemed interested in what that young woman had to say."

John scoffs. "You're one to speak. You were warming up quite nicely to one of the other Valenfort sisters. The one with dark brown locks."

"Ahh, Eleanor," Alexander replies with an arched brow. "I spoke with all of the sisters. Even the only brother, Thomas, who very kindly showed me a drawing he and Frances made together."

John nods before grabbing his head in discomfort and leaning against the railing, his balance shifting. "So, would you wish to marry this Eleanor?"

Alexander frowns. "You are quite drunk, sir."

John laughs humourlessly. "Quite."

"Is anything wrong?"

John glares at the dark garden. "You know the only reason we be here is because my father wishes for both of us to marry an eligible lady."

"Why is your father so invested in my personal life?" Alexander asks as he approaches John, leaning on the railing beside him. "You, I understand. But me? Why?"

"Probably because you are an outsider living in his house," John replies tiredly.

"Why not just ask me to leave?"

"I don't know, Alexander. Why not ask...ask-hmm...him, yourself?" John slurs.

Alexander sighs and steps closer to John, lowering his voice. "Let's go on a stroll. I think we both could use a breather from the party."

John tries to decipher where and why the mood of the conversation shifted, but he relents. They step down the stairs and walk side-by-side along the cobblestone path, darkened by the night sky as they distance themselves from the mansion.

"I apologise for my boorish behaviour. My head is swimming in champagne and I feel like I have not had a moment to think until now," John says after a few silent minutes into their stroll. They're both nearly encompassed in complete blackness by now, swallowed by the shadowy bushes of the gardens, away from the extravagantly lit estate behind them. The only light source being the moon shining in the starry sky. "Whatever we saw of each other this evening was an unfortunate display for the people around us."

"I must confess that we both play the part required of us a bit too well," Alexander replies, tucking his hands into his coat pockets. "Your father is convinced you fancy Miss Margaret Valenfort. He told me so early on in the evening." He sighs, shaking his head slowly. "Even to my own eyes did it appear to be that you only had eyes for her all evening, even as you tolerated her younger sister."

"Well, t'is for the best that my father believes I fancy a wealthy young socialite over my handsome colleague from the war," John rasps in a low tone, his nose brushing against Alexander's auburn curls as he leans closer. He revels in Hamilton's hitched breath, stopping them at once to tug him into a shadowy bush.

"John—" Alexander's voice muffles into John's mouth as he passionately kisses him against an old oak tree. He pulls back only to press wet kisses along Alexander's jaw, groaning in delight as he makes his lover quietly pant and moan. "You're being rather bold tonight, sir."

John grunts in response, loosening Hamilton's cravat to press more kisses along his neck. "Allow my lips to remind you of who had my attention all evening..." John trails his lips up Alexander's neck and pulls back to look down into his eyes. "Any moment I had to myself, my eyes would wander towards you."

"The feeling is mutual, my dear," Hamilton replies breathlessly.

"If you are remotely jealous of a woman, think again, my dear boy..." Laurens leans down to press a chaste kiss upon Alex's rosy cheek.

"You also need not worry over any lady I've spoken to this evening," Hamilton replies earnestly, gently cupping John's jaw and rubbing his thumb across his cheek soothingly. "For my heart sings to you."

John smiles sweetly before leaning down to lock their lips in a searing kiss of fiery passion. Their breathing becomes laboured as they continue to fight for dominance, both nipping and sucking until John's legs turn into a gooey substance. He slowly slides down, running his fingers along Alexander's sides as he gets onto his knees in front of him.

"What are you— oh," Alexander exhales deeply, rolling his head back against the tree as John presses a firm kiss against the growing tent in his breeches.

"It's been too long," John whispers as he slowly unlaces Alexander's breeches. "And Tuesdays are supposed to be our day."

Alex chuckles, rubbing his hand against his warm neck and biting his lip to resist the involuntary moan. "You must be very drunk tonight since you would never risk doing this sober. I must also be drunk since I am allowing this tomfoolery to continue."

John shakes with laughter, biting his wrist and snorting, trying to remain quiet. He wipes a few tears away before lifting his index finger to his lips, shushing Alexander with hooded eyelids before continuing his quest of unlacing Alexander's breeches.

"Anyone could walk by at any moment," Alex whispers.

"Shh, we are far from the house. As long as you stay quiet, none walking by should consider glancing towards the dark bushes," John replies, punctuating his sentence with one final tug on Alex's breeches, causing the man to cover his mouth as he struggles to resist the moan eliciting past his lips.

John's blood thrums hotly through his body, keeping his heart pumping and his excitement riveting with pure ecstasy. Hamilton's quiet mewling remains an impressive skill that both have acquired during their many years in the war. John is quick and efficient, bringing his Alexander to an explosive finish with his hand clasped against his mouth, leaving him to nearly slide down the bark of the tree in his euphoric state. John deftly pulls up Alexander's breeches and laces them with shockingly steady hands for an inebriated man as he. He stands up and wipes his lips with his sleeve before patting down his breeches of any leaves and dirt. John leans in, caging Alexander against the tree between his arms, and plucking him into a languid kiss.

"Christ," Alexander mumbles dreamily into John's neck after they part for breath. "You have yet ceased to amaze me, my love."

"Hmm, and now you may carry that memory with you as we return to the façade we have so delicately fabricated for my father..." John whispers hotly into Alexander's ear. Laurens smiles proudly when he hears him sigh, knowing he has fulfilled his scheme to consume Hamilton.

John and Alexander re-enter the party with an extra pep to their step. Alexander runs his fingers through his curls and smiles knowingly at John who suavely strides through the crowds alongside him with a strong aura of confidence that was not quite there when they initially retreated from the party. The duo approaches the two eldest Valenfort sisters and playfully pout when the two ladies giggle not-so-discreetly at Alexander.

"What is so amusing?" Hamilton inquires with an arched brow.

"Your cravat, sir, has gone loose," Eleanor replies, her cheeks tinted pink as she holds in her laughter.

Alexander flushes deeply and adjusts the cloth expeditiously. John tries to not stare at the action, recalling the taste of his skin in the darkness of the night. "Ahh, thank you, Miss," Alexander replies with a sheepish cough. "I had only wished to get some air and have foolishly forgotten that I had loosened it."

"Ah, yes. T'is rather hot in here," Margaret responds with a wave of her fan. "I do not blame you, sir, for desiring some fresh air in this crowded assembly."

"Were you in the garden?" Eleanor asks, inquisitive.

"Aye," Alexander clears his throat and grabs a champagne flute from a passing servant. "I must praise it for all its beauty."

"My favourite spot is most definitely the oak tree.

I'll have to take you to see it, sometime," Eleanor replies innocently enough. Alexander, however, chokes on his drink at the mention of the oak. Laurens and Margaret struggle to hide their laughter as Hamilton urgently wipes the dribbling champagne from his chin.

"Hmm, yes, I would, ahh..." he trails off his confusing array of words as Eleanor smiles sweetly at him. He startles as a small figure tugs on his breeches. "Ah, little miss Frances," he says, certainly relieved of the disruption. "What is it?"

"Thomas won't dance with me," Frances whines with pouty lips.

Alexander scoffs as if this sentence personally offends him to his core. "Well, how rude of him." He places his flute upon the fireplace mantle. "Would you give me the greatest honour and dance with me, petite fleur?"

Frances' mood shines as she procures a toothy grin; she nods vigorously and Alexander takes her hands. John watches with a warm heart as Alexander awkwardly fumbles with the tiny child, twirling her around and swaying with her as she stands on his feet.

"Oh, my. He is so wonderful with children," Eleanor praises with a hand splaying upon her chest, rubbing gently as she stares in awestruck at the adorably awkward sight of a grown man stumbling to dance with a vibrant six-year-old.

"Aye, he is," John replies offhandedly, unaware of his thoughts being spoken aloud until it be far too late to take his words back. "He would make the most excellent father," John adds quickly, hoping to mask his exposed vulnerability.

"No need to play up your friend, Mr. Laurens. My sister is already smitten," Margaret replies cheekily, earning a swift elbow to the ribs from her sister. John smiles amusedly at the sibling antics between the two ladies, watching fondly as Eleanor grumbles something into Margaret's ear. He slowly shifts his attention back to Alexander as he is bowing to Frances; she curtsies in response and Alexander watches with a knowing smile as little Thomas gains the courage to ask Frances to dance.

John's thoughts seize beyond the memory of Alexander's trembling body against his whilst socializing for another endless hour. As he hears polite laughter from the group, his ears still ring with the choked back moans of Alexander. When he kisses Margaret's hand in farewell, his lips still hold on to the lingering taste of Alexander's skin.

He carries an exhausted Frances out of the estate, her light breaths puffing against his neck as they stroll to their house. His father speaks to him along the way, but his thoughts only focus on the dream-like week in January where it was only John, Alex, and Fanny. Somehow, in his inebriated state of mind, he only thinks more clearly now than ever. He is tired of resisting his deep passions for Alexander and hopes to worship him every night. Or perhaps he is still running on his high from earlier, but who is to judge a hopeless man in love?

After a dull shuffle into their estate and a good-night exchange from Henry, the man retires into his room. Alexander retreats towards his own room but is halted by Frances. She reaches out to grab his ear-lobe and he chuckles at the strange action resisting his escape.

"Come tuck me in?" She whispers sleepily.

"Of course," Alexander replies earnestly. John grins and the two take her into her room.

After changing the sleepy girl into her night-gown, John tucks Frances into her bed; Alexander stands nearby with a lone candle. She yawns like a kitten as John presses a sweet kiss to her temple.

"G'night, daddy," she mumbles sleepily.

"Goodnight, my sweet girl," John whispers in response.

Frances peaks an eye open and reaches out to-wards Hamilton. He chuckles warmly, placing the candle on the nightstand by her discarded necklace and presses a hesitant kiss to her forehead.

"Bonne nuit, ma petite fleur..." Alexander mutters

into her hair before pulling away. He runs his fingers through her golden locks, lulling her as she sinks further into her cozy bed. She sighs with a tired smile, snuggling into her pillow.

"Sweet dreams, papa..." she replies softly— Alexander's breath hitches and he jerks his hand away from her. There it is again; that simple word. It could not possibly be mistaken for a simple jest from a child since she had muttered it in such a vulnerable state of exhaustion.

John stares at the flabbergasted Alexander; the red-haired man's eyes grow glossier by the second as he stares down at the sleeping girl, slowly grabbing his chest and rubbing it as if something had phantomly wounded him. John clears his throat and grabs the candle before retreating from the room. Alexander follows him out, both silently gazing at Frances whilst closing the door to encompass her in peaceful darkness. Alex stares at the floor whilst he wanders towards his room, only stopping when Laurens follows him and places a gentle hand on his arm.

"Alex?" He tilts his head, smiling at him. "May I stay with you tonight?"

Hamilton blinks, his smile growing gradually before he steps aside, allowing John to enter his room. John quietly closes the door behind him, places the candle on the dresser, leans down —cupping Alexander's jaw— and captures his desirable lips.

Chatpter 12

JOHN BECOMES AWARE OF THE LIGHT shining directly into his face and his excruciating headache. John peels his eyes open, only to squeeze them shut in discomfort. He rubs his eyes before curling into the warm body tucked in front of him. He nuzzles into the flaming locks flowing down the bare freckled back and presses kisses into the skin there as a way of distracting himself from the painful consequences of drinking one too many champagnes last evening.

He would be horrified for acting so foolish right about now if Alexander was not worth such a mighty risk. In truth, he may be ill from the drinks, but his soul is liberated as he snuggles into Alexander, smiling at the steamy candlelit memories of the previous night. John wriggles his legs against his lover's, revelling in the pleasant discomfort lingering in his bosom from their nightly basket-making activities, and continues to re-linquish his dear boy in lazy morning kisses.

Alexander hums sleepily but does not show any other sign of rousing. John continues his conquest, trailing his fingers along Alexander's abdomen. He smiles deviously into Hamilton's warm neck as the ivory-toned skin prickles beneath his wandering fingertips. John pulls Alexander until he lays on his back, smiling now with his eyes still closed. John leans down, cups his face, and kisses his lips. Alexander responds sluggishly, his mouth moving in slow motion as he finally gains the strength to pry his eyes open. John tilts his head away to gaze lovingly down at Alex, who glows like an ethereal being in the sunlight.

"Good morning to you, too," Alexander says in a gruff tone, his voice still hoarse with sleep.

"I had a wonderful time last night," John whispers against Alexander's cheek, nuzzling his face soothingly against the grain of his oncoming stubble.

"I don't know what came over you, but I'd very much wish for a night like that again," Alexander replies with a low, rumbling chuckle.

"In truth, the copious amount of alcohol I con-sumed last eve may have erased any filters I have set up to protect us from being caught," John admits. "But even now as I am painfully sober, I've not a single regret in my soul. I wish to cherish you with my love every day, even if t'is but a simple embrace."

"Don't declare any promises you cannot keep, now," Alexander replies with a grim expression.

"I truly mean it," John responds in earnest, leaning down to pepper Alexander with feather-light kisses. Alexander snorts fondly, urging himself to avoid giggling profusely as John cuddles and caresses his dear boy. "I was a fool to resist you, darlin'."

"Hmm, for once you are correct," Alexander says with a smirk, earning a flick on the shoulder from John's finger. "Do you think we succeeded in satisfying your father last night?"

John hums, rolling over onto his back. "I hope so. And as we still speak upon the topic of last night, I wanted to ask of you in accordance to what Frances had said—"

"Say no more, John. She was only jesting," Alex intercepts with a tense jaw. "T'is fine by me, I do not mind at all."

John frowns, carefully considering Alexander. "What about when she said it again before she fell asleep? She would have been far too tired to conjure up any humour—"

"John," Alexander says in a challenging tone. "Enough."

"Does it bother you, so?" John asks defensively,

his nerves tingling with anxiety.

Alexander sighs in defeat, covering his face with his palms and shaking his head. "No. Quite the contrary..."

"Then why deny it?"

Alexander hesitates, chewing his bottom lip. "Because if she truly intended to call me that —if she sees me as a father figure and plans to call me such a word again— we will have to tell her to stop..."

"What?" John sits up, leaning against the headboard. "Why would we have to tell her to stop—" as he says it, staring into Alexander's deep blue eyes, he suddenly recalls the existence of the outside world. If his daughter were to walk around town, calling Alexander 'papa'—what social repercussions would come of that?

"Oh." John stares vacantly at the blanket covering the lower half of his nude form.

"Aye."

"You have been as much a parent to her as I've been," John adds, looking down at Alexander again as he sits up beside him. "She is young and so in her naive perception—"

"We are both fathers to her," Alexander says determinedly, looking into John's eyes. "She has no concept of what consequences could come of her calling both of us father—and I do not wish to have that discussion with her."

"Neither do I," John sighs. "But regardless of all that, you still avoid the fact, here."

"What fact? That we're doomed to a life of secrecy?" Alexander grumbles. "I was already aware of such a thing."

"Nay, sir. The fact that Frances considers you to be a father to her—you have yet to tell me how that makes you feel," John replies cautiously.

Alexander blinks, his eyes wide and glossy with vulnerability. He shakes his head slowly, looking at his hands wringing together anxiously in his lap. John leans over to hold his hands, ceasing the perpetual motion.

"It makes me fearful, John," he whispers after a moment. "I've always wanted to be a father, but I never thought..."

John waits patiently for Alexander to complete his thought, but he does not. He only shakes his head before leaning against John's shoulder, fiddling with their entwined fingers.

"Well, hearing her call you 'papa' only solidified what I already knew in my heart," John says with a smile. "That you both are my family."

Tears roll down Alexander's cheeks. John wipes

them away with his thumbs before pulling Alexander into a slow and sensual kiss. They chuckle softly into the kiss and Alexander climbs atop John's lap to deepen it. John runs his hands down Alexander's back and begins to breathe deeply through his nose as the heat between them coils his growing excitement. He lulls his head back, giving Alexander better access to his neck to kiss and nibble as he pleases. The blanket slides down, exposing their bare skin to the glow of the rising sun.

A sudden rapping on the door extinguishes their flame, leaving them in a deep chill as they abruptly halt their movements with owlish eyes.

"Mr. Hamilton? Are you decent?" Henry's voice rings through the door.

In John's panicked haze, his eyes flicker across the room, looking at the clothes strewn about on the floor that paint a vivid image of what has transpired in here.

"No!" Alexander replies urgently. "Give me but a few moments, sir!"

The pair leaps from the bed in a frenzy and begin re-dressing themselves. Alexander dresses sooner than John and throws the crimson waistcoat and matching jacket into his wardrobe.

"I need those!" John hisses as quietly as he is able whilst shoving the end of his shirt into his breeches.

"No," Alexander whispers sharply. "You will exit through the window facing the garden and walk into the home from the back door. If your father catches you, he will question why you're still wearing your clothes from last evening—"

"Mr. Hamilton? Are you alright, sir?"

"Aye, sir! Just a moment!" Alexander replies loudly over his shoulder towards the door. He turns to see John opening the window leading to the side of the house and staring at the vines along the wall with frightened features. "You'll be alright?"

John wordlessly nods before turning to Alexander. Despite the situation, he smiles and leans in for a final quick peck with adrenaline flowing through his veins. He pulls back and carefully begins his trek down the side of the estate, gripping the vines along the brick with a powerful grip. Alexander closes the window and hurries to open his door as casually as possible.

Henry's features exude suspicion as he looks down at Hamilton. "I apologize for the early intrusion, but I was hoping you've seen my son? His bed appears to be empty and made as if he had not slept in it last evening."

Alexander leans against the doorframe, feigning confusion. "Huh, how strange. Perhaps he is already awake?"

"Where would he be at this hour?"

"I know not as I've not seen him since we returned to the estate last night after the party," Alexander replies smoothly.

"I had hoped to speak with him before you both leave to Congress this morning, so if you see him—"

"Worry not, Mr. Laurens. I will make sure John knows you require his presence if I see him before you do. I am sure he can't have gone too far at this hour. Perhaps on a morning stroll in the back gardens?"

Meanwhile, on the side of the home, leading into the back garden—John loses his grip on the vines and falls from the lower half of the wall, landing in the bushes. He hastily stands, wheezing and wiping the dirt from his breeches and shirt. His muscles ache and his head throbs, but he determines there be no serious damage as he can awkwardly stumble out of the bush patch.

Laurens pauses when he notices soft giggling; he sharply turns his head and gapes at Miss Margaret Valenfort who stands on the other side of the fence that separates the property from a pathway leading towards the park.

"What on earth are you doing?" she asks after finally calming herself enough to breathe.

"I can see how this may appear, but I promise

you there is a perfectly reasonable explanation."

"Is your staircase broken, sir?" she inquires with a sly grin.

"Ah, no... I was only trying to avoid my father," John replies sheepishly, rubbing his neck.

"Ah, I see. Perfectly reasonable," she concedes with an arched brow, angling her chin lower. "You must truly wish to avoid him if you're willing to climb down the foliage on the side of your home, sir."

"This not be my home. T'is only a place to live until I may return to my home," John corrects as he rolls up his sleeves.

"Oh? Where is your home, then? If you don't mind me asking?"

He thinks of nothing but his family when he replies with, "New York." John pauses —realizing he would usually say South Carolina— his immediate response to her was rather surprising for himself as it was for her.

"That is where you plan to run your Law Firm Esquire with Mr. Hamilton after your time in Congress, correct?" she asks with a tilt of the head. She seems strangely forlorn about this and John cannot quite place why he would read such an expression on her face. Perhaps they are becoming faster friends than he had previously realized.

"Aye, miss."

"I thought we were past formalities, John."

He chuckles, resting his hands on his hips. "You're right, Maggie. My apologies. I still attempt to uphold my southern gentleman upbringing, regardless of the fact that you have seen me stumble and fall on multiple occasions."

She giggles at this and John smiles, proud of himself for brightening her spirits again and subverting the subject matter from his and Hamilton's future life together in New York.

"Jack, what the hell are you doing?" Henry's thundering voice cracks through the light-hearted mood of the interaction between the two.

John looks over at his father wearily. "Ah, father. I was only out here to get some fresh air when I noticed Miss Margaret Valenfort walking by and we had merely greeted each other only moments ago."

Henry's face shifts from disappointment into one of...*amusement*? He smiles knowingly, raising his brow questioningly. "Of course. And she merely happened to walk by our property this early in the morning. How utterly convenient."

John blinks at Henry in befuddlement; who is this man before him as it be nothing akin to the father he knows? Margaret flushes deeply and John continues to gawk between the two of them, wondering what the hell he has gotten himself into. "Did you, ah, intend to speak with my father or have you come to embarrass me?"

"Have a good day, you two," Margaret interrupts firmly before walking in the opposite direction of the park, seeming to forget herself as she practically flees from the scene with tinted cheeks.

"You seem to have made a friendship with this young woman," Henry observes nonchalantly as John approaches him.

"I suppose, as she is our neighbour and we had visited her family home last evening?" John replies suspiciously. "What was it you wanted, father?"

"Ah, it was actually regarding Miss Valenfort and you," Henry replies earnestly, reaching out to pat his son's shoulder, and leading the both of them inside. "I have yet to see you so vibrant with another woman since Martha Manning."

John's stomach anchors him to his spot, halting the two of them in the back corridor. His nerves explode as if his humerus bone has been punctured by a nearby object. "Pardon?"

"All I am saying, son, is that if you were to pursue a relationship with this woman, I'll give you my blessing." John stares at his father in surprise. This is not where he thought this conversation would lead to at all. "Their family is quite notable and Margaret Valenfort seems to make you happy. And that is all I want for you, my boy, is for your happiness."

"What gives you the impression that she makes me happy?" John inquires bewilderingly.

"Do you recall the day I arrived?"

John swallows painfully; he is unable to forget it, unfortunately. "Yes?"

"Beyond my initial disappointment, Diana has since prescribed me another perspective."

John raises a brow, his dread only worsening his post-intoxication headache. "Oh?"

Henry smiles and John wonders when he had last seen his father smile in such a way. "When you played in the snow with your daughter, you were so full of life, son. I see now Miss Valenfort's presence that day, albeit how inappropriate it may have been, had brought out that spark for life in you, Jack."

Henry's words strike something within John's heart. Henry had completely forgotten Hamilton's presence that day—in truth, it was not Miss Valenfort, but rather Alexander's presence that had done the very thing Henry is referring to. Alexander and Frances are his family and the ones responsible for John's drive to continue living—Miss Valenfort is a mere footnote that had somehow forged her way into the forefront of

Henry's mind and in John's life.

It's no wonder Henry was so very eager to bring them to the dinner party last evening. John could scream at how absurdly this all panned out.

Thankfully, he does not.

"What are you saying, father?" John replies in a gravelly voice.

"I am saying that I support yours and Miss Valenfort's future courtship if that is where all of this is leading to." Henry's features twist into a firm one. "I hope that is where this leads to. We don't want a quick eloping like last time—and possibly offending her father and tainting yours and her legacies."

"Of course not," John says automatically. His heart is somehow simultaneously full and devoid of every emotion imaginable. "Thank you, father." John resists the urge to smack his tongue against the roof of his mouth as the words leave an unforgiving aftertaste.

Henry nods curtly before one final pat on his son's shoulder. "Now, get yourself dressed. I do not intend to keep you from your busy work in Congress. We can further discuss the details on how we may propose this courtship to the Valenforts later on?"

"Aye," John croaks weakly, nodding. He swiftly turns and walks towards the stairwell, his mind

already racing from one loose thought to another—
none of them being able to hold still long enough for
him to properly focus on them or anything around him.

"Oh, John. There you are!" Alexander's voice
chimes from the stairwell, interrupting John's dizzying
thoughts. "Your father is looking for you," he says as
he nonchalantly pulls the ruffled sleeves from his coat
cuffs, smiling innocently as if this be the first time they
have seen each other today.

"Ah, I've already spoken with him, Mr. Hamilton,
but thank you," Henry pops in from behind, reassuring
and annoyingly chipper.

John hurries up the stairs as Alexander jests over
his state of undress with his father, his mind swimming
in an agonizing hurricane of revelations. How is he
supposed to approach this situation without setting off
any signals regarding his inclinations towards a very
specific man?

John wishes to have never allowed Miss
Valenfort onto their property that day, for he had
unintentionally planted a seed that has been
blooming amidst his targeted attention on his secret
relationship. He had blinded himself on what had truly
been transpiring behind his back within his father's
plan for John's future. He'll have to tell Alexander what
is happening.

How is he supposed to avoid a possible courtship

with Miss Valenfort without rousing any suspicions in his father? What are he and Alexander supposed to do regarding Frances calling Alexander 'papa'?

Where the fuck did the missing money in the safe go?

John glares at his neatly made bed, a sore reminder of the pain in his head and his rear from last night's —and this morning's— events. He furiously whips the pillow at the far wall in his blind and rather sudden burst of rage. Control and freedom is an illusion perpetuated from his youth. Congress leaves him bitter with no real change beyond the separation from the British Monarchy. And now his father bears the burden of his reality; he and Alexander were doomed from the beginning and he had refused to accept it all.

Dying with glory in battle seems far more appealing to him as he scathingly dresses himself for another goddamned day in this hellish post-war life he has trapped himself inside of.

Chatpter 13

JOHN HAS TO TELL ALEXANDER ABOUT
the courtship proposal, but he chooses to push them
in the rear of his mind like most of his responsibilities.
Instead he sits in front of a blank sheet of parchment,
tapping the tip of his quill against the wood near the
inkpot in deep contemplation. One of the last things he
said to his sister before leaving was that he would refuse
to write to her for assistance as he would not require
it—but now as he sits here, staring at the page, he fears
he has no other choice.

Patsy has always been able to calm their father
down regarding his misplaced but well-intentioned plan
for John's future. She was the one who got him off John's
back long enough so he could study in   Geneva
and secretly explore his desires. Patsy always had John's
back and he had good intentions for her as well. Since he

last saw her before Frances' birth, she has gotten more reserved, and he wonders if she took his   advice to better fit into what society expects of them. But his bitter spite is keeping him stuck in this   perpetual state of being.

The thought of telling Alexander what is going on before he has any real plans to stop this from happening leaves him with no other choice. He must ask his sister for assistance here in Philadelphia. He finally lifts the quill over the inkpot and dips the tip in the black ink before beginning to scrawl his desperate plea for Patsy's assistance.

***

My dear sister,

I finally wave the white flag, surrendering myself for your urgent assistance. This not be in accordance with Frances, but rather our father—he arrived very suddenly in January and has yet to leave the premises even as I write to you. In truth, Patsy, I must confess things have gone well for all of us, but I require your immediate presence in Philadelphia.

Our father has this misplaced need to have me married to a local young woman by the name of Margaret Valenfort—a good girl, no doubt, but I know not know how to explain my lack of desire to marry as of yet to our dear father as he refuses to listen to what I have to say.

I pray you are able to talk some sense into him and explain how sudden this all is, for I do not wish to begin such a courtship with this woman so soon after not only discovering my wife's passing—but so soon after having Frances introduced into my life. We were perfectly content, just the ~~three~~ two of us—and our father has continuously disrupted the relationship with my daughter. I hope you see my perspective in this and write to me soon—or even reply by simply arriving at our Philadelphia estate.

Your niece fares well and misses you as much as I.

Your dear brother,

John Laurens

PS. Send mine, Frances, and Hamilton's best regards to our neighbour, Mrs. Rosmund. I hope you two are settled nicely and we hope to hear from you both soon as it has been far too long since any of us have kept in contact. I am aware I struggle to upkeep correspondence, but I must beg for your response as soon as possible.

***

John places the quill down, nearly knocking over the lone candle illuminating the dark study. He moves the candle away from his flailing hand before powdering the letter. He works quickly to have the letter enclosed as soon as possible before anyone might see—

"What are you doing?" Alexander asks from the doorway with folded arms.

John sighs in defeat as he presses the hot wax onto the parchment to seal the letter. "I'm sending a letter to my sister."

"What happened? What did your father say to you this morning?" Alexander saunters into the room, closing the study door behind himself.

"Why must you assume the worst?"

"Because you vowed to not write to your sister unless it was an absolute emergency," Alexander replies wearily. "And you've been in a sour mood all day."

John looks down at the letter and chews the dead skin from his bottom lip. "Something did happen this morning, but I don't believe you'll enjoy hearing about it."

"Did he...discover us?"

John snaps his head in Hamilton's direction with wide eyes. "Heavens, no! He expects me to propose a courtship with Miss Valenfort."

Alexander's features twist into an unreadable one as he leans on the desk beside Laurens. "Hmm, that sounds about right..."

John raises a curious brow, hoping Alexander will continue his thoughts aloud, but alas, he continues to stare perplexedly at the hardwood floor. "You don't seem surprised or even hurt by this."

Alexander shrugs noncommittally. "Why would I? It would be far too exhausting. This was bound to happen eventually. We don't even share a bed any longer these days so us marrying off to eligible ladies won't be any different than what we suffer through currently."

"I refuse to do it," John bites back with gritted teeth. "The thought of subjecting another woman into a loveless marriage nauseates me to my very core."

"Stop pretending to care about what is best for the women in this scenario. You don't give a damn about them," Hamilton snips in retaliation. "You only care about how this affects us which is perfectly reasonable—so stop pretending to care about the ladies to appear like a fucking gentleman."

"Fine," John grumbles. "The thought that I should have to subject myself into another loveless marriage sickens me."

"There you are—now that is an honest response," Alexander says with grim features.

"What do you expect your sister to do about this, anyway?"

"She aided me once before," John replies quietly. "She had convinced my father to allow me to go to Geneva on my own."

Alexander raises a curious brow and nods sluggishly. "Ahh, yes. Where you and Kinloch spent some time together." The way he says his name sounds like the vowels and consonants leave a bitter taste upon his tongue.

John scoffs. "That's beyond the point. She is calm and collected and can talk some sense into him for me."

"Have you ever tried to talk to him about your disdain to marry at this time or are you simply hiding behind your sister like a coward?"

John snaps his head in Alexander's direction fiercely. "You bite your tongue, sir."

"All I suggest is that you speak with him yourself, first, before sending that letter," Hamilton replies with a grimace.

"He is abundantly aware that I do not wish to marry," John retaliates. "I have voiced my wants and desires on multiple occasions and he still disregards them. Do not call me a coward."

"I apologize for calling you cowardly, but John,

when have you spoken to your father about such matters? I've not personally heard of these discussions taking place."

"I don't tell you everything, Alex," John snips back with rose-tinted cheeks. "They were discussions that we've had over the years."

Alexander groans, rubbing his face tiredly. "Alright, fine, but back to the matter at hand—I don't see how Patsy can somehow change his mind if you cannot do it yourself."

John fumbles with the letter before tossing it carelessly on the desk behind him. "I've no idea of what else I could do at this point. If I outright deny proposing a courtship, he will become suspicious."

"Then go through with the courtship if we shan't risk the possibility that he could discover us otherwise," Alexander replies with a shrug. "I could, perhaps, propose a courtship to her sister and then we could become brothers-in-law. That way we can stay near each other without raising any suspicions."

John's face twists in discomfort. "Absolutely not."

"Why not? It will be our cover story, like the old spying days in the war."

John examines Alexander perplexedly. "Just like that—you're willing to accept this without a fight?"

"Men like us don't receive what we wish to have," Hamilton grumbles bitterly. "We make do with what we are handed in this world to survive. We could still see each other in secret—we were not shy about our affair during the war when you were married. What would be different this time?"

"This not be a relationship built upon lust. I love you, Alexander, and I wish to be with you in other capacities beyond pleasuring ourselves below the waistband of our breeches," John whispers sincerely, lacing his fingers with Alexander's and tucking a stray curl behind his ear as they gaze into each other's eyes. "I long to do laundry with you and Frances, or play in the snow, or cook supper together. I wish for both of us to read bedtime stories to our daughter and hold each other in the night when we feel like we may be drifting away. We've made a family, the three of us, and marrying off into new families will rip away the only thing that holds my will to live."

Alexander's eyes glitter in the candlelight as tears build up. He forcibly wipes them away, yet one manages to escape, sliding sluggishly down his flushed cheeks. John leans in to kiss away the rolling tear on his cheek, only pulling away enough to look into his eyes. "The war was something to be survived. Our family and our lives beyond the war should be ours to have—I don't want to survive any longer. I yearn to live. With you."

"Oh, Jack." Alexander's voice catches, husky with affection. "You undo me."

Laurens cups his jaw and connects their lips in a chaste kiss. He smiles into it and tilts his head to deepen it, tangling his fingers in the small hairs at the nape of Alexander's neck. His queue falls loose as John's fingers tug and prod at the strand to elicit sweet gasps from his dear boy. Alexander's free-roaming hand slides down John's waistcoat and his fingers rest lightly upon the edges of his breeches, teasing the buttons as he turns the kiss into one even the French would swoon over. John's body bursts into flames with every touch Alexander—

CRASH!

"Oh my god!" Diana yelps in terror, causing the two men to leap away from each other.

John stares with a palpitating heart, wiping his wet lips with his palm as he registers the tea tray laying upon the hardwood floor; one of the cups had fallen away from it and cracked. He adjusts his breeches, utterly scandalized as Diana stands in the doorway, ogling at the two men in frozen bewilderment with her mouth agape.

"Diana," Alexander says hoarsely. "What in god's name are you doing here?"

"I—" she swallows, seeming to find her bearings as she fumbles onto her knees to clean up the mess.

"You were supposed to be working. Your father suggested I bring you both tea." As she speaks, the sound of faint footsteps in the distance gains speed as they near the stairwell. Her breathing and speech grow at rapid speeds. "I thought you were working. My hands were full. I should have knocked."

"Diana?" Henry's voice calls from the stairwell, laced with concern.

Hamilton kneels in front of Diana, grabbing chipped porcelain pieces further from her reach. "Allow me to help—"

"Is everything alright up here? I heard a crash," Henry's voice bellows as it grows nearer to the study.

"You saw nothing," Alexander hisses sharply, pointing the sharp edge of the chipped porcelain in her direction. She stares at it, wide-eyed, and presses her lips firmly together as Henry enters the study. The room begins to spin as Henry attempts to decipher the scene before him, dizzying John as he leans against the desk, stunned to his core.

"She lost balance of the tray and had dropped it by mistake," Alexander says smoothly, dropping the sharp piece of the cup onto the tray as if he hadn't threatened Diana with it moments ago.

"Aye, sir." She looks up at John and he nearly loses his constitution at the mere sight of her horrified expression. "T'was an accident."

Henry, oblivious to her expressions as he looks down upon her back, shakes his head and sighs. "My apologies. I had sent her in hopes to keep your spirits high as you work—I hope you were not too greatly disturbed."

Diana's features twist uncomfortably at this; Alexander promptly ignores her. "We were startled but t'is all fine and well."

Henry hums, looking at John. "Well then, if all is settled, I'll leave you to it." Henry chuckles warmly as he stalks out of the room.

Diana scrambles to her feet moments later with the tray in her hands. "Sorry to disturb you both. I'll be off—" she halts abruptly as Alexander closes the door on her, disallowing her exit.

"I'm afraid we can't let you go until you promise to keep this between us?" Alexander whispers, raising an antagonizing brow as he puts all of his weight against the door.

She breathes heavily and nods feebly. "Of course, sir. It was a mistake, sir."

"Try to knock next time you are about to enter a room with a closed door." Hamilton seethes with disdain as he speaks. Diana nods again, more firmly this time, before he forces a placid grin. "Glad we've come to an understanding." He opens the door and she rushes out without a hitch.

As Alexander closes the door again, John falls to his knees, clutches the potted plant in the corner, and expels his supper into it.

"Oh god!" Hamilton hisses in despair as he hurries to John's side. "My love" —he hesitantly places a hand on John's shoulder— "are you alright?"

Laurens shrugs the hand away and lowers his head shamefully. "Don't." He squeezes his eyes shut and mutters, "S'il vous plaît Seigneur, a pitié sur mon âme," under his breath.

"We'll be fine."

"We'll be damned to Hell," John snips in retaliation.

Alexander scoffs indignantly. "As if we already weren't before today? I thought you had given up on the morality of our relationship?"

"My father will kill me," John whispers with wide eyes, ignoring Alexander's words as he glares at the safe in the corner of the study. "He'll kill you and then me."

"She won't speak on it," Hamilton replies earnestly.

"Right, because threatening her was the proper thing to do in this scenario?" Laurens snaps, turning away as he stands unsteadily on his feet. "Who's to say she won't tell him out of fear for my father and child's well-being?"

"She's only a slave," Alexander says stoically, his cheek twitching. "He wouldn't believe her even if she did reveal to him what she had bared witness to. Your father would deny it in fear of his precious legacy being tarnished."

"She is not a slave," Laurens bites back, looking over his shoulder with a darkened glare that has Hamilton stepping back in trepidation. John glances away from Alexander and down at the letter he wrote to Patsy, sealed and ready to be shipped to York City. "And you don't know my father as I do." He grabs the letter and delicately hovers the corner of the parchment over the candle flame.

"What the hell are you doing?" Hamilton questions in a small voice.

"I am cleaning this mess we've made," John replies coldly. The letter catches flame and he tosses it carelessly into the fireplace, the hypnotizing sight reflecting in his hollowed eyes.

"But I thought that you..." He doesn't finish his thought.

John keeps his stony gaze on the flames as they envelop the plea for his sister's assistance. "You were right. Men like us don't receive what we wish to have."

He glances at Alexander with deep longing. "I can't risk yours or Frances' safety."

***

Laurens spends the night cold and alone, dreading the inevitable. He wonders how he could spontaneously perish as he dresses himself the next day. He drags himself down the stairs and finds the breakfast table already set with his father, daughter, and Hamilton sitting there, chatting amongst themselves.

"Ah, good morning, Jack," Henry chimes brightly as John tiredly sits across the table from Hamilton and beside his daughter. He grunts in acknowledgement as he places food onto his plate from the buffet in the centre of the table. "How was your night, son?"

John tries to not think of Alexander's lips upon his as he replies. "Fine." He pauses in his motions as Diana enters with a coffee tray; they make direct eye contact. "I actually thought a lot about what you said, father," John carries on, his gaze unmoving from Diana's as she places the tray on the table beside Hamilton.

"Oh?" Henry lifts a curious brow as he reaches for a coffee cup.

"Aye, sir." John turns his attention towards

his father, unable to look at Diana or Alexander as he speaks his next words. "I would like to propose a courtship with Miss Margaret Valenfort as soon as possible."

Diana fumbles with Hamilton's coffee cup, nearly spilling it on his arm. "I'm sorry, Mr. Hamilton!"

Alexander waves her off with a hum, his expression stoic and far-away as he stares out the window whilst sipping his coffee.

Henry smiles and pats John's shoulder encouragingly. "Wonderful news, son! I'll set up a meeting with Bill! I'm certain he will approve, no doubt. That young lady fancies you."

"Fancy?" Frances pipes in curiously, looking up from her plate as she had been playing with her food distractedly moments before. "What does that mean, daddy?"

"Nothing that concerns you, sweetheart," John assures her gently. "And food is meant to be eaten, Fanny—not to be played with like your dollies."

"Sorry," she mumbles before plucking a grape from her plate and popping it in her mouth.

As Henry boasts about setting up the meeting regarding the proposal, John avoids any eye contact with another person in the room, opting to gaze longingly at the sharp carving knife laying by the fresh bread.

Any moment he strays his gaze away from the table, he catches Hamilton looking away in that moment to stare out the window behind him, or catching Diana's strangely distressed expression as Henry goes on about this courtship's benefits.

"Oh, not to mention your daughter may have some future siblings. Perhaps a few younger brothers to carry on the good Laurens name?" Henry adds with a knowing grin, causing John to nearly choke on his bread.

"Let's not get ahead of ourselves now, father," John croaks out weakly. "We haven't even proposed a courtship yet. Let's not go into the topic of marriage as of yet."

"Why not discuss future marriage benefits now? That is where this will lead to, anyhow," Henry replies before taking a languid sip of his coffee. "A new wife and mother to help you bring more legacies into our household name."

"Oh, why don't you look at the time, it's getting late! We should really be off to work, John," Alexander interrupts sharply, standing jarringly from his seat and causing Frances to wince at the scraping sound from the chair dragging across the floorboards as he excuses himself from the table.

"Right, yes. I must go now father, but we may

discuss more later on," John says quickly, standing and kissing his daughter on the forehead before rushing out of the dining room after Alexander.

As they exit the estate, Laurens walks alongside Hamilton, slipping his hands into his pockets as they stroll down the pathway towards the park. "I don't believe we're expected to be in for another two hours today."

"I couldn't sit through that for another minute," Alexander replies gruffly. "Besides, I need to speak with James Madison now that Jefferson has left for France. I wonder if he may be willing to hear out our ideas regarding slavery and how to abolish it efficiently."

"What gave you such an impression that he'd listen to our proposition?"

"I can probably convince him. I'd rather waste my morning talking his ears out than listening to your father drone on about you having any more kids with this woman," Alexander admits, chewing the dead skin off his bottom lip. He winces when it bleeds and brings his finger to his lips, wiping the blood away. John tries very hard to not watch, keeping his eyes on the path in front of him.

"I see." They walk a few more minutes in silence. Hamilton's posture is far stiffer today as he walks nearly an entire metre away from him on the empty pathway. "You're upset."

Hamilton snorts, unamused. "Aye, sir."

"You told me you expected it to happen. That it would be far too exhausting to let it bother you so. That men like us do not—"

"And then you had to pour your heart out and remind me why our relationship is special—why it's worth fighting for," Alexander interjects harshly. "But then you gave up on all of that as if it meant nothing to you. I swear you were mighty convincing with that speech, sir."

"I meant what I said. Have you forgotten the part when we were caught? Or did that slip your mind?"

"By a servant," Alexander snaps. "We were caught by a fucking servant. She didn't say anything this morning. Actually, she seemed rather confused as to why you were so very eager to get married to Miss Valenfort."

"My father seems to think of her in high regard. He would listen to her, I think, if she said something," John replies.

"Your father? Really? Having high regard for a woman like her?" Hamilton laughs dryly, utterly humourless. "How many slaves does he own, eh? He only pays her to keep his liberated and spoiled son at bay."

John grabs Alexander's bicep and pulls him into

the array of bushes and trees, the park still dimly lit with the rising sun and thick fog rolling into the scene. He holds him against a tree and takes pause, unable to shake the thought of two nights previous when he had Alexander in a similar position.

"Why must you mock me? I know you're upset, but tarnishing my character out of spite is a new low, sir. Even for you."

"So you believe I already can go low, is that it? Am I merely a low life to you?" Alexander shoves John's arms away. "I am tired of this back and forth, John. You say you love me and promise to express that every day, and then the next day —nay, the next breath— you say we cannot be together and that we must suffer like every other man that might be inflicted with what we have. If you wanted us to marry off to ladies, you shouldn't have told me to break off my courtship with Miss Schuyler!"

John stares at Alexander for a moment, his throat constricting as old wounds are being dug into. "So you do resent me for that."

"I didn't before now," Alexander snaps. "Now I am a bachelor without an eligible lady that I would not mind marrying."

"What about Elanor Valenfort?" John inquires curiously. "What about the brothers-in-law plan you conjured up?"

"I do not feel the same for her as I did for Betsey," Hamilton confesses. "The Valenfort plan is a means to an end. If I were to marry a woman, I'd rather marry one that I do not mind sharing my company with."

John blinks and turns his head slightly. "Betsey?"

Alexander raises a brow. "Elizabeth. Miss Schuyler. Same thing."

"It's not the same thing," John says slowly. He breathes deeply, stepping out of Alexander's personal space. "Did you love her?" John asks quietly. "Did you ever love me?"

"Look at that ring you wear upon your finger and look around you, John. I chose you."

"You didn't answer my questions," John snaps. "Did you ever love me?"

"Of course I love you. I've loved you for years."

John breathes wearily. "Did you love her?" Alexander glares at John but visibly bites his tongue as he breaks eye contact, glaring at the ground shamefully. John steps back further. "My god, you loved her."

Alexander shrugs. "Why should it matter if I did or not. I wanted you more."

John scoffs and marches away. "Unbelievable!" He distantly hears Alexander following him, the fog around them thickening with the early spring chill. "All this time my suspicions were correct. I have made a terrible mistake leaping for you, it seems."

"And what about my suspicions of you? I know your shoulder looks worse than I last saw during the war. I heard whispers that you were honourably discharged after a foolish decision you've made in the dead of night!" John stops at once, freezing in panic. "Aye, sir. I know about the Combahee Skirmish. You really thought I wouldn't discover such a thing?"

Laurens turns his head ninety degrees, looking at the dirt path and avoiding Alexander's eyes, unable to speak.

"You were feverish," Hamilton continues in a wobbly tone, his voice cracking with bursting emotions he has seemed to repress until this moment. "You took your men out in the dead of night, took them to battle in the dark when you heard gunfire on your march. You were shot off your horse, lucky to only get a bullet in your goddamned shoulder again and not in the chest." The wind whistles as a tear slips past John's eyes. "You went in as if you wanted to die. I would wager that you read my letter that night and you still went into battle knowingly."

John turns around completely. "The thought of living in a world beyond the war frightened me," he admits in a croaky voice. "As far as I was aware, you wanted to find Miss Schuyler again and attempt to marry her because that would have better suited your needs than a spoiled molly like me."

"So you admit it then. You wanted to perish."

Laurens sighs, looking away into the hazy park and nodding slowly.

Hamilton kicks a stone into the blank abyss of the smoky mist, cursing loudly as visible tears stain his freckled cheeks. "So this is it, then? You were going to leave your daughter as an orphan? Leave me alone to mourn your demise as I marry off and have a family of my own, away from you permanently?"

"It would have been easier that way," John whispers.

"It would have been fucking miserable!" Alexander roars in retaliation. "In truth, I don't love Elizabeth Schuyler. I was growing fond of her and saw a potential love brewing, but then you wrote to me. You were the one who told me of a dream you had in which you met me as an older man with silver strands of hair by my ears, one where I had begged you to choose your life over what is safe. You chose me and I cherished that, waiting with bated breath until you returned to me! And you were going to fucking die anyway like a goddamned coward!"

Laurens doesn't think as he steps forward, reaching out and grabbing Hamilton's coat collar and pulling him into a deep and passionate kiss. Alexander melts into it, wrapping his arms around John and pulling him closer as they stumble into a tree.

"I'm sorry," John mumbles into Alexander's lips, hoping his words seep into his lover's skin to heal the wounds he had made. "You're right, I am a coward, but I don't know what to do. I swear on my mother's grave that I love you with every inch of my damned soul, so help me god" —he punctuates his sentences with feverish kisses— "I'm sorry. I'm sorry. Please forgive me, for I am a fool. How can I keep you and Frances safe without the risk of being caught?"

Alexander pulls back for breath, pressing his forefinger against John's lips. "There will always be a risk." He sighs, leaning his head against John's chest. "I understand you cannot avoid this courtship. But do not push me away. We can figure this out together. Just... stop pushing me away. Don't give up so easily, my dear Laurens."

John nods, holding Alexander close to his heart in an earth-shattering embrace. All the tension from years of secrets and lies finally falls loose between them as they say their peace. "I'm sorry I lied to you about my discharge from the army."

"And I apologize as well." Hamilton pulls back enough to look into Laurens' crystal blue eyes. "Next time we mustn't hold such baggage close to our hearts if we wish for this between us to work."

"I agree." John tucks a russet curl behind Alexander's ear. "I promise to share my heart with you."

"Like the John in that letter who was candid about his nightmares?"

"Aye, if you promise to do the same," John whispers.

"I do," Alexander replies breathlesslybefore pulling John into another tight embrace. The birds chirping around them remind them of their surroundings in the foggy —and thankfully vacant— park. They reluctantly break apart their embrace, but now with a solidified promise in their hearts.

**

John and Alexander walk into the estate with boisterous laughter as they jest upon the dreadfully bland day in Congress. As they step into view of the parlour, they halt when a man clears his throat. John turns in bewilderment at the sight before his eyes.

"Miss Valenfort?" Laurens asks, looking at her, her mother, then her father who sips a golden whiskey with a raised brow. He flickers his gaze to Henry, flabbergasted. "What is this?"

"You said you wished to have this taken care of as soon as possible, and Bill was more than eager to get this over with as well," Henry replies, patting Mr. Valenfort's shoulder in a far too friendly manner, one that insists a closeness that was not quite there at the Valenfort dinner party. "We've spoken a lot and I have offered a wonderful proposition for his family in your favour."

"Your father tells me that you wish to court my daughter," Mr. Valenfort says, approaching John with an intimidating flair. "Is this true?"

John swallows thickly, turning towards Margaret and watching her hopeful eyes bore into his tainted soul. He does not risk a glance in Hamilton's direction as he replies. "Yes, sir."

Mr. Valenfort turns to Margaret. "Well, t'is ultimately up to you, dearest. What do you say?"

She barely hesitates as she stumbles out a quick, "yes!" She clears her throat, seeming to find herself as she corrects her eagerness. "I mean to say that yes, I agree to your terms of courtship, Mr. Laurens."

Henry and Mr. Valenfort chuckle in celebration. "Wonderful!" Henry boasts proudly. "Glad we could come to an agreement upon this matter at hand."

"Hear, hear," Mr. Valenfort cheers as he raises his

glass of whiskey.

"Jack, come drink in celebration!" Henry declares excitedly as he begins pouring two glasses. "You as well, Mr. Hamilton! I'm certain you'd very much wish to celebrate your colleague's achievements?"

Laurens' blood turns to frost as he remembers Alexander's presence in the room. He wearily gazes at him and is shocked to find him smiling rather convincingly. "Of course, sir!" Hamilton turns to John as they receive their glasses of whiskey. "To your success, prosperity, and good health upon your future courtship!"

They all clink their glasses together, Margaret watching John with a wistful smile as he drinks half of his cup. He watches Hamilton in the daze of uproarious conversations between the men in the room; he seems light on his feet and undisturbed—in fact, he seems rather cheery. Laurens takes true notice of Mrs. Valenfort for the first time as she ushers Margaret away from the men. John observes his life slotting against his own merit yet again, the chess pieces sliding in the places Henry had devised all along.

John regrets burning that letter to Patsy.

In the hustle of the chatter, he manages to catch Hamilton's eye for a brief few seconds. Alexander gives him a knowing wink before carrying on his larger-than-life charm with Henry and William Valenfort, causing John to breathe in relief.

They'll be okay. They're still on the same team and nothing will tear his love from him again, no matter what transpires in their cascading lives.

Chatpter 14

LAURENS HAS NEVER COURTED anyone, and he fears that his ignorance upon the matter will slip through his performative attitude towards Margaret. Someone always chaperones their outings and he never quite grasps onto a topic of discussion with her. He fears he is beginning to bore her with his placid smiles and empty conversations as his or her father shadows them nearby, always a heavy presence.

John also wonders why Diana has not spoken about what she had witnessed; perhaps she took Hamilton's threat to heart, even though he truly knows it to be a rather empty one. Two weeks have gone by since the initial courtship proposal, yet he is certain they've been doing this for years. However, he minds not since he can always say farewell after a few dreadful hours and spend the evening with his daughter and Hamilton.

He smiles as he holds his teacup, dreaming of his family and longing to see them again. Delicate fingers wiggling in front of his face pulls him from his daze, anchoring him into reality again as Maragaret watches him from across the table with a raised brow.

"My mother went inside," she says, placing the cup on the table. "I must apologize, for I have not quite been myself these past two weeks. T'is only the fact that they keep watching us with such intensity that I feel as if I truly cannot get to know you as we have before the courtship," she admits in a conspiring tone.

"They only watch us because of my own father's insistence," John comments in a low tone as he places his cup down. "He is concerned about what we could do in private..."

"Why would he be so concerned? What would we do other than talk amongst ourselves?"

John moves closer to reply, but flickers his gaze to Mrs. Valenfort as she re-enters the sunroom. The two of them assume their previously stiff postures as she takes her seat at the nearby table. John wonders if this is what courting Alexander would be like if he were allowed to do so. He sighs in frustration as he goes to sip the rest of his tea, despising these high societal standards.

Mrs. Valenfort takes notice of the young couple's

discomfort with a raised brow; John internally kicks himself for letting his mask slip. She gives them a once-over before standing once again. "Oh, I had completely forgotten that I promised the twins I would take them to the park. Perhaps you two could finish here after I leave?"

John gawks at her and Margaret smiles gratefully. "Yes, of course. Go on, mother. We won't be much longer, anyhow."

Mrs. Valenfort eyes John for a moment, sending anxiously chilling tendrils down his spine—a warning, no doubt—then she nods curtly and excuses herself once again from the sunroom. John nervously holds the cup to his lips to sip from his tea but finds it to be empty—he sips on air, pantomiming the action to buy himself time to conjure up an excuse to leave.

"Finally. Alone at last," she whispers. "My mother can be reasonable sometimes."

John hums, looking away awkwardly as he still holds the cup to his lips for a beat too long before placing it down. "I appear to have finished my tea. I should return home to tend to my daughter's needs, I'm afraid."

"Wait!" Laurens halts as he stands, staring at the hand locking around his wrist, resisting him from fleeing. "I haven't had a chance to truly speak with you until now."

"What do you wish to say?"

Margaret shrugs, standing up and stepping closer to John. She laces their fingers together; he swallows thickly, wanting to flee like a redcoat with a white flag. "I don't know. Everything? Nothing? I wish they didn't watch us so closely. You have always been a perfect gentleman. I don't possibly know what we could do besides learning more about each other?"

John casts his gaze away and gently pulls his hand from hers. "There is something you don't know about me and my past. You see, my late wife and I were...ah...not married when we had conceived Frances. I assume your propriety is what our parents worry over."

Margaret raises a curious brow and tilts her head. "I thought you had to be married for such a thing to work?"

John stares at her, his soul sinking deeper into the depths of hell as his face flushes crimson. "Sometimes just doing the act can make it happen."

"Doing the act? What are you referring to?"

John yearns to throw himself into the Delaware. "Do you not...understand how a child is conceived?"

Margaret blushes deeply and shrugs half-heart-edly. "I was admittedly educated rather scarcely upon the matter. I was instructed that I would learn more when I got married."

Sweat trickles down John's forehead and he backs away. "There is a reason why my father is weary of us being alone together and I feel that we should not contravene with the rules in place, despite your mother being courteous. I would like to do this properly." He clumsily bumps into the doorframe and she furrows her brows in confusion. "I apologize, sincerely, but I really must go. I'll see you tomorrow." John distantly hears her saying farewell but he retreats from the Valenfort mansion in haste.

Laurens strides at a brisk pace to his father's house and enters with a clouded mind that soon clears up when he stops at the sight before his eyes. Hamilton is on his hands and knees in the parlour, neighing like a horse as Frances squeals with joy, gripping his coat collar with intensity as she points a stick from the garden outward.

"Quick, horsie! We must defeat the redcoats!" Fanny cries theatrically as Hamilton begins crawling around the room, purposely bumping her up and down so she may giggle and hold on tighter. He makes a peculiar clicking sound with his tongue which John soon realizes, amusedly, that it is meant to be his 'horse hooves' impacting with the dirt.

As they pass the sofa, Frances slices her stick across her dolly and it falls to the ground. She cheers triumphantly and Hamilton neighs, lifting to wiggle his arms as a horse would when spooked, causing her to fall on her rear and laugh hysterically.

"I've fallen!" she giggles from the floor.

"Aye, but falling never meant staying down for your father," Hamilton replies, reaching out his hand to help her up. "Your father has fallen off many horses in the war, and many times had been shot down—in his right shoulder!"

"Ouch," she replies empathetically. John realizes he has been smiling like a fool as his face grows sore. "He never gave up?"

"Never," Alexander replies earnestly as he sits on the sofa. She climbs onto his lap and he situates her more comfortably, still having not noticed John watching from the corridor. "Your father was very brave in the war, refusing to stop fighting for what he believed in."

"What about you?" Frances asks, waving her stick around in a strange attempt at a parry.

"Who, me? I spent most of my days in Washington's offices, writing boring correspondence for him."

"Lies, sir!" —Hamilton and Frances snap their heads in Laurens' direction as he saunters into the room— "I do recall you falling from your own horse in battle as well, Hamilton."

Alexander scoffs as Frances gasps in awe.

"Really, papa? You fought, too?"

"Not nearly as much as your father."

"You fought plenty," John corrects patiently. He sits down beside the duo and slips the stick out of Frances' grasp before she may smack his face with it. "Did you tell Frances about the time you had stolen canons with your militia?"

"Woah!" she gasps in awe. "Canons are the big boomers, right? That goes like—" Frances does a dramatic reenactment of her interpretation of a canon, expanding her arms abruptly as she screams a loud— "*boom!*"

John and Alexander laugh. "Aye, petite fleur," Hamilton replies between chuckles. "You are correct."

"Alexander was in the war since the beginning," John adds after a beat. "I only joined in seventeen-hundred and seventy-seven. I went straight to Washington's headquarters and met this fiery young man, passionate for change."

"That's how you met?" Frances asks, her head tilting innocently, her eyes big and curious.

"Oui, Fanny," Alexander responds, bouncing his leg to erupt a few giggles from her. "I was not very fond of him when we met, but we became friends rather quickly after our craggy beginnings."

John laughs, flushing like a schoolboy as he

recalls his embarrassing memories of that first day in camp. His hair had been powdered and he was wearing the finest silks, getting side-glances from the soldiers, whispers spreading around him as he approached the main tent. He had accidentally bumped into old Reed on his way into the tent and had been on his rough side ever since. And Hamilton had been arguing with said man, his face still pink from the heat and his fury. John had a fleeting thought that he desired to kiss those cheeks until they became redder, but had quickly dismissed the thought before shaking his hand in greeting.

Even as their start may have been rocky, he cannot deny that the first moment he laid eyes on Hamilton, he had been smitten.

"Aye, but soon enough I was welcomed into the aides' family—which, as I mention them, I recall Lafayette had convinced all of us aides to call Hamilton our petit lion," Laurens boasts jovially.

"Little Lion?" Frances giggles.

Alexander scoffs at John but finds himself grinning. "I know not why they called me such."

"You were the shortest of us," John quips back. "And fierce like a lion."

"Absolutely not! Meade was shorter by two inches!" Alexander declares, earning bubbling laughter from the Laurens'. John and Alexander take a moment to collect themselves. "Anyway, enough of the past. How was your day? When did you return?"

"T'was fine—I returned not very long ago," John replies with a shrug of his shoulder, allowing the subject to change.

"Where were you today, daddy? You leave a lot without papa," Frances inquires abruptly, yerking John out of his blissful haze.

"Pardon?"

"You've been leaving an awful lot and we have to wait for you to come home," she says as she bends over to pick up her dolly. "Where were you, daddy?"

John makes eye contact with Alexander and the two swallow deeply. "Ah, I was visiting Miss Margaret Valefort for tea today, Fanny."

Frances stops flopping her dolly around and hugs it, looking at John wearily. "Oh? Are you making new friends?"

John sighs, leaning over to straighten the dolly's dress to utilize his twitching hands. "Not quite, sweetheart. Miss Margaret Valenfort is, ah…" he tilts his head, pulling his hands to his lap, trying to figure out how to form his incoherent thoughts into words. "I am courting Miss Margaret."

Fanny looks at Alexander now, expectant with wide, youthful blue eyes. "Cowr-ting?"

"Coor-ting, dear. It's when two grownups famil-iarize themselves with each other before marriage," Alexander explains patiently; he absentmindedly bounces his knee as he continues speaking. "Your father is hoping to possibly marry her someday soon, and you'll have a proper mother and father again."

Frances frowns, shoving herself off of Hamilton's bouncing leg. "I already have a mommy," she snaps, hugging her dolly closer to her chest. "I don't need another mommy."

"Frances," John says soothingly, kneeling in front of her and holding her shoulders so she may face him properly. "Nobody will replace your mother. What Mr. Hamilton aims to say—"

"Papa!" she yells. "He is my papa!"

"No," John bites back. "He is Mr. Hamilton. I am your papa."

Frances whips her dolly at John's face and stomps on the floor. John stares in bewilderment at the beginnings of her tantrum. "No! You're my daddy! He's my papa! And I don't want another mommy!"

"Frances Eleanor Laurens," John roars, causing her to shrivel. "You will stop this!"

She folds her arms and harrumphs, shaking her head violently. "No!"

"Frances, listen to me!" John yells. "You will

cooperate with me on this. You will be kind to Miss Margaret—"

"No, no, no!" She squeezes her eyes shut as tears begin to spill.

John sighs shakily but keeps his expression firm. "—And you will cease with this childish game you've created by calling Mr. Hamilton papa, do you understand me?"

"It's not a game—"

"Stop this—"

"He is my papa—"

"No, he is not!" John roars, standing on his feet to look down at her, fueled with a strange array of frustration from his pertinacious child whom he cannot escape.

"I hate you!" she cries, sprinting out of the parlour whilst wiping tears from her blotchy face.

"Fanny!" Hamilton calls out desperately, chasing after her. "Come back! Don't leave your father like this!"

John follows behind, racing through the corridors before stopping jarringly as he spots Frances gripping Alexander in a tight embrace. He is on his knees at the end of the hallway, holding her with tears of his own slipping down his cheeks. John watches with watering eyes as Alexander rubs soothing circles on her back.

"Petite fleur, you must listen to your father. You have to stop calling me that."

She sniffles, pulling back to wipe her snotty nose. "But why?"

Hamilton sighs with a tremor to his breath. "Because I am your father's friend, and being good friends with your father does not make me your papa."

"But you treat me like daddy does," Frances whispers. "You tuck me in at night and play with me and show me how to speak and write like you."

"I know." He rubs his face, sniffling in defeat. "But you have to stop. I can't explain why, but you must. What will people think if you call me papa in front of them, hmm? I am only a friend of the family. I am not a part of it, so it might confuse people."

"But I love you like I love daddy," she mumbles.

Hamilton stares at her with wide eyes. Silence thickens the air around them.

In a blink of John's eyes, Alexander curls himself and expectorates a desperate sob, covering his face with one hand whilst gripping the floor with the other. "Papa?" Fanny gulps, folding herself around his quavering shoulders in a gentle embrace. "Don't cry, papa. I'm sorry I made you sad."

He only continues to wail in sorrow and John collapses to his knees, crawling to the two of them with a sharp pain in his chest. "I'm sorry," he mumbles with a hiccup. "I'm sorry. I'm sorry. Shh," he whispers soothingly, sniffling as he rubs affectionately into Alexander's back. He settles himself in a sitting position on the floor and cries into John's chest as he holds him. Frances shuffles between them and John holds them close to his stuttering heart that he has shattered with his own hand.

They sit together in a pile on the floor for endless moments before a hand gingerly grips onto John's shoulder. He stiffens his muscles and turns to face the person, staring in bewilderment when he discovers it is Diana, on her knees with deeply disheartened features.

"How much have you witnessed?" John whispers in a gravely tone, his voice worn from crying. Frances and Alexander look up at her with ample eyes.

"Enough to discern why you're huddled on the floor." She glances over her shoulder before turning back to them. "Your father is outside still, speaking with one of the neighbours. You should get up before he finds you like this." Diana quickly stands and offers a hand to Frances who dozily complies, rubbing her eyes exhaustively as she stands up and walks away, hand-in-hand with Diana, towards the stairwell. "I think it's time for a nap, little one. You've had a rough day, haven't you, darlin'?"

Frances hums affirmatively before they turn to ascend the stairwell. John helps Alexander stand up and the two wander into the kitchen to straighten themselves. They utilize the recently filled water basin by rinsing their faces of any evidence pertaining to their emotional outburst.

"I should leave before this becomes any more difficult to bear," Alexander whispers hoarsely.

John does not respond, knowing the deeper implications of such a phrase beyond simply leaving the room. Alexander waits not for a response; he wordlessly exits, his posture wooden and distant as he sulks away. He aggressively pushes the swivelling door open, leaving John alone with the *creak-swish* of the door whilst the hinges slow it down until there be nothing left.

John loses track of himself, his body going through perpetual motions for minutes, perhaps hours, until he finds his way sulking up the stairs, weighed with every step he takes.

***

"How does your daughter fare?" Margaret inquires as they stroll arm-in-arm down the stone pathway, their fathers a few paces ahead and mingling softly amongst themselves, his steps still heavy.

John pretends to not ponder over the way his daughter had ignored both him and Hamilton this morning after their emotional outburst the previous day. "She is fine."

A beat of thick silence passes them. Birds chirp in the trees, the nearby Delaware splashes with the current. "How about your friend, Mr. Hamilton?"

John's features remain utterly indifferent. "Fine. They're all fine."

"And what about you, John?" They pause by a peculiarly grand tree and he sighs, looking down at her as she pulls her delicate arm out of his. "You seem unwell today?"

His right shoulder aches but he disregards it. "I am fine."

"Haven't you gained a stronger vocabulary whilst in school?" She raises a curious brow; John notices their fathers continue walking around the bend, unaware that they have stopped. "Seriously, John. Are you alright?"

His throat disallows his scream of agony for them to urgently return. "We should continue walking before our fathers take notice of our absence," he says, instead.

"Stop avoiding the question," Margaret interrupts furiously. "You have been acting strangely since we've started courting each other. Acting as if you do not wish to be here."

"Because I do not, in fact, wish to be here," he snaps. As her eyes widen, he realizes his error.

Damn.

"No, wait. I had intended to say—" she turns around, shaking her head in annoyance. "Maggie, I apologize. I had not meant to—" he sighs in frustration.

"What is on your mind, John? Why do you not wish to be here?"

He stares at her. "I do wish to be here. I did not intend to imply otherwise."

"There was no innocuous purport, sir," she hisses, snapping her head around to look sharply at him. "You've expressed that you do not wish to be here in the most frank of terms—"

"I meant to say that—" he glances over her shoulder where he last saw their fathers disappear around the bend. He takes her by the shoulders and ushers her towards the tree, hoping to procure some sense of privacy in this public park. She looks utterly scandalized, blushing furiously as they situate themselves against the tree. "I had somewhat of a disagreement with my daughter yesterday after we had tea. She was rather upset and it's been haunting my mind ever since. I greatly apologize if my mood implies I did not wish to spend time with you."

Her features twist from irritable to one of sympathy. "Oh, John. I am so terribly sorry." She gently holds his cheek, smiling with great tenderness. "I am aware that you care for your daughter tremendously." Her eyes flicker to his lips briefly; his heart drowns. "You're an exceptional father, always looking out for her." Her hand slides to the back of his neck as her voice drops into a husky whisper. Before he may react, she pulls him down and firmly presses their lips together. She is quite chaste in her advancements, but John finds himself now being the scandalized one as her fingers tangle in his hair above his queue, deepening the kiss.

He wishes to enjoy it and to hold her close. John, instead, pushes her away in a panicked frenzy. "What are you doing?"

"Kissing you," she declares breathlessly. "You are the only man I know who goes out of his way to make sure his daughter is well and becomes visibly distraught when she is unhappy. No other man is willing to be so involved in his child's life whilst still working so hard to provide for his family, and I admire that about you, John."

Laurens is flustered, wiping his lips with his hand and coughing shyly. "Oh." He cannot bear looking into her eyes as her words truly settle into his mind. "Oh..." He loses his balance as his mind becomes an echo chamber. He has broken Hamilton's and his daughter's hearts but had somehow won Margaret's in the process. This is all so terribly wrong, yet it should be right. He should respond in haste, kissing her back with passion. He should ask for her hand in marriage right then and there as his heart swells with joy, planning to expand his family with this kind woman who sees something special in him.

"I can't do this," he whispers erratically. "I can't..."

She frowns in confusion, tilting her head and holding his trembling hand. "John? What's the matter?"

His soul screams as if it be dragged to hell for all eternity whilst he stares down at her. "I am so sorry. I cannot lie to you. You've been so kind to me, but I must cease this before it goes on too far." He squeezes his eyes shut with great shame, the only image behind his eyelids being one of peril and heartbreak as he recalls Hamilton sobbing on the floor, unable to withhold his despair from Frances any longer. "The argument I had with my daughter was regarding our courtship, Maggie. She doesn't want another mother and I do not know what to do—I feel utterly compunctious for having carried this on so long."

Margaret examines John closely, seeming to solve an elaborate puzzle in her mind. "I see how that can be difficult. Does she still grieve the loss of her mother?"

"Aye..." John looks away and Margaret gasps under her breath.

"Oh, John. Do you still grieve the loss of her mother?"

Laurens' gaze interlocks with Margaret's. Nobody had ever seemed to consider asking him such a thing when their parents had insisted on building their courtship. He speaks not a single lie as he replies with, "I do. I'd only discovered that she perished only a few months previous—on the date of my birthday, no less."

She covers her mouth with glossy eyes. "Oh, dear! You poor soul." John attempts to swallow the ball of needles forming within his throat. "Why propose this courtship if you and your daughter still mourn her?"

John sighs, depleted of all energy. "My father insisted. I did not want to tarnish your reputation with my own. Most are aware I had eloped with my late wife, and I did not want people to whisper about you simply because you stood by my company a few times."

Margaret smiles. "Ah, yes. Father's always must look out for their children. Although, sometimes, perhaps, even if they mean well, they intervene in the most inopportune of ways..." She leans against the tree, her hands pressing against it behind her back as she gazes off into the middle distance. "I also understand what it's like to be the eldest with far too much on your shoulders, and your parents expecting you to be married expeditiously to a flawless namesake."

"You don't appear to be upset over my revelation," John observes aloud, his voice laced with disbelief.

"How can one be upset when they can empathize, John?" Margaret replies earnestly. "If you and your daughter still mourn your late wife, I cannot endure this courtship any further. Or at the very least, not at present as you are certainly not ready for remarrying at this time."

John gapes dumbfoundedly at her. "What are you saying?"

She stares into his eyes defiantly. "We must end this. I refuse to marry a man whose heart belongs to another."

John's eyes swell in trepidation. "I b-beg your pardon? My heart does not—I do not—"

"I'm no fool, John. I recognize what a person who loves someone that does not or cannot reciprocate looks like. Trust me, sir. I know." She sighs with deep melancholy as if she attempts to say something between what she actually articulates.

"I've not a clue as to what you refer to," John

replies, attempting to remain collected and aloof. He is now plagued with nothing but over-analytical thoughts of his outward perception towards society. Had he been too affectionate with Alexander? Had she noticed?

"You still love her," Margaret states, deadpan. "It's alright, John."

He blinks, astonished.

Oh.

The beast within his soul claws away at his intestines for experiencing relief over her interpretation of where his affectionate devotion lies. "What do we do? This courtship must come to some sort of conclusion."

"Agreed." Her eyes light up and she pushes away from the tree. "Propose to me."

"What?" he chokes. "Did you not just say that you—"

"We're both aware that you were coerced by your father into courting me. He won't accept us merely breaking it off. Propose to me, and I will reject your proposal."

John rubs his chin with furrowing brows and flattened lips. "You're suggesting that I propose to you so that you may reject me?"

"Aye. Are you daft, sir, or did I not make that

clear enough?" Margaret holds his cheek, stealing his attention. She smiles with adoration and patience. "I am willing to wait for you if time is all you require."

"You would do that for me?" he whispers in a gravely tone. "Why?"

"Because I love you, John. And I want you to love me the same when you truly propose. I do not desire to marry a man whose heart is still yearning for another."

John is speechless, only able to articulate his pure unbridled joy by capturing her into a tight embrace. "Thank you," he breathes into her shoulder, dreaming of Frances and Alexander living with him in New York. "Thank you."

He does not see the tears that she wipes away before returning the embrace. "You're welcome," she replies, her voice cutting out into a raspy burst of emotion.

Chatpter 15

JOHN ENTERS THE HOUSE ALONGSIDE his father with a newfound confidence. Henry examines his behaviour and raises an inquisitive brow at his son as he unclasps his cloak and hands it to an awaiting Diana.

"You seem chipper," Henry observes; Diana inconspicuously watches the scene unfold as she hangs up Henry's cloak. "Did you enjoy your outing today, son?"

"I did." John smiles genuinely as he responds. "In fact, I have news."

Henry takes pause in front of the parlour, gazing at John curiously. "Oh?"

"I was wondering, father, if I may have your blessing to ask Margaret's father for her hand in marriage?" John bursts out.

Henry's eyes swell before his face melts into one of pure delight. "Oh!" His smile grows impossibly larger as he grabs John's shoulders to pull him into an embrace. John freezes momentarily, taken aback by the abrupt action from his father. "Of course, Jack! Oh, what wonderful news! I cannot wait to share this with Bill!"

John laughs jovially with his father, eager for the pieces slotting nicely into place in Maggie's grand plan. He melts into his father's tight embrace, feeling like a small boy again. He internally remarks that his father had not held him in such a tender way since he was young, and his face shifts into a rather grim expression before slipping away with the release of the embrace.

Henry holds him at arm's-length, slapping his wounded shoulder affectionately; John resists wincing painfully at the action. "My boy, I am incredibly proud of you. We shall celebrate with a drink!" As Henry stalks backwards into the parlour, John's features shift yet again, befuddled to hear such bold words spoken within his father's breath. Proud. His father is proud of him for proposing to a rather conventionally handsome socialite. John catches sight of Diana fleeing down the corridor with an unusual expression upon her face.

"Son?" Henry inquires wearily.

John spins dizzily towards the parlour, procuring a sheepish grin amidst his racing thoughts.

"My apologies. What did you say?"

"A sherry or whiskey?" Henry asks, lifting each glass bottle as he says their names.

"May I take a whiskey?" Hamilton's voice replies from behind John, emanating a waterfall of chills flowing down his spine. "I refuse to miss out on such a grand toast," he adds with a cheery tone, but as John examines him, he deciphers no emotion from his face; he is not frowning or smiling, utterly neutral as he approaches Henry.

Henry gleefully pours Hamilton a whiskey, too buried within his own excitement to take any notice of Hamilton's off-putting demeanour. John swallows painfully and follows behind to grab another cup for himself. "Whiskey for me as well, father," he says upon his approach.

After all glass cups are filled, they each lift them in a toast. "To Jack," Henry begins pridefully. "May God bestow upon you riches and good health throughout the duration of your marriage."

"I've not even proposed as of yet," John replies, hiding his nerves rather poorly behind a breathy chuckle.

"And I've no doubts that she will accept your proposal, son," Henry replies. "That young lady is quite smitten with you, my boy."

John manages to abort a knowing chuckle. "Well, thank you for your pep...posterous words of wisdom, father."

Hamilton and Henry proffer deep chuckles in response as they clink their glasses together. "I hope Miss Valenfort can handle your ridiculous puns," Hamilton quips cheekily.

"Soon to be Mrs. Laurens, no doubt," Henry adds coyly, nearly about to take a sip of his sherry.

"Wait," Hamilton interrupts, unable to leave John any time to internally process his father's words. "I have something to say."

John and Henry watch with curious expressions. "I only wish to grant you the best of wishes in your future endeavours with Miss Valenfort," Hamilton begins with a wavering smile. "When we met in the war, I knew we would be inseparable and work alongside each other to build the foundations of our country once we won her freedom. I truly wish you both all the best, John."

"Hear-hear," Henry cheers, re-tapping the lip of his glass to theirs before taking a long-awaited sip.

As the drinking ensues, John finds his glass empty after only a few sips. Perhaps he is already losing track of himself as he drowns in the thrill of such an insane plan. He has never been this excited to propose to a woman and probably never will be ever again.

"Daddy?" Frances interrupts from the corridor. John stares at her, his throat closing up at the sight of her.

Diana rushes behind her in haste. "Miss Laurens! We must get you prepared for your piano lesson!"

"What's going on?" Frances asks innocently as Diana holds her hand and ushers her away.

"Wait, Diana. I believe this is an appropriate time to share with her the good news," Henry states firmly as he places his glass down. Alexander and John share a timid exchange with nothing but their eyes as Henry kneels in front of Frances.

"Good news?" Frances beams. "Are we getting a puppy?"

John is willing to tame the nearest beast if it will keep her calm within the duration of this exchange. "Actually," Henry begins slowly. "Do you recall Miss Margaret Valenfort?"

Frances' features melt away like the snow they had played in many months ago. She flickers her gaze towards the two nervous men standing behind Henry, pouting. "Mhmm?" she hums in acknowledgment, nodding her head.

"Your father is to be married to her, so she will be your new mother," Henry replies. "And hopefully soon, you will have little brothers and sisters to look after."

John closes his eyes, bracing himself for her tantrum.

"Oh. Okay." John blinks in bewilderment as Frances shrugs half-heartedly, looking at Alexander over Henry's shoulder. He offers her a weak, but encouraging, grin. "May I go to my piano lasso now?"

"It is 'lesson', not 'lasso'," Henry corrects sharply. "And yes, you may go."

John watches the hollowed shell of his lively daughter turn around and sulk towards Diana. Her back straightens and her eyes downcast with a blank expression on her face; the only indication of any feeling inside her vessel are her hands as they vigorously bunch up in her skirts. He prefers her dramatic outbursts over this emptiness. In fact, both Hamilton and Frances are acting in such a vacant manner, that he wonders if they had already spoken before now, as if to prepare for this news to be dropped upon them.

Diana steps forward and hesitates at the entryway as Frances stalks out of the parlour and waits in the foyer. "Henry, should you be drinking? You've already had some this morning—"

"I'm fine Diana. There's no need to dote upon me now," Henry brushes her off, taking a sip of his sherry to punctuate his statement. He absently rubs his chest and she puts her hands on her hips, scoffing.

"Sir, if you do not take care of yourself, I'll be out of work. Don't coddle yourself with the thought that I dote for emotional purposes." She points accusingly at his hand rubbing his chest. "You're having chest pains as we speak, aren't you?"

Henry laughs and John stares at the exchange in silent befuddlement, giving Alexander a look who also responds accordingly. "It's nothing to worry over. Your job is secure. As is my heart." He pauses to take another sip, as if he wishes to piss her off further; he waves his hand theatrically as he lowers the cup and swallows. "Now, go prepare Frances for her lesson. Leave me to drink in celebration with my boy and who I assume will be his best man?" As Henry says this, he turns to look at them for clarification.

Alexander feigns a grin and nods vigorously. "Of course."

"Right then. Carry on, Diana," Henry dismisses her in finality. She sighs before turning to lead Frances up the stairs. John and Alexander sip their drinks with wide eyes as Henry pours himself another glass of sherry. John will never comprehend the bizarre relationship between his father and his own health; as well as his relationship with this peculiar housemaid.

***

John stands in front of the mirror in his bed

chambers, fixing his cravat tie in a perpetual loop. His mindscape seems to no longer process time passing by as he realizes the past day is like a numbing blur in comparison to his striking nerves at this moment. He startles at the sound of soft knocking on his door frame and gazes at Hamilton in the reflection of the mirror.

"Hm, come in," he grumbles, turning his attention back to his tie. Hamilton closes the door behind him and approaches from behind, appearing in the mirror with a forlorn expression. "I actually wanted to speak with you before we leave."

"About your proposal, I presume?" Alexander replies, his eyes carrying an exhausted aura that John hadn't seen since the war.

"You needn't look so worried. I can assure you that everything will be fine." Alexander scoffs and John raises a brow. "I have a plan."

"A plan?" Hamilton folds his arms over his chest defensively.

"She'll say no," John confesses, giving up on his tie and turning to face Alexander.

"I—pardon?"

"The plan," John whispers conspiringly. "I hadn't been able to share the details with you whilst my father was around" —he searches over Alexander's shoulder to double-check that the door be closed. "It entails me asking for her hand in marriage and she will reject me in front of our fathers, thus allowing the opportunity for my father to leave me alone after such an embarrassing display."

Alexander snorts amusedly. "And what makes you so certain she will reject your proposal? We are all aware she's in love with you."

"I'm certain it will work because it was her idea," John replies cooly.

Alexander's lips putter like a trout out of water; utterly bewildered. "I'm sorry, did I hear that correctly? This absurd idea was her's?"

"It will work."

"Why would she suggest such a thing?" Alexander pales as he says this. "Jesus Christ, John! Did you tell her about us?"

"God's, no!" Laurens replies incredulously. "Why the hell would I do that?"

"Wait, why else would she suggest this plan?" Alexander blinks quickly and stumbles backward a step. "I am confused."

"She's aware that I am not ready for marriage," John elucidates calmly. "She believes me to still be in love with my late wife. So, she offered to deny my proposal since she '*refuses to marry a man whose heart belongs to another*'. Her words, not mine."

"I see..." Hamilton eyes him suspiciously. "What if this is a trick on her end to convince you to propose when you clearly do not wish to do so? What will you do if she says yes?"

John, foolishly, had not considered that. "She wouldn't do that," he argues. "Maggie would not do such a thing to me. She is kind."

"Maggie, eh?" Alexander echoes in a dry tone laced with envy. "You've given her a pet name, 'ave ya?"

John startles at hearing his native accent slip into his speech. "I was blending in."

Alexander steps closer, arching his brow challengingly. "You were quite friendly with her."

"Don't act the jealous fool, now. You know that I am in love with you, Alex," he retaliates in a sharp whisper. "Mag—Margaret is a friend. She would not sabotage this for me."

"Well I suppose you've got yourself trapped inside a hellish situation no matter the outcome," Alexander replies haughtily. "If she says yes, then we see this was all a ruse to lock her into a marriage with the handsome and rich Southern Gentleman, John Laurens." He pauses for theatrical effect. "And if she says no... Well, then you are the bastard who convinced a naïve young woman into rejecting you out of love."

"Love?"

"If she loves you John, she'll say no," Alexander whispers as he subconsciously begins tying John's cravat. "And that will make it far worse for leading her on."

He grabs Alexander's wrist as he finishes tying the cloth. "I wouldn't have ever required doing such a heinous act if it weren't for my father's overbearing pressure."

"Perhaps you should learn to stand up to your father like a man instead of playing games with people's hearts," Alexander snaps in retaliation, pulling his arm away. John shoots daggers into Alexander's retreating form but says nothing—because he is right.

"What about our duty to abide by the law?" John questions as Alexander reaches the door.

He hesitates with his hand lingering on the door latch. "And what about our plan to override such laws?" He turns his head cryptically. "We work in Congress now. We had desired to make change. But perhaps you're right in being realistic. In truth, I never thought this could work, but you had somehow convinced me that it could."

"It can still work," John replies. "Please, trust me."

Hamilton sighs, bowing his head. "I always have." He exits the room.

Chatpter 16

JOHN MAY LOSE HIS CONSTITUTION ON
Margaret's shoes—or, perhaps, in the potted plant in
the corner of the Valenfort's sunroom. He hovers the
teacup against his lips as he watches Frances nibble
from the biscuit that Alexander had procured for her. He
flickers his gaze to John briefly and offers a   reassuring
grin, somehow settling his nerves amongst the roughest
patch within their relationship. Henry and Bill converse
lightly and Margaret utters no sound as she sips her tea
silently, not making any eye contact with John; she must
be dreading what's to come as well.

John wastes no more time as he places his teacup
down and clears his throat. He knows his father and Bill
had already discussed the proposal. All that is left is to
perform the show he and Margaret had planned for the
afternoon. John stands as the people at the table give

him their undivided attention.

"I, ah, have something I wish to say, if that is alright," John nearly growls. He clears his throat again, realizing it is incredibly dry. He resists the urge to take a nervous sip from his tea.

"Yes?" Margaret asks, standing as well out of politeness.

John scrambles his brain for words; he had not even considered how he would phrase this *'big moment'* like the imbecile he truly is. "Mr. Valenfort, it would be my greatest pleasure if you were to graciously accept my proposition for you, today."

Margaret raises a curious brow as Bill stands up, smiling brighter than ever. "Relax, John. Your father already spoke of assets with me. Please, this is entirely for her."

"Pardon?" Margaret asks with faux ignorance, looking at her father inquisitively before searching John patiently. "What is all this about?"

John holds her hand and swallows deeply. He refuses to glance in the direction of spectators. "Margaret Valenfort," he begins, his heart thundering within his ribcage. "Would you do me the greatest honour and take my hand in marriage?" He tries to not cringe at how similarly phrased his sentence was to Alexander's proposal, but he shields his inner thoughts with a placid grin.

Margaret stares at John, her eyes glossy. She gazes at Frances indecisively

, causing John to panic as he sets sights on his family who watches with curious expressions. Margaret chews her bottom lip and Bill furrows his brows in bewilderment. She says nothing.

"Peggy, is everything alright, dearheart?" Bill whispers into her ear.

Henry stares stoically at John, nodding firmly to urge him onwards. John merely shrugs in response to his father, feigning confusion as Margaret pulls her hand away. "Margaret?" John queries in a low voice. "Have I offended you?"

"No," she mumbles. She sniffles and steps out of her father's reach. "I apologize," she blubbers somberly. John's spine is swallowed with fire and ice as the fleeting thought of her saying 'yes' invades his mind. She wouldn't do such a thing. She's only playing it up for the others, surely?

"What do you apologize for?" John replies wearily.

"I can't... I refuse your hand," she sobs, grabbing her handkerchief to wipe her tears. "I'm so sorry," she wails as she runs out of the room.

John blinks in surprise, wondering if she is falsifying her reaction, or if she truly cannot hold back her tears. He attempts to withhold his giddy interior, hoping to combat a smile as it dawns upon him that she followed through with the plan. The reigns of hell's grasp tightens around his soul at the thought.

Henry rises from his chair cautiously and puts a hand on John's shoulder. "Perhaps it is only nerves?" Henry suggests, seemingly attempting to console John.

"She ran out of the room saying no," John croaks, hoping he is playing along well-enough. "I don't believe that to only be nerves, father."

"What in God's name just happened?" Bill grumbles in utter confusion. "I was certain she…" he awkwardly looks over at Alexander and Frances who sit at the table, silent as mice. "I'll go speak some sense into her."

"No," John interrupts, reaching out to the retreating man. "Please, I do not wish to upset her any further. Perhaps we should vacate the premises as she is rather emotional at this time. I do not wish to crowd her."

"That's very courteous of you, John, but we already made a deal," Henry growls harshly. "Go speak with her. She should be thrilled to receive a proposal from my son."

"Father!" John snaps, enraged. "That's quite enough. If she does not wish to marry me, then she has every right to refuse my hand. This is not your decision to make."

"You're right, son," Henry replies, raising a brow. "It's yours. I can't believe you're acting so docile right now."

"Perhaps we should leave and get some fresh air?" Alexander suggests abruptly, interrupting the father-son dispute. "John is correct. We should not overstay our welcome." Alexander holds out his hand to Frances who graciously accepts it. "Let's go, petite fleur. We'll wait for your father outside."

As John moves to follow them, Henry stops him with a firm grip on his shoulder. "I don't understand, son. You should be fighting for the love of your life."

"I'm sorry, Henry, but my daughter has the final say," Bill states firmly. "You should leave before this mess worsens. I sincerely apologize for any inconveniences."

"Thank you for your understanding," John replies, bowing politely before striding from the estate.

He walks briskly until he catches up with Alexander and Frances, and the trio begin their trek back to the house, unwilling to wait for Henry. John wordlessly takes Frances' hand and leads her to the dirt road.

"What's wrong, daddy? What happened?"

Frances questions with wide, naïve eyes.

"Margaret Valenfort declined my proposal," John replies stiffly, keeping his eyes on the path ahead of him. "I will not be marrying her as we previously thought."

"Oh," she replies, her lips curling upward. "That's good."

"Frances!" Alexander gasps incredulously. The group halts in the road, their property in view further down the street. "Be polite!"

"Why should I? I didn't want them to be married," she replies bluntly.

John is unable to resist any longer; he begins to laugh. The pair stare at him perplexedly as he calms himself. "You are a stubborn girl."

Frances only lifts her chin defiantly and John smiles endearingly at the sight. He kneels in front of her and grips her shoulder. "I'll let you in on a secret if you promise not to repeat my words to anyone else." Alexander raises a brow as Frances smiles and nods excitingly. "In truth, I also did not want to marry her. So, Margaret saying no was an absolute relief."

Frances exhales and tilts her head with pursed lips. "If you didn't want to, then why do it?"

"Your grandfather wished for it," John mumbles in response. "I tried to tell him we were perfectly fine on our own, but he would not listen."

"He sounds like he's negligent with your wishes, daddy," she says solemnly.

That word. She had learned it ages ago and as she misuses it, she is somehow still correct in her observations. Pride swells within John for his daughter's brilliance and clever attitude. He pulls her into an embrace, gazing up at Alexander over her shoulder. His lips quirk upwards on one side with his hands casually settled inside his coat pockets.

"How are you so intelligent?" John asks her rhetorically as he lifts her up, resting her against his left hip so he may carry her the rest of the way.

"I dunno. I think you and papa put some smarts into me."

Alexander and John unanimously chuckle at her absurdly adorable response, turning around the corner to enter the property with livelier moods than when they had left earlier. Diana meets them in the foyer expectantly, her features twisting in discomfort as she gazes at the longcase clock by the staircase.

"That was awfully quick. Did it go well?"

"She said no," John replies flatly as he lowers Frances onto her feet.

"Oh." Diana looks over Hamilton's shoulder at the open door. "And how did your father take this news?"

"Not well, but that's to be expected from him," John says whilst closing the door.

She studies the three of them with folded arms. "You're certain she said no, or was it you, Mr. Laurens?"

John balks in front of the parlour, staring at Diana as his body convulses an icy sensation through his blood. "Excuse me?"

Before anyone is able to respond, Henry rushes into the house, slamming the front door behind him. "I made a deal to speak with Bill. Will you join me?"

"Enough of this, father. She said no."

"Everyone else said yes," Henry snaps in retaliation. "I don't understand why you aren't fighting for her!"

John scoffs, shuffling into the parlour and grabbing a glass. "I do not wish to force a woman to marry me when she does not wish to do so. I'd rather treat this with more delicacy and less impulsiveness, father. I thought you of all people would respect that." Henry abruptly slams the glass out of John's hand, shattering it upon the hardwood floor. John glares at his father whilst Alexander subconsciously steps in front of Frances, blocking her from the parlour.

"Henry!" Diana's voice booms from the corridor. "Watch your temper. Your condition—"

"I am fine, Diana," Henry gruffly interrupts, his tone already quieter than previously. He turns to John and sighs dejectedly. "I will make this right, Jack." John kneels down, ignoring him as he picks up the pieces of glass. "You deserve to be happy. I only wonder why you refuse to allow yourself to be happy?"

"Forcing someone into a marriage they do not wish to be permanently signed to by law will not bring me happiness, father," John replies gruffly.

Henry rubs his chest and nods silently. "Alright, son. I will still speak with Bill this evening in case it was only nerves that compelled her to say no. But I will not push if she truly does not wish to pursue it."

John sighs in relief, standing up with the broken glass tumbler in his open palm. "Thank you."

Henry hums, still rubbing his chest before stumbling away. Alexander shuffles out of his way, looking sheepishly at the floor for having witnessed the dispute. Frances grips Hamilton's coattails from behind, spying up at her grandfather with wide eyes. Henry turns towards Diana and pats her shoulder. "I'll be leaving soon. For your peace of mind, I will take some of that experimental medicine I bought a while back—if you are able to grab it for me?"

"Of course, sir. That's what I'm here for." She curtsies quickly and hurries up the stairs.

"Medicine?" John queries in a small voice. "How ill are you, father?"

"I'm only taking it for everyone's peace of mind. I'm perfectly fine, John," Henry replies offhandedly. "Damn medicine cost me a near fortune—about forty-five dollars, or so. Had to take some money from the safe upstairs to give to Diana so she may procure the medicine at the market," Henry rambles, irritated as he recalls the memory.

John's skin prickles with gooseflesh; he could slap himself for not considering it sooner. The missing money in the safe. How had he not considered that his father took the money out, himself? Henry obviously would not mention such a thing so as not to worry his family. John tightens his fists and winces, realizing too late that his left hand still holds glass shards in it. "Fuck," he whispers under his breath as his palm begins to bleed.

"Be careful, Jack," Henry scolds as Diana walks down the steps with a strange pill in her hand. "Dispose of that glass before you harm yourself any further by mistake."

John huffs gruffly as he passes them to throw away the glass and rinse his hand. Before he turns the corner, he watches Henry pocket the pill and mentions something about taking it when he meets with Bill before grabbing his hat and cloak.

***

After the glass has been disposed of and his hand be cleaned and carefully bound, he ventures out into the corridor to find it empty. He glances into the reading room and finds Alexander sitting at the piano they had purchased for Frances' lessons, tapping a few keys languidly as he picks up the glass of whiskey resting atop the instrument to take a languid sip. His coat is absent, only sporting his waistcoat; his sleeves rolled up to the elbows. John lightly knocks on the door, absently re-fastening the binding on his palm as he discovers it to be too tight. Alexander's eyes flicker towards John and he smiles, placing the glass down and closing the lid of the piano to protect the keys from dust.

"How's your hand?"

"Fine." John saunters into the room, removing his coat and draping it over the chair. He gazes out the front window. "Where is everyone?"

"Well, your father left to go speak with Mr. Valenfort, as you know," Alexander replies as he stands, arching around the piano and grabbing his cup on his way towards John. "And Diana offered to take Frances on a walk through the park behind the estate to calm her down so she won't be too excited for supper time.

Your father put on quite the scene earlier and it startled her."

John nods slowly, sealing his binding before leaning against the piano. "So, t'is only you and I in this godforsaken house?"

"Aye, sir." Alexander raises a brow as he takes one last sip before placing the glass on the table beside the window. He grips the curtains and closes them, his posture far too casual for the way his eyes darkly scan John's physique. "I suppose your proposal worked out exactly as planned."

"I told you it would be so, but you refused to listen," John quips back lightly.

"I trusted you. It was her I did not trust," Alexander admits as he slips between John and the piano, leaning against it with his neck strained, acting as if he were only stretching when John knows innately what he's truly hoping to accomplish with such an action.

"Are you still jealous of a woman?" John teases in a sing-song tone, stretching his arms on either side of Alexander, pressing his fingertips on the piano—caging the smaller man. "You know that I still wear your ring. You have my heart in your possession, my dear boy."

"Mmm," Alexander leans up to press his lips against John's ear. "Prove it."

John dips down to capture those delectable lips, sighing in content. He smiles as he cups Alexander's jaw and tilts their heads to deepen it, thrilled at the prospect that his binds to societal expectations have been tamed. "I was thinking," —John whispers against Alexander's jaw as he lazily unlaces his cravat— "of us living in New York. Finally starting our law firms. Just you, me, and Frances."

Alexander hums, his eyes closed and his grin wide as John slips his cravat off of his neck. "Mmm, how wonderful that sounds."

"We may return to congress later on. Once my father is no longer here to burden us with his presence, that is," John carries on as he tosses the cloth and un-buttons Alexander's waistcoat.

"Your father isn't all too bad. The courtship was what had been unbearable," Alexander replies, allowing John to slip his waistcoat off of him. The fabric thuds lightly as it lands on the hardwood floor. "Sneaking around with you is rather exhilarating. Keeps things fascinating, at least."

"I'd rather not sneak around," John says quietly. He leans in and kisses his lover with ease, practically melting his body into Alexander's. "When we're alone, we can do whatever we please."

"What are we to do, then? Now that we're alone?"

John grunts, pulling Alexander into a passionate kiss. He pulls him away from the piano and pushes him onto the sofa, immediately removing both of their shoes before crawling over Alexander. They laugh as they nuzzle their faces together and roam their hands freely under their shirts, overjoyed with an intense heat building up between them.

"Jack," Alexander moans as John kisses down his neck, pulling his shirt aside to expose his collarbone. His hands grip John's hair, pulling him back up to his lips so that he may capture them once again. John rolls his hips into Alexander's groin and the pair moan unabashedly, holding each other closer as they continue to rut against one another until a smooth rhythm forms.

John pushes his loose hairs back and unfacens his breeches. Alexander lowers his hands to unbutton his own before pulling John's face close enough for him to kiss. John awkwardly shuffles the flaps of Alexander's breeches apart and yanks the cloth down to his thighs. Alexander chuckles warmly, throwing his head back in pleasure as John pushes his shirt higher up his abdomen so he may expose him entirely.

Laurens places wet kisses along his husband's exposed neck, rolling his hips against him again. Hamilton moans loudly as their hot skin presses firmly against each other with each thrust. John holds onto him as if he be an anchor, disallowing his ascent into the heavens as he drowns in ecstasy. That familiar coil builds more tension as he continues thrusting his hips in full strides now, mumbling sweet nothings and grunting breathlessly into his lover's ear.

"Yes, yes, yes," Alexander whispers, his voice rising in pitch as he exposes his neck, tilting his head as far back as it may go. His russet curls loosen from their queue as he practically digs his head in the juncture between the cushion and the armrest of the sofa, his blissed-out features illuminated by the few wall-mounted candelabras in the room.

John stares at him in awe before slowing down to lean in, pressing a tender kiss upon his lover's lips. He strokes Alexander's freckled cheek affectionately, smiling down at him as he begins panting. "I've got you, my love," John mutters sweetly, cuddling him closer as he focuses entirely on bringing Alexander to his capstone. John kisses his sweat-coated skin and revels in Alexander's squirming; his nails gripping into John's loosened waistcoat as he reaches for the peak of his pleasure. John chuckles warmly into the juncture of Alexander's neck, overcome with—

"What the hell are you doing?" Henry roars from the open doorway, his booming voice coursing through John's skin and shattering his demeanour as he shrivels with degradation. He shields Alexander with his entire body, staring down at him with wide, trepidatious eyes. Alexander shrinks within himself, practically melting into the sofa as he lays frozen underneath John's weight, only able to search his ample blue eyes for solace.

John wearily raises his head to look into his father's piercing dark gaze, his face shifting from ice-cold into a burning crimson as humiliation and guilt settles within. "I—ngh," —he swallows painfully as his throat closes up— "father, I can—I can explain…"

Henry's eyes squint in disgust as they remain on the two men laying on the sofa, his hand gripping the doorframe visibly tensing. "I'd rather not hear the details, boy. Get up."

John shakily moves his head side-to-side, subconsciously gripping Alexander tighter to shield his propriety from his father's judgemental sneer. Henry scoffs, looking down the hallway with a grimace. "Get. Up." He tiredly rubs his face. "And dress yourselves."

John watches his father for another moment, realizing he still looks determinedly down the hallway and no longer at them. John shifts and pulls Alexander's breeches up before re-lacing his own in haste. The two scramble off of the sofa, nearly falling over as Alexander picks up his waistcoat and cravat by the piano and they fumble with their shoes. John brushes the wrinkles of his own waistcoat until it lays flatter upon his chest.

John turns as his father does, and tears begin to prickle behind his eyes. He blinks a few times, resisting the urge to sob as his father eyes them both with revulsion. "I wish to speak with my son alone," Henry rumbles, his eyes narrowed on Alexander.

He hesitates, looking to John for assurance—

"Get. Out!" Henry snarls, enraged. Alexander stumbles awkwardly past Henry as he shifts out of his way. Before he may utter a word, Henry slams the door in his face, leaving John utterly alone with his fuming father.

"What do you have to say for yourself?" Henry interrogates, his tone unrelenting.

"I thought you weren't home," John mumbles defeatedly.

"I'd returned not a minute ago. As I was about to call out your name, I overheard the noises emanating from this room," Henry replies, seething. He begins to pace, huffing as he watches John with wild eyes. "I'd thought, perhaps, that you might have been with a common whore, but this was far worse." Henry stops pacing two metres away from John. "I never thought I'd say this, boy, but I'd rather walked in on you with a woman!"

John looks away, crossing his arms with a twisted expression. "Sorry to disappoint your expectations, father…"

"Disappoint?" Henry yells, smacking the chair furiously. "Son, I am far beyond disappointed! I am horrified!"

John squeezes his eyes shut shamefully as tears begin to flow against his will.

"You have committed one of the darkest sins!" Henry growls.

John wipes his face, sniffling. "We were just— our love is not a sin—"

"Love?" Henry chokes, astonished. "What I had bared witness to was not love, Jack. That was lust."

"You're wrong," John retorts, his eyes red-rimmed and his features swelling with his flush of emotions. "Now that you know, I may as well admit my true feelings to you. I love him!"

Henry gags, causing John's stomach to curl with shame. "A man cannot love another man in such a way. What of the values I taught you?" Henry blinks in astonishment. "Have I failed you, Jack?"

"Oh, you taught me your values quite efficiently, father," John replies. "My values just do not align with yours any longer."

"That man is devil-incarnate, tempting you to follow his sinful ways," Henry garbles madly to himself, running his fingers through his fly-away hairs. "My boy, have you lost your damn mind?"

"No, father. For the first time in my life, I am

thinking clearer than the most beautiful day after a storm," John replies, sniffling and wiping his face dry. "You said you wished for my happiness—and Alexander, he is my happiness. I am at my best when I'm with him, and I cannot control these feelings. It's not a sinful urge to love someone wholeheartedly."

"My god, you're delusional," Henry mutters with disbelief. "Jack," he whispers tenderly, seeming to calm his exterior. "My son, listen to me. This man will be your undoing." He carefully steps forward and cups John's face with such paternal affection that it gives John whiplash, nearly losing his balance. "I can fix this. I can fix you. If you let me, I can make this problem disappear—"

John sharply tugs himself out of his father's gentle hands, his face scrunched with disgust. "Stop meddling in my life, father. I don't need to—to erase this. It's not a problem—I am not broken. You cannot fix what isn't broken!"

"How can you not see he is taking advantage of you, son?" Henry replies, shockingly mellow. "You may have been on top of him tonight, but he has you under his thumb."

"Fuck you," John spits out, utterly discgraced. "How dare you presume the worst of him? Have you considered that I could have initiated this relationship?"

"That doesn't necessarily imply that he's still not taking what he can from you," Henry retaliates, crossing his arms and raising a challenging brow. "Have you considered that he might be falling to his knees for you so that you can provide him with great luxuries?" John narrows his eyes. "Does he pay for that house in New York? Or do you?" John fumes with rage. "Do you shower him with gifts?"

"No—"

"I suppose his actions are unsurprising. The apple doesn't fall far from the tree," Henry mocks in a seething tone. "He's just like his whore mother—"

"Enough!" John snaps, stepping closer to cage his father against the wall and smashes his bound fist against the wall. "You will not speak of him or his family in such a way!"

"I only speak the truth, son," Henry spits back, shoving his son out of the way, causing him to nearly tumble. "That man is a filthy rake and you know it!"

"You refuse to listen to reason!" John cries out angrily. "Can you put aside your archaic beliefs for five minutes and actually listen to what I have to say instead of assuming the worst?"

"Archaic?" Henry gasps. "Son, now you speak blasphemy if you believe the values of the Lord is—"

"You're out of line," John interrupts, pointing his

finger accusingly at his father. "You always taught me how God made us in His vision. If who I am is a sin, then why would he make me this way?" John pleads desperately. "I cannot choose whom I love, and I've fallen in love with him. And I know he loves me, too. If you are unwilling to accept who I am, then...." he trails off, uncertain of what to say next.

"You still chose to lay with him. The choice to be with him is the sin, Jack," Henry explains carefully. "If you had repressed it and learned to live a virtuous lifestyle—"

"You think I chose this inflection towards men?" John gasps, grabbing his head in despair. "Dammit, I've tried to repress these feelings but I can't help it! I love him! I don't understand how you cannot accept this! I am your son! Not a criminal. I thought you would trust me in this."

"Fine," Henry replies slowly with a dark glint to his eyes. "If you refuse to listen to reason and continue to choose to live this sinful life, then consider yourself cut off from my aid," Henry barks with finality. "No son of mine will be a molly."

John's eyes water as he frowns. "I don't need your name or your money. We can survive on our own. Just the three of us!"

"Three?" Henry's eyes enlarge as the revelation dawns upon him. "Dear god, you've infected your daughter with this knowledge as well?"

"God, no!" John interjects heatedly. "But what she does know is how much we care for her and we are fully capable of looking after her ourselves. We functioned perfectly fine without the assistance of you or your frivillous luxuries."

"Get out of my house!" Henry yells, stomping his foot down and gripping his chest.

"Alright, then." John turns sharply to approach the door.

"And you can forget the fortune you were to inherit. You can consider yourself removed from my will entirely, you hear!" Henry grunts, gripping his chest tighter. "I will not support you or that avaricious criminal any longer!"

"Fine by me!" John replies dismissively, waving his hand.

"You should be lucky I won't see to your fucking hanging, boy!"

"Good riddance," John snips back, turning harshly to scowl at his father one last time. He pauses, furrowing his brow at his father's theatrics, watching him grip his chest. "What's wrong with you?"

"You're..." Henry groans in pain. "You're breaking my heart, Jack..."

"Oh, don't be so dramatic, father. You chose this." John huffs bitterly, echoing his father's harsh words back at him, and opens the door to retreat. Henry collapses onto his knees and John swiftly spins around, raising his eyebrows in bewilderment. "Father?"

"Jack...." Henry barely holds himself upright with his wobbling arm that grips the floor. His other hand desperately claws at his chest as his eyes bulge from his sockets in despair. "My...chest..." Henry groans. "It's like a thousand knives..." he trails off as he topples over onto his side, curling into himself.

John rushes to his side, kneeling beside him and cradling him gingerly as his father wails in pain. "What is—What do I do? What's happening to you?"

"Son," Henry chokes out, weakly reaching into his coat pocket. "My medicine. I forgot in my—ugh!—haste to speak with...mmm...Bill..." he pulls out the pill and drops it on the floor as the pain overcomes him again.

"Dammit, father!" John cries out. "We can—what can we do?" Henry struggles to respond and John begins to truly panic. "Alex!" he cries out in agony. "Help!"

"Ja-h-ck..." Henry grumbles tiredly.

Alexander appears in the doorway, out of breath and gripping the frame with alert features. He looks ready to throw a punch but seems to reset his stance as he catches sight of the scene unfolding in the room.

"Find a doctor! His heart!" John begs, and Alexander nods quickly before disappearing down the hall and presumably out the front door in an urgent rush.

John returns his attention to his father cradled in his arms, his eyes filling with tears as he holds him closer. "Shh, papa. It's going to be alright. Help is on the way…"

Henry, despite his pain, smiles weakly. "You've not…called me that in so long…"

John shakes his head. "I'm sorry… Please, stay with me."

"No," Henry coughs, tensing and gripping his chest with the utmost despair as the pain seems to build relentlessly. "I am sorry. You know, I've always wanted to do right by you children…?" John sniffles as his father takes a moment to catch his breath. "I think I'm dying, son."

"No, you can't be—"

"I knew this day would come…I just thought I'd have more time to….make things right…" John stares in bewilderment as his father continues to struggle. "I wanted to see you happy and—argh!—secure before I… went to be with your mother…"

"Papa? What are you" —John sniffles, letting out a sob— "what are you saying?"

And as Henry looks into his eyes, epiphany strikes. His father's sudden need to relentlessly meddle with his life the past few months. His careless behaviour regarding his health. He was ready to die. He was trying to set John up with a secure family to ensure his legacy carries on without him. "You can't go. I need you."

Henry smiles warmly. "No, you don't. You know exactly....exactly what you're doing..."

"What about everything you said?" John quivers delicately. "I thought you hated...that I..."

"—In truth, son...I'll always," —Henry chokes painfully, seizing up within John's arms.

"Father?" John cries as Henry stares up at the ceiling with glassy eyes.

"Ellie?" Henry whispers so quietly, John almost misses it. John waits patiently for what he is to say next, his mind sinking into the depths below as his father lays uncomfortably still. His chestnut eyes go lax, his gaze unfocused as each eye lazily falls upon a different spot of the room.

"Papa?" John mumbles, desperately shaking him. "Wake up!" He lightly taps his father's cheek and repels at his lacking reaction. "Papa, wake up! Please! I'm sorry! I'm sorry!" He cradles him closer, sobbing openly. "I take it back. Please! I take it back! I need you to—"

"Mr. Laurens!" John sharply juts his chin towards Dr. Ramsay and Hamilton, both standing with owlish eyes in the doorway. "Good god!" Ramsay mutters in distress as he hurries to Henry's side. "Release him!"

John places him down carefully and watches hopefully as Ramsay carefully examines his father. John watches expectantly, furrowing his brows the longer Henry goes on without moving. "Do something, dammit!"

Dr. Ramsay sighs defeatedly and cautiously closes Henry's eyes. "I'm sorry, but I detect no heart-beat or breath."

"You just sat there with your head next to his! Try again!" John fumes. "You have to do something! He can't just—he can't be...."

"I apologize, Mr. Laurens, but I was too late." He shrugs. "Even if I had come sooner, I don't know what I could have done to save him. This was a preliminary disease of the heart. It was bound to happen eventually, knowing his worsening condition."

John shakes his head. "We were merely talking... and then he..."

"Perhaps the tone of the discussion could have stressed his heart? It's difficult to say as everything seemed to stress that man," Dr. Ramsay replies patiently.

"It's my fault..." John whispers in shock.

"Absolutely not," Ramsay cuts in, placing a firm hand on John's shoulder to capture his attention. "This was not your fault. It matters not if you argued with him tonight. His heart giving out could have happened at any point. It's unfortunate that it happened now, but you cannot possibly blame yourself for this."

John stares emptily at his father's corpse. Alexander places a hesitant hand on John's shoulder. "I'm so sorry—" John twitches away from his grip, glaring daggers at him over his shoulder. Alexander searches his eyes, visibly torn as he sulks further into the floor beside John.

Dr. Ramsay moves his attention to Alexander. "Mr. Hamilton, would you procure a sheet to wrap the body? We can take him to my practitioner's office in town. I mind not doing such for the Laurens family, but I'll require your assistance with removing the body."

Alexander nods feebly and retreats from the room. John remains on the floor, unmoving, his features neutral as the shock of it all begins to truly consume him to the point of complete numbness. He sits for a long time, watching as his father is wrapped gingerly in a white linen sheet. Hamilton gags and covers his mouth as he attempts to help Ramsay carry Henry out of the house.

"I can't...I can't do it," Alexander mumbles,

covering his mouth in shame as he nearly loses his constitution at the site of the linen-covered corpse.

As John watches Alexander nearly retch away his meals, he is stricken with the truth. His father is dead. They were caught and it killed his father; he knows this for certain. The one person he would risk his life for kneels beside his father's corpse, holding his pride and dignity like a soldier in the battlefield. How foolish was he to believe that he could run away with Alexander? How foolish to think he could let go of his familial duties as the eldest man of his family?

John cannot go anywhere with Alexander. Even in death, his father still controls his life.

"We're home!" Frances' chipper voice rings from the foyer and slices jaggedly through John's dissociative thoughts.

John urgently turns to Alexander. "Keep them away from here," he begs.

Alexander rushes from the room and stops Frances outside of the door before she may enter. "We must stay clear of this room, petite fleur."

"What's happened?" Diana asks from the hallway.

John slides himself closer to the sofa and leans his back against the base, pulling his knees up to curl himself inward. He listens as Alexander talks in circles outside the door, slowly leading them further away so that the pathway may be clear for his father's body to be removed.

Akin to a fragile glass, the façade of their life is now shattered. John sighs in resignation; how could he allow himself to fall into Hamilton's web of fantasies yet again? He is aware that this was only temporary, but when he had arrived in Philadelphia, Hamilton had made him perceive that they were to stay together forever.

John spirals further until he is left with nothing but his echoing last words to his father before his final breath, wishing desperately for it to all be one long nightmare.

Chatpter 17

THE LEAVES RUSTLE IN THE GENTLE
breeze, the sky a shade of purple aconite as the sun sets.
John's eyes hurt as he stares at the sky for too long, not
quite understanding why he sees brushstrokes in the
blue hue of the atmosphere. He looks over, laying upon
the textureless grass with a deadpanned Hamilton
staring back. He furrows his brows, opening his mouth
to speak, but utters nothing. He opts for touching his
face, the skin rather smooth. His hair has become like
water, flowing around his fingers as if they're heatless
flames in the breeze.

Alexander smiles, proffering a ripe red apple
from his side. John wordlessly accepts it, taking a
simple bite. As the crunch echoes, Alexander mounts
himself on top of John. He flushes as he lies upon the
grassy field under the mighty oak, his pleasure the only

sensation coursing through his body as Alexander begins to move. He sighs contentedly, gripping Alexander's hips to encourage his hips to move faster. Alexander grips John's face and kisses him passionately on the lips,   enhancing him into a hazy state.

"Sinners!" a faceless mob hisses abruptly in the wind around them, causing John's heart to squeeze.

They are surrounded by a slew of spectators screaming in outrage as Alexander speeds up, pinning John to the earth's floor. He sinks into the grass, the blades binding his resistant wrists as he squirms and struggles in a frenzy. He rolls his head over to face his father, holding Frances' hand in the front of the crowd, both unspeaking amongst the screaming mob.

"Disgusting!"

"Unholy!"

"Monsters!"

John cries in despair, silently begging his daughter to look away as Alexander continues his rhythm, amping up the graphic display for the cruel onlookers. His voice is lost beyond his reach, only able to form the words with his lips. He focuses on Frances' eyes, pleading in forced silence for her to cover her eyes.

To look away.

Henry holds a rope hanging from the tree; he swings it forward and passes it to her, his eyes locked onto the men committing sodomy upon the grass in the centre of the crowd. As Frances grips the rope and tugs, something brash and scratchy tightens around his neck. Alexander halts as he is suspended into the air by a noose, John following soon after Frances yanks on the rope even further.

John extends his hand out to Alexander and he reaches back, their hands mere centimetres out of touch. John turns his attention to Frances, choking on blood as he attempts to plead for his life, praying for her mercy on his soul. '*Look away,*' he internally screams. '*Release us!*'

The sun sets into a grey fog, the crowd vanishing in the blink of an eye; all but Frances and Henry. Her grip on the rope remains firm as Henry walks away, undisturbed and painfully casual. A slimy creature crawls up John's legs, looping around his body as it rises until the beast faces him; a serpent, licking his face with its forked tongue.

In the distance, blue lightning expels from the heavens and disrupts the scene, rumbling the earth with the crackling boom of the following thunder. The blue light strikes trees in the distance, slowly approaching the tree John hangs from with his lover. As the final tree may be struck, it's his child who is stricken instead, causing the rope to loosen and release him.

John falls into the abysmal green grass below, his heart stuck behind within the grandiose oak as he continues to fall further until his eyes see no more.

THUD!

John gasps on the hardwood floor of his room, his ample eyes wildly examining his environment and clawing pitifully at his neck. He finally comes to his senses, listing off the things he takes notice of. Bed. Wardrobe. Window. Sunlight.

Crackle—**BOOM!**

He listens to the rain pelting against the windows and roof, shivering because of the chilly breeze emanating from the fireplace. Water leaks through, rolling down the crimson bricks and onto the burnt wood that had been lit the previous evening.

It was only a dream.

John cranes his neck as he gazes upon the remaining suitcase in his room, kicking his legs to untangle them from the mess of linen sheets upon his bed. He awkwardly rolls over until his numb legs hit the floor, groaning into the wooden floor as he lays flat on his stomach. Debility prevents him from moving any further, the moist pressure in the room nearly lulling him into another sleep until a door slamming down the hall re-snaps his eyes into focus.

John grunts, ignoring the cotton-stuffed

sensation in his head as he sorts himself out of his state of disrepair. He resents his imaginative mind for cursing him with vividly disturbing nightmares, longing for the days of boyhood when he would conjure up exciting tales within his expressive dreamscape.

These days, John has no positivity left in his subconscious, but thankfully his conscious mind is able to suppress his inner darkness that sluggishly stains his soul like a sheet of parchment coated with spilled ink. The words of beauty writ upon the page are now indecipherable as the stain consumes it until there is nothing left to find.

John completes his morning routine habitually, his deft fingers effortlessly completing his cravat's knot before shuffling across the room to resume his packing. All letters have been sent and all errands in Philadel- phia have been settled. He has dreaded this day for the entire week but also longed for it to come as soon as possible, unable to face him even in a passing glance. Just the singular thought of Alexander nauseates him for countless reasons he has not the time to dwell over.

He closes his suitcase with a resounded sigh, pinching the bridge of his nose before rubbing out the crusty bits from the corners of his eyes with his index and thumb. His father is already being shipped down to Mepkin in South Carolina to be further preserved on their family property until he may arrive for a proper funeral.

He cringes at the thought. Shipped. As if his father is an inanimate object to be sent through the post.
Only a week previous he had been alive. Only a week
previous he had discovered his son to be a molly. Only
a week previous he had declared John as being 'dead to
him' before perishing himself. And now John remains
here, the eldest son of the family, left with his father's
will that he had yet to correct before his departure from
his life. John wanted nothing and was left with
everything.

All that remains for John to handle is saying
farewell to his previously desired future, and
shattering his daughter's heart with the harrowing
truth; her grandfather is dead and he is never coming
back.

John snarls at his suitcase, utterly enraged as
he lifts it with a low grunt before retreating from this
hollow room that had been nothing but a prison cell for
him over the years. He stumbles as he nearly impacts
with a body, far too frazzled to give them the time of
day before he turns sharply on his heel and marches
down the corridor towards the stairwell.

"John?" He ceases his muscles atop the stairs, his
shoulders tensing as his voice croaks desperately from
where they had bumped into each other. "I only— May
I speak with you?"

John turns around, placing his suitcase on the

floor by his feet and staring at the corner of the study door, unable to meet his eyes. "Aye?"

"Is today the day you disembark?"

"Mhmm," John hums in acknowledgement, yerking his head up and down once, sharply.

Silence screams at the two men, distanced by the elongated hallway between them. "Have you told her yet?"

John exhales deeply, closing his eyes and shaking his head. "I don't know what or how to," — John grimaces with discomfort— "I've no words."

"Perhaps I can assist with the discussion?" Hamilton suggests meekly, and John finally looks into his eyes, profoundly grateful for the first time since—

"Sure, if you wish."

"Of course I wish to help," Hamilton replies incredulously, yet his voice holds none of his previous ardour. He sounds rather soft these days—as if he is walking delicately on thin ice, tapping his toes ahead to test its strength and infrastructure before treading onwards. "Whatever it is you require, I am always here for you. You're aware of this, right?"

"Aye, of course." John pinches his lips together thoughtfully, roaming his eyes at the wooden railing. He rests his hand on it, rubbing his thumb against the smooth grain to anchor his floating attention span. "I've waited far too long, haven't I?"

"You've been preoccupied," Hamilton replies patiently. "We all have."

John gazes at him disquietly, his expression twisting into rapid anguish. "Why not push back as you typically would?"

Hamilton crosses his arms over his chest, raising an irritated brow. "You're not the only one who needed space this week. It was difficult for us all."

"He wasn't your father."

"No," Hamilton agrees, releasing his arms and shoving them into his coat pockets. "But he was yours. And I know you believe it to be your fault no matter how often I assure you that it is not—because that is what you do, Jack. You blame the world's mortality and sins upon yourself, and carry this great burden on your shoulders no matter how much I desperately attempt to claw it away from your grasp." He sighs, resigned, and leans against the wall temperately. "You cower at the mere sight of me and shrink away, further into the depths of your mind whenever I reach out. I worry for you, my dear."

"Well don't," John replies mutely; he leans down and picks up his suitcase. "It will only drain you to worry. I'm sure I will be able to move past this. I only require the time to sort it out on my own."

"You never informed me of the duration of your trip," Hamilton intercepts rather jarringly, seeming to latch onto that final statement. John rolls his eyes in annoyance. "You're doing it again; dismissing me whenever I mention the fact that you have yet to give me a time limit on your visit to South Carolina."

"I'll only need to remain there as long as it takes to bury my father to his precise specifications and settle his inheritance with my siblings." John shifts his weight, slipping the suitcase from one hand to the other to relax his arm.

"How long will that take?" Alexander inquires deliberately, shoving away from the wall to approach John. "Months?" He tilts his head, his eyes blown wide and his lips curling downward into a dull grimace. "A year? Two? Five?" He stops only a metre away, looking up defiantly. "Forever?" he adds softly, finally.

"I don't know," John replies gingerly. "One thing I can state for certain is that I will return to you." Alexander perks at this, his demeanour greatly subdued compared to his quintessentially buoyant character. John had foolishly ignored his needs, unaware of how amplimatic this situation had become; it had severely affected Alexander's eudemonia, leaving nothing more than a vacant shell of who he once was. "I will always return."

Alexander nods, eyes downcast. He twists his

hands around his wrist, chewing the dead skin from his bottom lip. "Okay," he replies.

They make their trek down the staircase and find Diana and Frances in the dining room. John puts his bags with the pile at the front door and the pair of men sit across from Frances as she eats her breakfast.

"The coach should be here soon," Diana comments as she sets a plate for John and Alexander.

John waves his hand in front of his plate before gesturing to the seat beside Frances. "Please, sit down and eat. It will be a long trip and you've already done so much."

Diana takes pause and furrows her brows at John before relenting, setting a plate up for herself before sitting beside Frances. The head of the table remains vacant and the three adults examine each other worryingly as Frances eats her food, oblivious to what is going on.

"Frances," John begins. He clears his throat and puts his fork down, capturing her attention. "There is something we have yet to tell you about our trip."

"What is it?" She tilts her little head, her lavender pendant shifting as she leans back from the table.

"Well, for one, Alexander will not be coming with us." She frowns, her eyes flickering to Alexander who ducks his head in shame.

"Why not?"

John sighs, exasperated. "Because we will be going to our family plantation in South Carolina."

"Is that where grandpapa went off to?" she inquires innocently, her food stealing her attention.

"Yes," he replies gruffly. T'is technically not a lie. "He will be there."

"Why can't papa come with us?"

Alexander swiftly takes over, putting his fork down gingerly. "Because you will be taking care of family business and I will remain here to finish my work in Congress. I am certain you will return to New York when I have set up our law firm in your father's absence."

"Oh." Her lips press into a thin line. "Okay." She turns to Diana before looking at her father. "Why did grandpapa leave without us?"

John covers his mouth and is unable to hold back his whimper. Frances' confusion only deepens as he struggles to keep his composure.

"Petite fleur, your grandpapa...he left early because—"

"Your grandfather has passed away," John states firmly, blinking away his tears. "We're going to South Carolina to bury him."

"What?" Frances looks around, puzzled. "I don't understand—"

"That was abrupt, sir," Diana scolds with a grimace. "You tell her now before we depart?"

"I should have told her sooner," John retaliates.

"Grandpapa is....gone?" Her voice is meek and Alexander reaches his hand across the table, patting hers affectionately.

"Aye, ma petite lavande," Alexander whispers, his eyes interlocking with her pendant. "Je suis très désolé. Mes condoléances à toi."

She shakes her head in disbelief. "He's gone like mama?"

John can only nod as his throat constricts his speech.

"Why?"

John tiredly rubs his face and shrugs. "I don't know, dear. God has made all of us mortal."

"But I wasn't finished with him," she grumbles, crossing her arms bitterly. "Why didn't we have more time?"

"I said I don't know!"

Silence flows throughout the room, all people at the table only able to stare at each other or at their forgotten meals.

"Finish your breakfast," John says with finality. "It's going to be a long trip today. We won't have a chance to eat again until we're on the ship."

"I'm not hungry."

"You will be. Now eat," John snaps exhaustedly.

"Patience, Mr. Laurens," Diana soothes. "That was very big news you had dropped upon her."

"I didn't ask for your opinion," he retorts coldly.

"Your father's passing is a terrible thing. It's affected all of us," she replies calmly. "I understand you're upset but do not lash out on me, sir. I will leave if you do so again."

John stares in bewilderment at her boldness. She resumes eating her food, seemingly unaffected by his outburst. "My sincere apologies, Diana. I had not intended to offend—"

"Eat your breakfast, Mr. Laurens. As you said, it'll be a long trip to South Carolina." She swallows another bite of her food before continuing. "And you are forgiven."

***

After they finish their meals and finish packing Frances' belongings, the coach they had called upon finally arrives before eleven. Diana begins packing the carriage with the coachman, Frances attempting to help valiantly. John turns around at the front entrance, looking into the expansive estate, staring into the endless corridors. Alexander appears in the doorway, watching them pack the coach with a forlorn expression upon his freckled face.

Frances runs up to him and gives him no warning before she collides into his legs, nearly knocking him off his balance as she embraces him tightly. "I'll miss you, papa."

He kneels down to meet her eyes, smiling at her brightly. "I will miss you too, petite fleur." He pats her shoulder and raises a brow. "Write to me. Don't put that writing skill you've acquired to waste."

She nods enthusiastically. "Okay, papa."

He leans in conspiringly, glancing up at John. "And make sure your father writes to me as well. He's terrible with keeping up with his correspondence."

"I will."

"That's my girl," Alexander boasts proudly. She wraps her arms around his neck for a proper hug and he returns it graciously. They reluctantly release their embrace and she silently slips out a locket, placing it inside Alexander's palm. He gazes at it for a while, opening it and gasping lightly.

"I figured you would want it, even though it doesn't really look much like him," she mumbles, her hands gripping and rubbing anxiously at her skirts.

"Thank you," he murmurs before putting the treasured item inside his coat pocket. Alexander slowly rises to his feet again as she sulks towards the carriage with her head down, only looking back at him once before climbing the step with the coachman's assistance and sitting on the bench inside.

"Is that everything?" Diana inquires, resting her hands on her hips by the boot of the carriage. John notices her expression is quite knowing, and turns to face Alexander at the same moment as him.

"I think I forgot one thing and then we can leave," John replies before entering the house. He closes the door behind him and Alexander stands there patiently as John examines him.

Alexander extends his hand for a friendly shake, his smile gentle and reassuring. His empathy sings loudly in such a simple action; a silent assurance that Alexander does not expect anything more from him at this time. They drugingly part as their eyes search each other with profound longing.

"You had better write to me, John Laurens," Alexander says in a gravelly tone.

John smiles. "I will." He tenderly brushes a loose curl behind Alexander's ear— hesitates—then pulls away reluctantly, turning around and opening the front door.

Don't look back.

His body weighs him back as he attempts to distance himself from the house, performing his aloofness as he walks with clinical dexterity.

Don't look back.

John approaches the awaiting carriage and steps up on the small foot ladder attached to the base, gripping the inside of the door with a white knuckled fist. He glares at his hand gripping the carriage, directly at his ring shining in the sunlight.

John looks back.

Alexander appears tremendously small in comparison to the enormous estate framing him. He watches John enter the carriage with his lips tugging into a grim expression. John closes the door and Diana knocks on the window of the cabin to alert the driver to disembark.

John's body jolts with the abrupt motion of the carriage as the horses pull it down the road. He stares at Alexander as he speedwalks to the edge of the property, watching as the carriage rolls further away. John turns his body to peek through the back window; Frances waves solemnly at the retreating form of Alexander and he raises his hand in response, arching his arm widely until his form is no longer in sight.

"I'm gonna miss him," Frances mutters as she turns around to slump into her seat. Her head plops onto John's shoulder after an egregious bump in the dirt wobbles their balance. He puts an arm around her, holding her close, and chewing the inside of his cheek. He glances out the window as the houses pass by; his eyes linger on the Valenfort estate. Margaret watches longfully as their carriage rolls roughly behind the trotting horse. John's eyes do not linger.

"Me too."

Epilogue

April 17th, 1783
New York Harbour, New York

My Dearest Uncle

I had received your letter dated the 20th of January. I am grateful to hear that all is well across the sea with my beloved aunt and siblings, Polly and Harry. I knew Harry would be able to woo over that lovely dove he so dearly wrote about. I never thought he would humble himself into the domestick lifestyle but I am surely proud to hear it. And if Polly still refuses to wear the skirts her aunt sews for her, perhaps you may settle by gifting her some of my breeches from boyhood to wear underneath her skirts as a compromise? Surely the poignant heat alone would put her senses in order and she would begin acting responsibly as any Laurens should.

I wish I could tell you we fare well over in the United States, but I write to you with a burden upon my shoulders. You must send my siblings over the sea urgently since we must read over our father's will and bury him according to his very specific instructions, else we are to be, quote "disowned". He had passed on two weeks prior—his heart had seized on him even after we had insisted he take proper care of his health. I am with my daughter, Patsy, and our servant at the post—set to board the next ship to Charlestown within the hour.

And to think, I had arrived here only 7 months

prior to begin my new future with my business partner.
I suppose some things were not meant to be. I promised
him I would return but I do not know how long I am to
spend in South Carolina. I am the eldest—as it is my duty
to look after our family now and I will wear this badge of
honour with great pride. I will make my father proud, and
in turn, hopefully you as well. I apologize for the short
and abrupt urgency of this letter. I hope to hear from you
soon.

My sincerest condolences for your loss of your
dear brother.

Yr. dear nephew,

John Laurens

PS. Send a bouquet to my dear wife for me. ~~I
should have been there for her.~~

To Be Continued...

Aknowledgements

I will probably miss a bunch of people and I also don't have enough space to thank everyone but I will try my best. I guess I can start with the classic: not to be cheesy, but YOU, the one who decided to purchase this book and read it to the end. Thank you so much. I am so grateful for your support!

- I would like to thank my siblings by name: Emily, Amanda, Danielle, and Ravin. All of you have been my biggest support throughout my life and I am extremely grateful for it! I wouldn't be where I am without you guys. Thank you!

- I guess I should also thank my mom Jennifer and my dad Alan for literally creating me and raising me and also supporting my creative endeavors. Thank you!

- My French editor/consultant, Ren Chalpin. Thank you so much for correcting my dodgy French and giving me fantastic tips for how to make the French dialogue as expressive as possible! (If there are any errors that slipped through the cracks, they're my fault.)

- My American History research consultant Lyrus Knight. You've helped me in all sorts of ways and I am blessed to have a History Major post-secondary student that I can send direct messages to in the dead of night when I could not find any sources. Your backlog of John Laurens correspondence was extremely useful and I thank you so much for sharing your long, intensive research with me!

- Another wonderful historical research consultant I have to thank is Izz. (Aka Amazing History Nerd, or That History Tumblr User that found a hilarious self portrait that Hamilton drew of himself in one of his chequing books.) Thank you for helping me find sources so I can make sure I knew the history before I purposely messed with it!

* Most of my research could not have been discovered without those previous two history nerds who dedicated so much time to researching this fascinating topic. You all also helped me find great resources on my own and it was amazing to find more stuff beyond the Library of Congress site. *

- I wanna thank my beta/test audience readers as well as my editors. Your feedback was extremely useful!

- I wanna thank all of my teachers that have encouraged me through the years from Elementary School all the way to Post-Secondary. I specifically want to name: Tim Chalmers (my grade 12 writer's craft teacher),

Deborah Spiotti (my grade 12 drama teacher), and Paul McGuire (AKA "Chappy" - the high school chaplain/ guidance counselor). I had a lot of encouragement from my teachers growing up and I felt it would be ridiculous to not mention them.

- I wanna thank all of my friends. You all know who you are. Thanks for indulging me.

- I also want to thank all of my followers on social media. There's a lot of you that I can't name, but rest assured, you all know who you are and deserve an honourable mention.

I literally could not have finished this book without these wonderful people. **Thank you!!**

About The Author

CE Parker was born and raaised in Ontario, Canada; nestled somwhere near a giant waterfall that may or may not be a world wonder. She prefers writing about herself in the vaguest of terms and in the third person. She has been writing avidly since she was 13 and finally decided to publish her debut novel at 24. In her free time, she enjoys watching movies & shows, listening to/working on music, spending time with her siblings, as well as drawing and staring off into the eternal abyss. She's always had a passion for history, time travel, "what if?" stories, and longed for LGBTQ+ historical content to the point of making some representation for herself. ~~CE Parker *might* be a person, but it's easily debatable.~~

She also refused to take an author photo, so she opted to put in a childhood photo since she looked way cuter back then, anyway. The author also goes by Hen. Despite her love of writing, *"About The Author"* sections are the bane of her exsistence.